1916 Angels over the Somme

Book 3 in the

British Ace Series

By

Griff Hosker

Published by Sword Books Ltd 2014
Copyright © Griff Hosker First Edition

The author has asserted their moral right under the Copyright, Designs and Patents Act, 1988, to be identified as the author of this work.

All Rights reserved. No part of this publication may be reproduced, copied, stored in a retrieval system, or transmitted, in any form or by any means, without the prior written consent of the copyright holder, nor be otherwise circulated in any form of binding or cover other than that in which it is published and without a similar condition being imposed on the subsequent purchaser.
A CIP catalogue record for this title is available from the British Library.

Cover by Design for Writers

Dedication

Anthem for Doomed Youth
What passing-bells for these who die as cattle?
Only the monstrous anger of the guns.
Only the stuttering rifles' rapid rattle
Can patter out their hasty orisons.
No mockeries now for them; no prayers nor bells;
Nor any voice of mourning save the choirs,
The shrill, demented choirs of wailing shells;
And bugles calling for them from sad shires.
What candles may be held to speed them all?
Not in the hands of boys, but in their eyes
Shall shine the holy glimmers of good-byes.
The pallor of girls' brows shall be their pall;
Their flowers the tenderness of patient minds,
And each slow dusk a drawing-down of blinds.

Wilfred Owen

Chapter 1

June 25th London

I had a week left of my convalescent leave and I was looking forward to spending more time with Nurse Beatrice Porter. I had blessed my wound for it had brought me in contact with the woman I knew I would spend my life with. I had been presented with a medal by the King himself and another by a high ranking French diplomat but they paled next to the joy of Beatrice and what she had brought to my life. She had filled a void I didn't even know I had. I now knew that she felt the same way about me. Even better was the fact that she and my sister, Alice, had met and got on like a house on fire. My life could not get any better. The walks in Hyde Park and the laughter made my heart lift. It all ended on the 25th of June.

It began normally enough. I was woken by the night shift with a cup of tea. Since I had been walking out with Beatrice the night staff had all been much nicer and more attentive towards me. They were all male orderlies and they would chat to me about the war at the front. I suspect they felt guilty that they had what was deemed a cushy number here in Blighty. It made my life more pleasant. I had been incapacitated for the first week but I was much improved. I could now dress myself and so after my tea I would wash, shave and then dress. I had never paid much attention to my appearance until I met Nurse Porter but now I trimmed my moustache and used a sharp razor to make sure I looked as smart as possible for the arrival of Nurse Beatrice Porter.

My day really began when the day shift and Nurse Porter in particular, arrived with our breakfast. The two of us always felt like naughty children for she managed to bring me something special each day; one day it might be a flower, another, a newspaper, sometimes just my toast cut a special way. It was our little game. She had to avoid the glares and starts of the matron and the sister but we were masters of the po face when they were present.

She had just brought my tray in with a huge smile on her face when Joe, the orderly from medical records came hurtling through the door.

"Captain Harsker, sir, a telegram!" He handed me the brown envelope and stood back.

Beatrice and I both shivered; telegrams never brought good news. My mother had only had two and they had both told her of the deaths of her sons. Who had died? Joe stood expectantly at the door. "Well go on sir. It must be important."

I took the knife from the breakfast tray and carefully opened the envelope. I took out the telegram as though it was wired with explosives. I read it and my heart sank. I looked at Beatrice while wishing that Joe would disappear. Annoyingly he said, "Well sir, what does it say?" I gave him an irritated look and he spread his arms. "It's not me sir it's Matron, she was in the office and she said I should wait in case there is a reply."

Matron had taken a great deal of interest in me since I had been awarded the Military Cross by the king. I sighed, "I have been recalled to active service."

Beatrice forgot herself for a moment, "They can't take you! You aren't ready to go." Aware that she had spoken before Joe she looked around at him and then said to me, "When?"

I folded up the letter and stepped on to the floor. "Joe can you pack my bag for me?"

"Of course sir."

He went to the cupboard containing my clothes and my kit bag.

I looked at Beatrice. "They are sending a car for me. It will be here in less than an hour."

Her hand went to her mouth. There would be no romantic goodbye. No lingering kiss. We would not even be able to hold hands. While Joe was in the cupboard I took a step towards her but at the moment when I was going to grab her hand and kiss her, Matron appeared at the door.

"There is a staff car for you downstairs, Captain Harsker." She sounded impressed. She took in Joe packing my bag and

Beatrice standing there. "Nurse Porter, lend a hand there. Captain Harsker hasn't got time to lollygag with you. Come on girl!"

I could said a few choice words to the silly old dragon but it would not have helped Beatrice. I went to fetch my toilet bag. As I placed it in my kitbag my fingers touched the back of Beatrice's hand. I saw the sudden flush. It was as close as we were going to get to a goodbye kiss.

Joe annoyingly fastened the bag up quickly. He put the toilet bag in the outside pocket. "There you go sir! All sorted! I'll carry it down for you."

I stood, feeling like a spare part. Matron said, "Well Nurse Porter get the bed linen off we will have new patients soon." She put her arm around my back to guide me from the room. "And you, Captain Harsker, are too important to remain here. Your country needs you. You have to return to the front."

"Er what about forwarding letters?"

Matron and I turned at the same time. "What Nurse Porter?"

"I was just saying, Matron, that I will need a forwarding address to send the captain's post to him." I saw the glower on matron's face and then Beatrice played her trump card. "Lady Burscough said she would write to the captain."

Matron's attitude changed in an instant, "Of course, a sensible idea. Would you be so kind as to write the address out for your letters, Captain Harsker?" She actually smiled at Beatrice, "Quick thinking Nurse Porter."

I grabbed a piece of paper and, after writing the address of the airfield added, '*And I love you, xx please write.*' I folded it and gave it to her. She opened it and nodded. "Thank you, Captain Harsker and good luck."

"Thank you, Nurse Porter, for all that you have done for me."

I was propelled through the door by Matron using a hand which could have done service in a blacksmith's!

Joe had spread the word and there were two lines of nurses and orderlies outside the doors as I left the hospital. They all applauded and began cheering. Even Matron joined in. When I got to the door of the car Joe said, "Your bag's in the car sir. I hope to see your name in the paper with another twenty kills eh sir?"

I nodded and turned to speak with them, "Thank you all. You have made my stay here more than pleasant. I feel as though I have stayed with dear friends." I spoke to them all but my eyes were on Beatrice.

I stepped in to the car and back into the war. The door slamming shut seemed ominous. The driver, a corporal said, "We'll have to get a move on, sir. There is a bit of a flap on."

He put his foot down and we sped through the London streets. I suddenly noticed that it was a very luxurious staff car. "Whose car is this corporal?"

"Why it is General Henderson's sir. He sent it special for you. There's something happening in France and they need you back there. I am taking you to the airfield at Greenwich. There's an aeroplane waiting to take you over to France."

I closed my eyes. I had not had much of a rest. The thought of flying over the chilly Channel did nothing to make me feel any better. I suddenly remembered that I had no flying gear. "Hang on Corporal, I haven't got a flying coat. I'll freeze up there."

I heard a laugh, "The general thought of that sir. You'll find my greatcoat next to you. You can use that."

"But what about you Corporal? Won't you need it?"

He tapped his nose as he looked at me through the driving mirror, "Don't you worry about that, sir. I'll end up with a better one. And there's a flying helmet and goggles there too, sir. The general thinks of everything."

"He does indeed, Corporal, he does indeed." This efficiency was not what I wanted but I would have to live with it. Now resigned to being back in France I began to work out what it meant. There could only be one real answer, an offensive and they needed every experienced pilot they could lay their hands on. I suspected that the promise of a new bus would have to go by the board. It would be the old Gunbus for me.

7

The airfield at Greenwich was a familiar one. I had flown from here before. The corporal took my bag out and then held the greatcoat, goggles and flying helmet. He handed me my hat. He saluted. "Good luck, Captain Harsker," he pointed to the medal ribbons on my chest, "you'll be after a V.C. next, eh sir?"

Then he jumped in the car and roared off towards Central London once more. I put the greatcoat on to free up one hand. I jammed the goggles and the helmet into the greatcoat's pocket and trudged over to the office. The duty sergeant glanced up and, seeing the corporal's greatcoat returned to his lists and said, "What can I do for you corporal?"

"Er that would be Captain Harsker and I believe I am flying today."

The sergeant leapt to his feet and saluted, "Sorry sir, I should have recognised you. It was the jacket that threw me." He pointed to the end of the airfield where there was a Gunbus waiting. "It's over there sir. I'll go and get the duty officer."

He disappeared into the office and a young lieutenant came out. He shook my hand, "I say, what an honour, Captain Harsker, a real ace. I saw the photograph of you with the King. I wish I was over there flying with you chaps. The knights of the skies and all that; it sounds like jolly good fun."

The reality was somewhat different to the public's perception. It was not the lieutenant's fault. "I believe I am flying today?"

"Er yes sir, Lieutenant Carstairs is your pilot. He is joining your squadron." I looked around to see if I had missed the pilot. "Oh he is on his way from town I believe."

"Well I was rushed here and told that it was urgent, where is he?"

The lieutenant looked embarrassed and the sergeant found his paperwork more interesting. "Er Jamie, that is Lieutenant Carstairs, wanted to see a show in town last night so…"

"I see. Well I shall wait by the Gunbus. Sergeant, make sure he gets to the bus as soon as he arrives. I do not like hanging around for second lieutenants who just want a good time." I glared at the young lieutenant, "There is a war on, apparently!"

The sergeant grinned at the lieutenant's discomfort, "Righto sir. I'll chase him up the minute he comes through the gate."

I hefted my bag onto my shoulder and began to walk down to the aeroplane. I jammed the bag into the front cockpit and took the opportunity to examine the aeroplane. It was factory new. I hoped that the mechanics had serviced and run it. The men who built them did not have to fly them. I did not relish a swim in the icy Channel. I put my cap in the cockpit and donned my flying helmet. I walked around to the engine and saw, to my relief, that it was fitted with the Rolls Royce Eagle engine and not the older Gnome. I peered in to see if there were any modifications.

I heard a voice, "Well don't just stand there, get the damned thing started, I haven't got all day! The sergeant said you had been here for some time, come on airman; I have a war to win!"

I looked up and saw the pilot. He had seen me near the engine wearing the corporal's greatcoat and assumed I was a gunner. There was something about him I didn't like. He reminded me of Second Lieutenant Garrington-Jones who had been a very arrogant pilot. I decided to play along and find out what kind of pilot he was.

I held the propeller and shouted, "Contact!"

"Well let me get in the damned bus!" I smiled and waited. "Righto, Contact!"

I spun the propeller and was delighted when it caught first time. I raced to the front and whipped the chocks away. Annoyingly the young pilot was not waiting for me to climb in before moving. Luckily I had done this a few times and I quickly scrambled on board.

He was not a good pilot. He tried to lift up three times before he succeeded. Luckily the FE.2 did not need a great deal of grass and eventually we were in the air. We wobbled alarmingly as he, I assumed, tried to look at the map and fly the aeroplane. This did not bode well! He should have planned his route before we took off and not while we flew. Also, the first part of the flight was easy, you just followed the Thames. When we reached the sea it might be interesting.

Even when we were over the sea and could see the French coast in the distance, his flying did not improve. I turned in the cockpit and saw that he was eating while we were flying! It begged the question why but explained his lack of control. Gordy and Ted were more than capable of eating and flying in a straight line but my two fellow officers had hundreds of flying hours under their belts.

When we crossed the French coast I breathed a momentary sigh of relief and then my heart sank. He was heading due east and not south east. He was taking us over the German lines. I turned and pointed to the south east. I shouted, "The airfield is that way."

He looked down at his map and shouted back, "Are you sure?"

I nodded, "I am based there!" He glanced down at the map. Each second wasted was taking us closer to the front and to the German fighters who hunted there. I shouted urgently. "South east Lieutenant Carstairs!"

He banked the aeroplane and I had to grip the sides to hold on, "You had better be right, Corporal, or you will be on a charge!"

I sat in the cockpit feeling increasingly angry. It was bad enough to be yanked away from Beatrice without a goodbye but to have to suffer this unprofessional pilot was too much to bear. I would have words with this arrogant young pilot when we landed. I just wanted to get down in one piece. I began to look for familiar landmarks. I saw some of the old damage from early in the war, the burnt out buildings and shell holes. They began to increase as we neared the airfield. When we passed the church with the two towers I knew we were close. I risked turning again. "It is two miles ahead. Keep on this course." He nodded and I saw that he was gripping the stick with both hands. The shell holes had shown him that we were close to war now.

The windsock fluttered in the wind indicating to the young lieutenant the direction of the wind but he chose to ignore it. He brought us in too quickly and, as we bounced up a gust of wind caught us and almost upended us. When the front wheels hit the ground and stayed there I breathed a sigh of relief. He did not park the aeroplane, he abandoned it. I leapt from the aeroplane and took off my flying helmet and my greatcoat. I donned my hat and walked around to the rear. I heard retching and saw the lieutenant being violently sick. I saw the mechanics wandering over. I waited until he had finished and he began to turn.

He was pointing an accusing finger at me when he took in my uniform and my pips. The finger and the hand turned into a salute. "Sir!" I just stared at him and the mechanics behind him were grinning as they saluted. "Sorry sir if I had known it was an officer..."

"You would not have made such an ass of yourself? I find that hard to believe, Lieutenant Carstairs. I am certain that you would have made just as big a fool of yourself even had you known. When you have helped these chaps to put your aeroplane in the correct place I will meet you in the adjutant's office."

The mechanics all saluted as I strode by. "Good to have you back, Captain Harsker."

"Lovely photograph sir."

I smiled at the familiar faces. They were not the cause of my ire. "Thank you. Would one of you take my kitbag to my quarters when you have finished? No hurry."

It was good to be back but this time my return was tinged with sadness. I had left with unfinished business and I knew that I would need to write a letter as soon as time allowed. I noticed, now that we were down on the ground, that the squadron must be flying as there was just one aeroplane standing forlornly at the far end of the field. All the rest were gone.

Senior Flight Sergeant Lowery looked up and saluted as I entered. "Glad to see you back sir. Things have been a bit hectic here." Over his shoulder he shouted, "Captain Harsker's back sir."

Captain Marshall came out with a beaming smile on his face. He shook my hand and then said, as he saw that he had shaken it rather forcefully, "Sorry, how is the wound?"

"Don't worry Randolph it is fine. I think they just gave me another week's convalescence to be safe."

"Yes it was damned unfortunate to have to call you back but there is an offensive coming up and the Colonel needed you here." He glanced at Sergeant Lowery and said, "Come into the office. Get us a cup of tea eh flight?"

"Sar."

Once in his office I sat down and lit my pipe. It helped me to think. Randolph pointed to the photograph of me and the King cut from the newspaper. It was pinned to the wall. "Good photograph by the way. It did morale the world of good to see the King present you with the medal." He pointed to my uniform. "They look splendid."

I had been called back and I did not need pleasantries. I needed to know the reason. "What's up then?"

He stood and went to the map. "As you know Verdun was a bit of a disaster for the French. Well truth to tell it still is. They are still fighting down there. The powers that be have decided that we should attack in this sector," he pointed with his swagger stick, "the Somme, to relieve the pressure on our French allies. The offensive looks big. There are thousands of troops moving into position and we have to keep the German aeroplanes away from the front. We would like the attack to be a complete surprise."

"Have they any new aeroplanes yet or are they still relying on the Eindeckers?"

"A couple of Fokker biplanes, the D1 but we can handle them. It seems the DH2 and FE 2 are the only British aeroplanes which can handle them."

"Any casualties?" It was a question I hated to ask but it was an important one.

" One of the new boys from Gordy's flight caught it. We are expecting his replacement soon."

I gestured with my pipe, "The boy wonder is parking his aeroplane."

"From your tone I take it you are not impressed with our new recruit?"

"He was my ride over." I chuckled, "I was wearing a corporal's greatcoat I had borrowed and he assumed I was his gunner. I went along with it to gauge him."

"And?"

"And I am glad that he is in Gordy's flight. He was late to the airfield. He had been out drinking all night. He hadn't planned his route. He cannot fly in a straight line and he has no navigational skills whatsoever. He tried to fly to bloody Berlin! Apart from that he is perfect!"

Randolph laughed, "Well Gordy is the man to sort him out."

"How has he been lately?"

Gordy had had a slight drinking problem. It had affected him adversely and the colonel had asked me to have a word with him. It had tested our friendship but he had improved and we had become firmer friends as a result.

"He seems fine now. Every time he gets a letter from home he is a different man."

"Aren't we all?"

"Well if you pop along to see the colonel, he will be pleased to see you." He nodded to the window. "I think I see our new pilot coming. He does not look a happy camper!"

I went to the last office in the building and tapped on the door. "Come."

Colonel Pemberton-Smythe was old school. He ran the squadron by the rules but he was a good commanding officer. When his son had been gassed he had spent some time at home but, since his return, he had had renewed vigour. He beamed as I entered. "Good to see you, Bill." He held his hand out and I shook it. "Wound all healed?" I gave a shrug. "Yes, well we had no choice in the matter. We are one of the few squadrons which can

13

hold its own at the moment and we have a big push on the Somme. It begins July the first. It will make Loos look like a sideshow."

"But will it succeed?" Loos had been successful but we had only gained a few miles of land. The cost in human terms was appalling.

"Who is to say but we need to keep the skies clear of German aeroplanes. That is all that we can do; our job. We are doing better. Some chap shot down that Immelmann fellow; the ace the newspapers in Germany were going on about but they have another ace now, Boelke and he is downing our chaps at an alarming rate. We know we are winning because they are on the defensive. They intercept our chaps over No-Man's land or their own lines and they never risk our guns. With the winds from the west it means the pilots who crash behind enemy lines become prisoners, while the German downed air crew are rescued. It is a difficult situation. Still, as I said, our squadron only lost one pilot since you left."

"I know it is only a couple of weeks but it seems longer."

He gestured with his pipe at my ribbons. "What is the King like?"

"He seemed pleasant enough but he was only in the ward for fifteen minutes or so. Just enough time to give me my medal, shake my hand and have a photograph taken."

"Ah well one problem you may have now is that you are known as an ace. Some of the Germans seem to like hunting our better pilots. Seems damned unsporting to me but you should know this. You may find the enemy seeking you out once they know you are back in the air. I daresay they have intelligence chaps reading our newspapers just like we read theirs."

"I see." I shrugged. I can't see how it makes life harder. As far as I was concerned every German was trying to kill me anyway."

We both heard the throb of Rolls Royce engines. "Looks like the chaps are back. No rest for the wicked I am afraid, Bill. You will be up in the air tomorrow. It is the twenty seventh of June. The big show kicks off in a day or so. We need to drive the

Hun from the skies. Tomorrow we have to keep an umbrella of wings over our infantry."

I could see from the look on his face that he was thinking about his son and the men he had fought alongside. "We won't let our lads down. I saw enough of their injuries when I was in the hospital in Blighty. The nurses were like angels caring for them. We will become the angels in the skies and watch over them."

Chapter 2

I went to the field to watch my comrades land their aeroplanes. As I passed Captain Marshall's office I could hear Lieutenant Carstairs getting a ticking off from Randolph. Young pilots had to learn. This was neither a public school nor a university. The air war was far more brutal and unforgiving than the newspapers made out. If you read the reports we all had a lie in, flew for an hour or so, shot down a couple of German aeroplanes each and had a nice meal when we landed. The reality was that if we landed safely without losing an aeroplane we felt we had succeeded.

I noticed, as they landed, that a couple of the Gunbuses had suffered some damage. I counted just eight returning. It was selfish of me I know but I breathed a sigh of relief when I saw Johnny Holt and Freddie Carrick land safely. I recognised the rotund figure of Lumpy Hutton as he clambered from the front cockpit. My gunner was safe. I looked astern and saw my old gunner, now a pilot, Charlie Sharp. With the new pilot and me we had just ten aeroplanes and no spare air crew. I could see this offensive being more difficult than Loos had been.

I waited until the pilots and gunners had checked their buses. It would determine the work schedule. I was lucky, I had no doubt that Lumpy would have been keeping an eye on our bus and we would just need an hour or so to make sure everything was as it should be.

They strolled over together. I tapped out my pipe on the heel of my flying boots and put it in my pocket. When they saw me Lumpy, Freddie and Johnny ran over to me.

Flight Sergeant Hutton looked delighted to see me. "Great to see you sir!" He turned to Lieutenant Holt, "Looks like you'll need a new gunner Mr Holt."

Johnny shook his head, ruefully, "I know Lumpy. I hope you will give him some of your sage advice."

"Of course sir." Lumpy looked at me. "I'll get changed out of my flying gear and check the bus sir."

"Get something to eat first. There's no rush."

Freddy pointed to Major Leach, "We have been in the major's flight." He hesitated, "But we will be glad to be back with you sir."

"And I am glad that you are both in one piece."

"It has been a little hairy sir but, from what we hear, we are having an easier time of it than many others."

"You are right. I think we have got the best of the aeroplanes here. They might look a bit strange but they have the beating of the Fokker."

"Yes sir and they have a new one; a biplane. It is a little faster than us at lower altitude but it turns better than the Eindecker."

"You are seasoned pilots now boys. I am lucky to have you in my flight."

They went to the mess with their heads held high. Major Leach waved as he and Sergeant Sharp passed. "We'll catch you later, Bill. We have to do some paperwork now. Charlie here has just made Second Lieutenant."

"Well done Charlie!"

"Thank you sir."

Ted and Gordy had crept up behind me and both of them slapped me hard on the back, "Well done Captain, sir! A medal from the King!"

If the day ever came when my success started to give me an ego my two friends would soon puncture that particular balloon. "You know I could have you two on a charge of assaulting a senior officer."

Gordy rubbed his hands, "Lovely stuff. A week in my tent waiting for a court martial would be just the job."

"And now you are reminding me of my court martial, I don't know with friends like you two who needs enemies!"

17

They both put their arms around me and Ted said, "Seriously it is good to have you back. We lost two more new pilots today. It is getting serious."

"Well I was flown in this morning by your new pilot, Gordy, and I have to tell you that he did not impress me. Lieutenant Carstairs has many faults. You will have your work cut out with that one."

"Well at least he is a body. The major and I have just one other pilot in our flights. We knew it was bad news when they recalled you."

Ted who was, without doubt, the most pessimistic man I had ever known was also one of the kindest men and he asked, "How is the wound by the way?"

My hand went to the shoulder. "It is fine but I reckon it will ache in the damp and the doctor said I am now destined for arthritis and rheumatism."

We walked in silence. Gordy said, "They are old men's complaints. Personally I shall be quite happy to get those two." He looked meaningfully at our small stand of graves which were clustered at the far end of the field. "Because that means I will have survived the war."

I changed into overalls and I spent the afternoon with Lumpy. The ground crews had had a couple of weeks to replace all the damaged parts of our damaged bus and cannibalise some of the parts from crashed aeroplanes. The result was that she was as good as new. We had the advantage that the engine was now well run and Lumpy and I knew all her idiosyncrasies. We took her up for half an hour. She didn't need it but I did. I had barely managed to land the aeroplane after I had been wounded and I knew that it was like riding a horse after a fall. You had to get back in the saddle as soon as possible. When the propeller stopped turning I breathed a sigh of relief.

Lumpy waited for me next to the wing. "Well done sir. That couldn't have been easy."

"It wasn't."

He pointed to the medals. "They look good sir."

18

"I am sorry that you didn't get one. You deserved it for saving my life."

"I was mentioned in despatches and that will help me get promotion."

When I had been in the cavalry I had served with many soldiers like Lumpy. They were what made the British Army what it was, the best in the world. He was one of the reasons that I knew we would not lose this war. It might take time but we British, and especially the likes of Lumpy, were stubborn and dogged fighters. We just didn't give in. That evening I went into the mess feeling more optimistic than I had for some time.

That evening I made sure I was dressed for dinner. Sometimes we were a little casual but I had made myself smart for Beatrice for the past week or so and it had become a habit. It made me walk a little taller.

I noticed, as I sat next to my two best friends that Charlie was sitting with the other flight lieutenants. They were all talking in an animated fashion except Second Lieutenant Jamie Carstairs who did not look happy. Randolph had told me that the young man had not taken criticism well. He made excuses for all the things he had done wrong. I had warned Gordy. That was the worst kind of attitude. My view was that if you did something wrong you owned up to it, changed and then moved on.

I soon forgot him when the Colonel stood and spoke. "Gentlemen you may smoke." He turned to the sergeant, "Keep the doors closed eh Flight? We have things to talk about."

There was a buzz of anticipation in the mess. I knew that I had been privy to more information than many. It would be interesting to see their reactions.

"Gentlemen, tomorrow morning is a momentous day for the British Army. We will be beginning our first major offensive since Ypres and Loos. Tomorrow eleven divisions of British Infantry and five divisions of French will advance towards the Albert-Bapaume roads. Our job from dawn until the battle is over is to maintain air superiority. We must deny the Germans the skies over the Somme." He smiled and pointed his cigar at me. "As

Captain Harsker said, we must be the angels protecting the infantry. I like that metaphor. You need to see yourselves as the men who protect our brothers in arms on the ground. We will fly two patrols a day. Major Leach will lead his and Lieutenant Thomas' flights in the morning and Captain Harsker will take the other two flights out in the afternoon. In the second week, if the battle is not won we will reverse the timings. I know we are short of pilots and aeroplanes but I have been assured by General Henderson himself that we will be given everything that we need to wrest control of the skies from the Hun. We are expecting more pilots and aeroplanes when they become available."

There was much cheering and banging of glasses. Major Leach stood and his Scots' voice boomed out, "Shut up you noisy buggers!"

Silence fell in the smoky mess. "Now a word of warning; Intelligence has told us that the Germans have reorganized their squadrons into Jastas, or hunting packs. We know that they like to stay on their side of the lines but they will attack in numbers. They will have plenty of fuel and support. That will make life difficult for us. Our skills as pilots will make life impossible for them."

This time Major Leach gave up as the buzz of conversation drowned out anything else he might have said.

Gordy lit a cigarette, "Well, Bill, it looks like you are stuck with me."

"I am not worried about that. I know you and Ted better than almost any pilot in the squadron. I am happy to be given the afternoon flights, it means the Germans will have the sun in their eyes."

Ted groaned, "And that means we will have it in our eyes in the morning. Great!"

"We will need to watch the front line; from what the colonel told me they are trying to draw us over their lines."

Gordy nodded, "That's how they got my new lieutenant. It was his second flight over their lines and he followed one of them." He shook his head. "He never stood a chance. He forgot my orders not to go chasing them."

"Remember we will be outnumbered. We might have to use the circle."

"With just five aeroplanes? Will it work?"

"We will have to wait and see." I suddenly noticed the new officer out of the corner of my eye. He was sitting alone. "He is the joker in the pack. You will need to keep your eye on him."

"As he is the only one left in my flight that shouldn't be a problem." Poor Gordy did not seem to have much luck with his new pilots. He had lost three whilst I still had both Carrick and Holt. They were almost the most experienced pilots in the squadron now and yet a few weeks ago they had been nervous young men just out of flying school. You grew up quickly at the front; or you died.

As I left the mess I wasn't too sure about Gordy's assessment of Carstairs but I had other things on my mind. I had letters to write and the first one would be to Beatrice. Our walks in Hyde Parks and hurried conversations in the ward were not enough. I needed to tell her how I felt. We lived a precarious existence. I did not want to die before telling her how I felt. When I had written Beatrice's letter I would write home.

I was woken by the shelling at the start of the offensive. I heard later that it could be heard in Hampstead Heath. All I knew was that it woke me. I sat up with a start. The constant cracking told me it was not a summer storm. I stood and looked at my table; I saw that I had just written the one letter to Beatrice. I had fallen asleep after signing it. I felt guilty. I would write home when I returned from this afternoon's mission. I addressed the envelope and took it to Randolph's office. As Adjutant he got to censor all of the letters we sent. He was a gentleman and a fine chap but I was not sure I would want him reading my innermost thoughts. I had, however, no choice in the matter.

He was at his desk when I entered. "A letter home."

He took it and was about to put it with a pile of others when he saw the address and felt the weight. "A girl you met in Blighty?" I nodded. "His face softened. He was a married man as was the colonel. "I will be discreet, Bill. You can trust me."

"I know Randolph it's just… you know?"

He smiled, "I know. I had the same thing with Gordy when he met his young lady."

I felt better after that. I was not the only love struck young pilot. I knew, however, that all such thoughts had to be expunged from my mind or else I would be jeopardising not only my own life but also the lives of my pilots!

We watched Major Leach and the other flights as they took off. The five aeroplanes seemed a pitifully small number to me. Ominously, we heard the constant crump of artillery shells as the German lines were pounded. We would have a better idea of the success of the attack when we flew over in the afternoon.

I spent the morning with the pilots and gunners I would be leading. Carstairs apart, the pilots had all flown with me before and knew my ways. I was aware, however that we had two new gunners. They deserved to have the same information as their pilots. "Today we begin the first of many such patrols over the battlefield. We will fly in two columns. Lieutenant Hewitt will lead his flight and I will lead the other." I pointedly looked at Carstairs. "You, Lieutenant, will play follow my leader with Lieutenant Hewitt. Where ever he goes you follow. You do not deviate one inch from that position."

"What if I am attacked?"

Gordy snorted, "You have a gunner, Sonny Jim and a gun fore and aft. You stick to my tail! If I look around and find you are not there then you will be in for it my lad!"

The new officer looked a little petulant as he said, "What happens if you are shot down?"

Gordy coloured bright red, "Then you had better pray that I am dead or else I will come and kick your backside all the way from here to Blighty! You keep me safe!"

The others chuckled but I knew that it was a fair question. "In that event you follow Lieutenant Holt and my flight." I could see the new gunners looking at each other nervously. "If things get a little hot there we have a defensive formation we use. It all depends on us flying in a circle so 'follow my leader' is a good practice. Make sure you have plenty of ammunition and that you have checked your guns before you fly. It is a little hard at five thousand feet with a bunch of Huns attacking you. One last thing, avoid following them over their lines. All we need to do is to keep them from our side of the front. Any questions?"

They all shook their heads. I pointed to Lumpy and Sergeant Laithwaite. "These two sergeants are the most experienced in the squadron; you new lads have a chat to them." I was pleased when the two new gunners almost ran to speak to the old hands.

I began to fill my pipe as the others wandered off. Gordy joined me. "I see what you mean about Carstairs. I hope he doesn't turn out to be another Garrington-Jones."

"We will have to make sure he doesn't then. Perhaps a taste of combat will change him a little."

"Perhaps."

We stood by our Gunbuses waiting for the return of the rest of the squadron. The big guns had stopped and we could just hear the ripple of distant machine gun fire. It was many miles away and seemed, remote somehow. I knew that it would become much closer and soon. The sight of five aeroplanes heading for the field was a welcome one. They had all survived but we saw much damage on many of the aeroplanes. The Gunbus had an enormous wingspan and was a big target for the German gunners.

When they had all landed we went over to speak with Major Leach and Ted. "It is a little hot over there, Bill. The advance looks to be going well. They have taken the first set of German trenches." The Major shook his head, "The trouble is that brings us closer to the Hun. In the last half hour this morning they sent more flights against us. Luckily we were on our way back and they were reluctant to follow us." He gave me a meaningful look. "They will be ready this afternoon so take care."

"Yes, sir." I turned to Gordy. "Fly just above me, say two hundred feet and astern of Johnny."

"You have something in mind?"

"They had a few books in the hospital and one of them was about Trafalgar and how Nelson would sail across the line of the enemy. It meant the first ship took the most damage but then the whole of the fleet could bring their guns to bear. If I get the chance we shall do that. I will try to turn and take us across their front. They have a fixed machine gun. It would mean we could use both sets of our guns."

"I am not sure what you mean exactly but I can follow." He jerked his thumb at Carstairs. "I just hope he can."

We took off and headed east. The flashes in the sky ahead told us that the battle was still raging. I was pleased that the troops on the ground had made progress; perhaps the generals had got it right for once. I took us quite high to avoid any ground fire although I hoped that they would be too busy with our infantry to worry about us.

I heard Hutton's voice in my ears. It was not his usual one. It sounded sad and distant. "Sir, just look down there."

I glanced over the sides. We were just passing our trenches. I could see pairs of stretcher bearers north and south with wounded men. Worse than that was the sight of so many men lying huddled together; they were dead or dying. They were not near our trenches but a hundred and fifty paces from the German lines. There were bodies draped over barbed wire and huddles of bodies in craters. They might have made great gains but the cost had been horrendously high.

I heard Hutton again, this time talking to himself. "Poor buggers."

"Keep your eyes peeled, Lumpy. We'll be over their lines soon enough."

Even from this height we could see the flash of machine guns. A brown smudge of men was marching resolutely forward. It brought back memories of the Marne and Le Cateau. It took real courage to do what they were doing. I knew that their sergeants would keep their lines straight and exhort them to keep moving. Although it was the right command it must have been all too tempting to turn and run back to safety.

"Sir, biplanes!"

"Arm your Lewis." I cocked the one in front of me. The rear facing one was in reserve. I saw that they had been waiting for us and there was a squadron of them. They looked like the Fokker the colonel had told me about. They were slightly faster at lower altitude. I would keep the trump of higher altitude for emergencies. They were coming at us in a staggered V formation. The lead aeroplane was the lowest. I had to assume that these had the interrupter gear of the Eindecker and could fire through their propellers.

"Right Sergeant, I intend to turn north as soon as we come into contact. You keep firing at their line and I will fire over your head. I will gradually climb."

"Righto, sir."

One of the reasons we made such a good team was that I kept him informed about my movements. I had been a gunner and there was nothing worse than for a pilot to suddenly move without warning. You wasted ammunition and lost sight of your enemy. I did not have to tell Lumpy when to fire. He could judge that as well as I could. The leading German must have been eager for he fired too soon. A couple of holes appeared in the wings but no damage was done. Lumpy fired when we were a hundred feet from the first aeroplane. I added a burst from my gun and between us we hit the engine which began pouring smoke. Even as I turned I saw the leader of the Jasta plunging to his death.

Lumpy turned his fire on to the second aeroplane. As I turned a third Fokker came into view and I gave a short burst. My target had open sky before him and my bullets rattled against his engine. Smoke appeared and he peeled off to the east. He would make it back to his field but he was out of the fray.

There were no enemies before me and I glanced to the east. Lumpy was still firing short bursts. Our speed and the lack of a solid fuselage made it hard for them to cause much damage. I saw that the rest of the flight was also performing the same manoeuvre. I increased the rate of climb. It was risky as it slowed all five of us down but it gave a more stable firing platform and it would enable us to give them a shock when I turned.

"Sergeant, are we in line astern?"

"Just about sir."

"Good, I intend to swing to the east and dive on them. We will make a north south pass."

I heard a chuckle, "That'll come as a shock to them."

I waved my right arm out of the side of the cockpit. It was mainly for Gordy who was slightly above us. I knew that Freddie and Johnny would soon follow. I glanced to the side and saw that the German biplanes were trying to reorganise themselves. I think they expected us to head west as the Major had done.

"Righty, Lumpy, here we go."

I had noticed he had changed to a fresh magazine. The other one was not empty but a fresh one would enable him to fire for longer. I banked and began to dive towards the ragged line of Fokkers. The increased speed would protect us but we would not have long to make a hit. As the first one came into view I fired a short burst. He was not expecting that and he banked to avoid a collision. Sergeant Hutton was able to rake his undercarriage as he flew close by and the aeroplane plummeted to the earth.

The Fokker Jasta had lost its formation whilst my manoeuvre had given us a solid defence. The German pilots tried to attack us but every time they came close there would be a machine gun firing at them. We had not used our rear gun but I suspected that Carstairs and Holt had.

A pilot with a red painted propeller launched his biplane at us. Lumpy emptied his magazine and then began to change it. I had only fired half of my magazine. When the pilot saw Lumpy changing the drum he must have thought we were a sitting duck. I pulled the trigger when he was a hundred yards away and held it down. I saw his body judder as the .303 rounds pumped into him. He spiralled lazily down to No-Man's land where a pile of smoke marked his demise.

I checked the fuel gauge, we were running low. "Sergeant get on the rear gun, it's time to go home!"

"And I was just getting warmed up."

"Unless you have a can of go go juice with you I think we will head back."

"Righto." I turned and we headed west towards the airfield. I glanced below and saw the Tommies waving and, I assumed, cheering. They were too far away to hear. I gave them a cheery wave in return as did Lumpy. Had he not been on the rear gun then I would have given the wings a little waggle.

Sergeant Hutton put his face close to mine. He shouted, "You won't believe it sir but that new lad has carried on east."

"What!"

"Don't worry sir; Lieutenant Hewitt has gone after him."

I cursed the fool for disobeying orders. I would let Gordy chew him out. He was in his flight after all. I knew that I had been more than lucky with Holt and Carrick. I could have been given a Carstairs or a Garrington-Jones.

We were almost flying on fumes when we landed. I was the first one to climb out, Lumpy always found it a struggle. As usual I began to check the propeller and engine for damage. There appeared to be none. When Lumpy clambered down he checked the undercarriage and wings.

"We did all right there sir. Just a couple of holes in the wings. The lads'll soon have them fixed."

I nodded, "We are not due off until tomorrow afternoon anyway."

"Well sir that is another two aeroplanes for you and one and a half for me. By my reckoning you have eighteen hits now. That puts you up there with that Captain Ball and Major Hawker."

"Do you keep count for me then Lumpy?"

He said, seriously, "Of course I do. When this war is over and I get to the missus and the kids I want to be able to tell them how I flew with the leading British ace."

"Then you will have to change your pilot."

"I don't think so sir. You have an instinct. That shot today when the Hun came into your sights. He was there for a heartbeat and you nailed him. You can't teach that sir and I should know

27

I'm a gunner." Realisation seemed to dawn and he grinned from ear to ear, "And so were you. Perhaps I should become a pilot like you and Sharpie eh, sir?"

"There's nothing to stop you, Sergeant."

"Oh yes there is, sir. I'd be bloody useless." He looked over my shoulder. "I'll get these magazines exchanged, sir."

I looked around and saw why he had left so diplomatically. Gordy was marching Lieutenant Carstairs over to me. I could see that they were both red faced and words had already been exchanged.

They stopped in front of me. "Captain Harsker, you know what this idiot said to me in mitigation of his action in disobeying orders? '*If everyone else was too afraid to go after the Germans he wasn't. He was an Englishman!*'" I could see how annoyed Gordy was. "I have a mind to give him a damned good thrashing."

I knew that when we were sergeants that we had both dealt with inferiors who did something wrong, but it didn't work that way with officers. I held up my hand to calm Gordy down. When I spoke I did so quietly. "Lieutenant Carstairs that comment is a slur on every pilot in this squadron and Lieutenant Hewitt in particular. I think he is owed an apology."

I was giving him a chance. He nearly refused the opportunity. I saw his eyes widen and then he must have seen the look of determination on my face; I meant it.

His look did not match his words. "Sorry Lieutenant Hewitt, I was upset."

Gordy shook his head. "See if you can talk some sense into him, sir. A pathetic apology like that just makes me want to smack him one." He stormed off leaving a white faced Carstairs watching his back.

"He means it too you know. Lieutenant Hewitt is not only one of the best pilots in the squadron and a very good friend of mine he is also as tough as they come. If he knocked you down you would stay down."

"I am not afraid of him sir."

"Well you should be because he saved your life today and every time you go up your life will be in his hands."

"I can look after myself. I saw your aeroplane shoot down four Germans and I know I could do as well."

"I could not have done that on my own. I was relying on the other four Gunbuses behind me. You would have lasted five minutes and you would have killed not only yourself but a new gunner."

I could see that the thought had not occurred to him. "How do you know I would have been shot down sir?"

"If I went to your aeroplane now I would find enough fuel to fill a gill glass. We came back not because we were afraid but because we were running out of fuel. Did you keep an eye on the fuel?"

"Well sir, no sir I mean there is so much to do and…"

"And you are new so we make allowances for you. Lieutenant Hewitt and I do not give orders on a whim. They are based on combat in the air for the last year. Trust me, Jamie, we know what we are doing."

He nodded, "Sorry about yesterday sir. I behaved badly and I know it. I should have recognised you. I saw the picture in the Times."

"Don't worry about it. Now if you have checked your bus get some food."

I saw his jaw drop. He must have suddenly realised he had just walked away from his bus. He looked over his shoulder where the mechanics and his gunner were going over the wings to check for damage. He began to run. It was only a glimmer but there might be hope for the young man yet.

Chapter 3

I was heading to my quarters when Randolph waved me over. "Sorry about this Bill but the Colonel wants a little debrief to see how the day went."

I was tired and ready for a drink but I knew it made sense. "Righto. Be right there."

It was just three of us in the office, the Colonel, the Major and me. Major Leach pushed a glass of whisky over to me. "You'll like this it's a Laphroigh. Lovely little number from Islay itself. It's very peaty, mind. Here's mud in your eye!"

"Cheers!"

I sipped it and he was right. It was fiery and tasted very smoky. It was a lovely drink and went well with the tobacco I was smoking.

"How many did you get today, Bill?"

"Two Fokkers, colonel. Sergeant Hutton got a couple too."

Archie shook his head and laughed. "No wonder he couldna wait to get to your front cockpit! He only got one when he was flying with Jonny Holt and none with me! How do you do it?"

I shrugged, "I don't know."

The colonel leaned forward. "No Bill, we need to know how do you do it? It is obvious to us that you fly and lead a different way to us. You are unique. You came from the cavalry by the way of a front cockpit. Archie and I learned to fly back in Blighty. You do things your own way. Could you come up with some ideas?"

"I'll give it a go Colonel but I just do what seems right at the time. I don't think about it."

"Well while you are sipping Major Leach's malt give it some thought." He shouted, "Captain, come in here a moment please."

Randolph came in, "Yes sir?"

"Bill here is going to make a list of what he does. Write it down and we'll put it in some sort of order. Is that all right with you, Bill?"

"If you think it is any use then I will." That is how we came up with the rules we flew by. The Colonel called the list Captain Harsker's checklist but, thanks to Ted and Gordy, they became better known as Billy Boy's Bullshit! They meant well and they liked them but it didn't do to let anyone's ego get too big. The rules were simple and they were displayed in the Officers' Mess. Lumpy Hutton also procured one for the Sergeants' Mess too. He was proud of his pilot.

1. **Try to get the upper hand by being decisive.**
2. **When possible keep the sun behind you.**
3. **Use altitude to help you.**
4. **Fire at the closest range you can and only when the enemy is in your sights.**
5. **When possible try to attack from the rear.**
6. **When an enemy dives on you fly to meet it.**
7. **When you are over enemy lines never forget your way home.**

It took an hour but they all seemed pleased. "God Bill but they are so simple and yet they make sense." Archie downed his whisky and poured us all another one. I knew there had to be something else. "So, today, what did you do?"

"We went in line astern with Gordy at a slightly higher altitude. We went straight for the leader and then I flew across their line so that we could all bring our guns to bear. Then we climbed and used our height to dive on them. By that time we were low on fuel."

"Simple enough. Archie turned to the colonel, "Bill is right, Colonel, fuel is the issue. It takes forty five minutes to get over their lines and we only have three hours endurance. We only achieve that if we conserve fuel by flying straight and level. Every time we climb we are burning it at too great a rate. We can manage a bare thirty minutes of combat."

"I am afraid we can do little about that. The replacement pilots will be arriving by the end of the week and I have asked for spare pilots and aeroplanes. Perhaps that might make a difference."

I didn't think that it would, we would still only have the same time over the German lines, but we had little choice in the matter. We had seen the slaughter on the Somme. If our flights could alleviate the deaths and the suffering then we had to keep going. At least we had lost neither craft nor pilot and that had to be good.

That evening Lieutenant Carstairs was sitting alone. I wandered over to Johnny and Freddy. "Try and make the new chap welcome eh lads?"

"We did, sir, but he is a little stand offish."

"Try again. I think he just feels alone here. Be full of good humour and jolly him along. If it doesn't work after tonight then let him stew in his own juices."

They both grinned. They were fine fellows. "Of course sir." I saw them take their plates and sit on either side of him. I joined Ted and Gordy and by the time the mess orderly had brought my food I saw the three of them chatting away. When Charlie Sharp joined them I felt much happier. Charlie had become a pilot as I had through the front cockpit. He knew what was what.

Gordy sniffed, "I still think a clip round the ear would have done him more good."

"That works for the likes of us Gordy but these lads from privileged backgrounds who went to public school are different. They have been brought up in a strange way. Besides we need every pilot we can get."

"You are telling me, Bill. The Major and I were knocked about a bit this morning and the three lads we have with us aren't a patch on your two. That's why we scored a duck this morning and your lads shot down five." He gestured with his thumb at my medals. "No wonder King George gave you that lot." He poised with the fork half way to his mouth. "Here do you get money for having a medal?"

"I doubt it, Ted. If you do I haven't seen any yet."

"A pity that. And you are entitled to a wound stripe too. A couple of them I should think."

"It was just a scratch."

Gordy laughed, "Mary told me the truth. The doctors and nurses were worried for some days before you recovered." He suddenly nodded, as though he had remembered something. "That is right, Mary said that you and the pretty nurse appeared close." I am afraid I could not hide my blushes and he and Ted almost fell to the floor laughing at my acute embarrassment. "At last the man of iron shows a softer side!"

I looked at my plate, wishing that the ground would swallow me up. Ted said, "That is a good thing, Bill. We are happy."

Gordy nodded. "Mary liked her." He spread his arms. "What more can I say?"

"Thanks chaps. It has changed my perspective on life."

"Well I hope he doesn't take away that which makes you a killer, Bill. We all need that."

I shook my head, "I think today showed I can still kill."

Gordy nudged Ted in the ribs, "You should have seen us today. We went across the front of the Germans. They had no chance because they weren't expecting it. We had every gun on them! As we flew across the pilots could all fire and when we turned our gunners could carry on. With so many bullets you have to hit something. And of course their fixed gun means that have to be facing you to hit you."

"They will be expecting that tomorrow, Gordy. We will have to come up with something new."

"You'll manage it I am sure."

During the morning we checked and double checked our guns and our buses. Even Carstairs seemed a little more interested in the aeroplane which might save his life. Captain Marshall came over to speak with me. He looked serious. "A chum of mine from

H.Q. was just on the telephone to me. The casualties yesterday were bad. Twenty one thousand officers and men were killed yesterday. One Newfoundland Regiment lost seven hundred and ten men out of the eight hundred who went over the top. The Warwicks, my cousin is in that regiment, had five hundred and twenty men killed and over three hundred wounded out of eight hundred and thirty six who attacked. It is a bloodbath."

I was appalled. "Can we carry on sustaining so many casualties?"

He gave me a cynical look, "Do you think the generals actually go with their men, Bill? They will keep on keeping on, as they say. There is still an endless supply of volunteers. We have to do our bit but, my God, I feel sorry for the poor buggers down there."

"We'll do all that we can Randolph and I hope your cousin is safe."

As he walked away he said, "I will live with him being alive at the end of the month."

I decided not to tell the others. It had upset me and most of them were younger that I was. I wanted them confident when in the air. I just determined to do the best I could. My problems and worries were as nothing compared with the men in the trenches and crater holes.

It was with some relief that I counted five aeroplanes landing safely. I knew that Archie and Ted had taken on board my comments and flown differently. Their cheery smiles told me that all had gone well.

We took off and headed east. The new front line looked to be holding but Lumpy and I were still appalled by the men we saw being carried back on stretchers. "The poor sods are still suffering!"

"They are that."

The skies over the German lines were, amazingly, empty. We patrolled our sector and there was nothing. Sergeant Hutton had sharp eyes and he spied something. "Sir, there on the Bapaume road. German infantry and they are enfilading some Tommies!"

I saw what he meant in an instant. The grey uniformed Germans were behind the hedgerow and firing at the infantry who were advancing east. The Tommies would be massacred. Although we had been told not to venture behind the German lines this, technically, was the front line. "Let's get rid of them!" I waved my right arm down so that Freddie knew what I intended. Gordy would realise what I was doing as soon as I dived.

I cocked my Lewis while I banked. We would use both machine guns at the same time. This was not an aeroplane which was moving all over the place. We would be firing at static German infantry who would not be watching for us. I took us down to tree top height and we zoomed along the road. Hutton and I both opened fire at the same time and the first Germans were slaughtered. They were knocked down like nine pins in the village pub. Those further up the road dived for cover but Hutton followed them with the Lewis. He tracked them and kept firing until he ran out of bullets. There was no place to hide and the trees and hedges provided scant cover. We kept flying and firing until my ammunition ran out.

I began to climb as Hutton reloaded. I turned and saw the others beginning their climb after their strafing run. As I began to descend I took out my Luger. I would not have time to reload but I could send nine German bullets back to their home. At less than fifty feet we screamed along the death ridden lane. I held the gun over the side and fired every two seconds. I had no idea if I hit anything but the bullets were going in the right direction. I saw two metal eggs dropped over the side and knew that Lumpy had dropped grenades. I hoped the ones behind had realised otherwise they could be badly buffeted by the blast.

We climbed and I looked to the right. The British infantry had taken advantage of the diversion and were racing for their objective. We had eliminated the threat. I heard the two crumps as the grenades went off and I climbed. We circled until all the others were in line. I could not see any smoke or major damage from my flight and we headed back to the west. We had not shot down any

German aeroplanes but we had helped the infantry. I would take that trade off any day of the week.

When we landed Archie met me. "Did you see any German aeroplanes?"

"Not a one."

"Neither did we. Perhaps we frightened them yesterday."

"Perhaps or they could be regrouping. We shot up some German infantry."

"Good." He put his arm around my shoulder. "I think you are right about the Germans. They are methodical and they do plan well. I think they will try to jump us tomorrow."

I nodded, "I agree."

"Have your flight take off fifteen minutes after mine. We might be able to surprise them. If I get my flights to go into the circle when they attack, then you could launch an attack from height."

"You mean number three from my list."

"Exactly." He pointed to the mess, "Now the new boys have arrived. We have four more pilots and aeroplanes but I intend to leave them here. They will be a back up for the day after tomorrow. I don't want to risk the news boys if the Germans are planning something."

We had reached the office and we went into Randolph's den. "Any news on the attack today?"

His face clouded over, "It did not go well and we made no more progress."

Archie shrugged, "We keep on doing what we do. We are doing our bit. I know that a handful of biplanes is not much in comparison with the casualties on the ground but I am afraid, laddies, it is not a level playing field. By denying the enemy the airspace we stop him targeting his guns. We are saving lives."

"I'm sorry sir but I saw those stretchers coming back. We are not saving enough lives. We need to do more."

Archie shook his head sadly, "If you can see a way then I am all in favour. Until then we keep on plodding away."

I left the office feeling a little depressed. I had been happy to have successfully returned from the operation with no losses but now I wondered what we were doing here. After I had washed, shaved and changed I went to the mess. I needed a drink. Ted and Gordy were already in there. They had left one of the more comfortable seats for me.

Ted held a glass out to me. "I thought I would treat you." I cocked my head questioningly. "Gordy told me about the raid on the German foot sloggers. Well done. We just tootled up and down wasting fuel."

"I am not certain what good it does. The infantry had a bad day today and made little or no progress. Yesterday we shot down a handful of aeroplanes."

Ted smacked me on the knee. "And you call me a pessimist! And today you stopped a British battalion from being massacred." He shook his head, "You are a daft bugger! Do you want to win the war all by yourself?"

I took a swallow of the whisky. It was not a great one. This was no malt but it warmed as it slipped down. "I want to make a difference. Don't forget I have been on the ground and know what it is like. How those blokes do what they do is beyond me! I was on a horse and I could get out as quickly as I got in. They have to march slowly against machine guns and if they fail in their attack, suffer the same machine guns on the way back."

The three young pilots who had flown with us came in and asked the mess orderly for a beer each. Gordy raised his glass to them, "Well done today, lads! A good day's work and no losses."

Johnny shook his head, "I didn't enjoy today, sir. It didn't seem sporting."

I felt myself reddening. Perhaps it was the whisky. "Sporting?"

"Yes sir, we just machine gunned them and they had no chance to defend themselves."

"This is not a bloody game at Eton or Harrow or wherever the hell that you went! This is war and the Huns down there were slaughtering our boys. Was that sporting? The sooner you get those silly public school ideas out of your head the better. Our job is to shoot down as many German aeroplanes as we can, destroy as much war material and kill as many Germans as we can. The sooner we do that the sooner we win this war and get back to Blighty!"

Johnny looked close to tears, "Sorry sir. You are right."

I realised that I had ranted a little and so I smiled, "You are a good pilot, Johnny, and you will do well in this war but you need to be more ruthless and stop treating all this as some sort of game. This is not a cricket match against the Headmaster's eleven!"

He nodded and the three of them scurried off to a corner of the mess well away from our gaze. Ted shook his head, "I heard that most of those foot sloggers going over the top are led by blokes just like those three."

"And they are the ones to die first."

"You are missing the point, Bill. The men follow them because they think they are Toffs and know more that they do because they had a better education. That just isn't true." He lowered his voice, "Look at us three. We are all working lads and we were sergeants. Compare that with some of the chinless wonders they had leading us. Would we still be here if Major St.John Hamilton-Grant was still in command? We would all be dead."

"Archie and the Colonel are all right."

Ted nodded, "You are right, Gordy, but are either of them as good a leader as Bill here? No! Who came up with the rules about combat flying? Bill. Who has more kills than anyone else? Bill. And who would any pilot follow if they were given the choice? Bill." He downed his whisky; others were coming into the mess. "Bill was right to have a pop at Holt. They all need to wake up and realise this is no game."

There was a subdued atmosphere in the mess that night. Captain Marshall asked me why the men appeared so down. "The lads who flew with us today were unhappy about machine gunning those Huns." I shrugged, "I sent them away with a flea in their ear."

Randolph nodded. He took a message from his pocket. "I was going to pin this up on the notice board tomorrow but I think it might help them realise that what we do is important if I read it to them."

He stood and tapped his glass with his knife he looked at the colonel who nodded.

Captain Marshall held up the piece of paper. "I have here a note sent to me by Colonel McCartney of the 17th Liverpool Battalion. They are one of the Pals Battalions. I will pin it on the board tomorrow but it might be useful if you hear what the Colonel has to say." He began to read,

'I understand that your squadron flies the FE 2 Gunbus which patrols our sector. I would like to applaud the courage and the zeal of the five aeroplanes which, today, saved the lives of many of my boys. We were being attacked in the flank and it would have gone ill for us had those five aeroplanes not destroyed the attacking Germans. We took our objective and only lost a hundred and fifty men in the process. That low figure was due, in no small measure, to the heroism of your pilots. When we come off the line I will call in to thank them personally.

Colonel Patrick McCartney, Officer Commanding.'

There was silence as he finished. I was taking in the fact that a hundred and fifty men had been lost out of a thousand strong battalion and these were considered light losses! As Randolph sat down the colonel stood. "Well done, to those pilots who flew under Captain Harsker today. The adjutant is right. Our war is not just against the German aeroplanes but the German infantry too."

There was a buzz of noise. "They aren't far from your neck of the woods Bill."

I nodded. "A good stretch of the legs. That makes me feel better knowing that they were neighbours."

"Aye and as they are a Pals Battalion they would be lads like us."

We ate for a while in us each of thinking of home and men we knew who might have already died in the bloody fields of the Somme.

"We are following the Major tomorrow, Gordy. We will be leaving a short time after they do. We think the Germans might be planning some retaliation. We have knocked them about a little over the last couple of days. We will be going in high to watch for the enemy fighters and we need the advantage of height. If we attack then we will do it in two columns. You take Carstairs to the port of me. It will give us a fine cone of bullets. I think making the first kill in any combat makes the difference."

He nodded, "I have noticed they mark their aeroplanes differently from ours. I think you got their leader first, you know the one with the red propeller, the other day?"

"You are right. It might be worth noting who we are fighting; keep a sort of record. I know that they have some good pilots. When I was in the hospital the newspapers were full of the names of their better pilots. It seems the German newspapers like their heroes."

Before I turned in I went to find Sergeant Hutton. "Better warn the other gunners, sergeant, that we are flying earlier tomorrow. We will be supporting the Major."

"Righto, sir. I'll make sure they are up bright and early then to check the buses and the ammunition. Did I hear that the foot sloggers we saved today were the Pals?"

I shook my head, the news had got to the Sergeant's Mess almost instantly. Was there some kind of ESP going on? They seemed to know what we all said as soon as we said it. It was uncanny. I smiled at Sergeant Hutton who was rarely this serious. "Yes why?"

"The wife's cousin is in one of them." He shrugged, "It makes what we do more personal like. They are ordinary blokes like me. See you in the morning, sir." He strode off to his quarters. And I wondered how many other people I knew were in the trenches of the Somme.

Chapter 4

We sat on the grass by our buses as Major Leach led his five aeroplanes east. The next fifteen minutes seemed to drag. It seemed to me that I ought to address the men. I remembered Lord Burscough doing so before we went into action when I was in the Yeomanry. I stood, "Remember chaps, today you will have to think on your feet. We have no idea what might be waiting for us. Unless you get a signal from me or Lieutenant Hewitt, it is still *'follow my leader'*." They all nodded their understanding. "Let's get aboard and remember what we do in the air will save lives down below."

It took some time to reach our cruising altitude. At the height we flew all sound from below was drowned out by the mighty engine throbbing behind us. We could see far below the strike of shells and the flash of muzzles. What we were watching for was the rest of the squadron.

"There sir! A mile away to the south east."

I saw that Major Leach had formed a circle and there looked to be more than fourteen aeroplanes swooping down on them. The Germans, although they had ambushed the Major, were in for a shock. I turned so that we would approach them from the north east. The bright sun would be behind us and we would have the advantage of height. I watched as Gordy slowly drew level with me. Flying fifty feet from my wing he gave me thumbs up. We both knew what we were doing.

I saw that they were biplanes, mainly Fokkers, but there were a couple of different ones too. I noticed that all of them were flying faster than the FE 2s which were circling still. That was ominous. The Eindecker had never been able to out run us; it looked like these could.

"Ready Sergeant? I will fire my gun at the aeroplane ahead of us."

"Right sir. I'll see if there is a better target."

41

I took that as a compliment. The sergeant was assuming that I would hit the aeroplane I aimed at. We were going as fast as the Gunbus could fly when we swooped down on the Huns. I saw one aeroplane with a yellow tail plane. It made as good a target as any. The Germans were diving on the squadron's aeroplanes and then trying to swoop underneath. The gunners were all defending each other but I could see damage on many of the wings and Lieutenant Green's bus had a little trail of smoke coming from the engine.

I waited until we were just fifty feet from the yellow tail. I gave a short ranging burst as I slowly lifted the nose. Once I hit I gave a longer burst. The effect was to stitch a trail of bullets until they struck the pilot in the back and the aeroplane spiralled away. Lumpy fired as soon as I did and he hit the tail of the next aeroplane in line.

I banked to starboard and another biplane, not a Fokker this time, came into my sights. I saw it for barely a heartbeat but I pressed on the trigger and saw that I had struck it. Lumpy fired half a magazine and he must have hit the fuel tank for the aeroplane exploded in a fireball throwing us up into the air. I fought the Gunbus to regain control. Luckily it was a stable aeroplane and we soon began to fly straight and level.

The Major and his aeroplanes were still in their circle and heading west. It was a slow process but a safe one. We had the option of joining them but I felt we had the upper hand. I began to climb. I noticed Lumpy changing his magazine. He never wasted any time. He wanted to be ready to fire as soon as he saw a target. As soon as he had reloaded, and as I banked, a Fokker began to climb to attack us. Hutton leaned around as far as he could and fired a short burst. Sergeant Laithwaite's gun behind joined in and as I completed the turn the two sergeants had him in a cross fire. The bullets penetrated the engine and I watched as the propeller stopped and smoke began to pour from the engine. It started a deep death dive to the ground. The pilot had no chance.

"Well done, Sergeant."

"Up ahead sir."

I looked and saw two biplanes diving at me. I lifted the nose and aimed for the one on the left which would soon be in my sights when I completed my turn. "Lumpy, take the one on the right!"

The two aeroplanes began firing. They were trying to emulate the two sergeants and get me in crossfire. However I could fire at both of them. I heard the tear of canvas as their steel tipped shells ripped into my wings. I waited. Lumpy fired before I did. When I opened up a moment later the Fokker tried to bank away. It was a mistake. In this game of dare he had blinked first and paid the price. My bullets tore into his fuselage. I watched as he continued his dive towards his own lines. He would land but he was out of the combat. Lumpy had also damaged the second biplane and it too began to limp east.

I watched as Lumpy changed magazines and I dived after the two fleeing enemy aeroplanes. Our bullets had slowed them down and we began to catch them. I hoped that my two pilots were still watching my tail. I took a chance and fired at eighty feet. I saw my bullets rip into the tail of the German. The damage caused by Lumpy had already made it unstable and when the controls were shot away it just dived into the ground. I banked and began to climb. As I did so I heard the rattle of a Lewis gun and saw Johnny finish off the Fokker I had damaged.

As we turned west again I saw that Major Leach had left the circle and was leading three of his aeroplanes towards the fleeing Germans. I slowly pulled the stick around so that we, too, were heading east. We were a little behind the others but I watched as two more Germans were destroyed. When Major Leach turned west again we began to climb. We would make a protective umbrella high above the others.

I saw Lieutenant Green's bus on the ground. He and his gunner looked to have survived but I could not see on which side of the lines they had landed. The front line on the third day of the Somme was a very fluid affair. I could see that, as we flew over the infantry, the static lines of a few weeks ago had gone. It looked to me as though they were fighting in woods, across hedgerows and over roads. That would be close combat and ugly. We were lucky to be soaring so high above the ground. And then I thought of the German whose aeroplane's engine had been hit by Lumpy and me. His death would not have been any better.

As soon as we landed Sergeant Hutton and I checked over the aeroplane for damage. It looked to be the wings and the tail which had been hit. They would not take long to repair. The newer Gunbuses did not have the tripod wheel and I was grateful for that. The front wheel used to get shot up too easily for my liking making the landing very difficult.

I headed for the adjutant's office when I landed. I had a report to give and I was keen to hear what the Major had to say. He was just finishing when I entered. "Well done, laddie, although it was a wee bit dangerous to head over their lines."

It was as close to a dressing down as Archie could manage. "It was a calculated risk, sir, and we managed to down two more of the enemy. It's a war of attrition on the ground and in the air now."

"Aye, you are right and the Gunbus is a solid little plane. They can soak up a lot of damage."

"But those Fokkers are much faster than we are and they had another new one there too."

Randolph flourished a sheet of paper, "A Halberstadt. We just had a memo from headquarters."

"That means we have to fly smarter."

"It does indeed, Captain Harsker."

I pointed to the map. "The same sector tomorrow then?"

Captain Marshall shook his head. We have to send the four flights out on reconnaissance tomorrow. The brass want to know where the front line has reached and what the Germans are doing just behind their lines."

Archie sank into a chair. "Great, that means I'll have to take two virgins out tomorrow."

I walked over to the map. "Which is the patrol which will be the easiest?"

Randolph joined me, "Here, Bazentin le Petit and Mametz woods. They are the closest to the airfield."

"Then why don't you patrol that with the virgins. The rest of us all have the experienced pilots anyway."

"I don't like to do that Bill."

"I know but Freddie and Johnny are the most experienced pilots. They can handle the pressure."

"You are right and Randolph, see if you can find out what happened to Lieutenant Green eh?"

We were about to leave when the Colonel came in and angrily slammed a letter on the desk. "Those damned brass hats have not got the first idea about esprit de corps and pride in a regiment."

Archie and I had no idea what had upset him but Captain Marshall read the letter and said, "It seems that Number 11 Squadron is so successful that they are giving that number to a brand new squadron of Gunbuses. They are straight from Blighty. It is hoped that the cachet of the name will give the new pilots confidence. We are to become Number 41 Squadron."

I knew what the colonel meant. I had had real pride in my yeomanry regiment and it had had a history going back to the Napoleonic Wars. "Well sir, it isn't as though we use the number 11 a great deal. I think the men will get used to it." The colonel shook his head, "Besides we can create a name for ourselves. Why don't we use the name, 41 Squadron?" They all looked at me as though I was cracked. "The Germans identify their aeroplanes and leaders. We could paint the number 41 on the tail and then the flight number on the cockpit. That way the men won't worry about the number 11. We could even make the 4 and the 1 interlink to make them look distinctive; it could become a sort of squadron insignia."

I saw Randolph nod and when Archie spoke I knew I had his support. "I think it is a good idea. And the flight and number will help us when we are in the air. It is worth a try sir. It is just a lick of paint after all."

We waited expectantly, "Very well go ahead." He stuck his jaw out pugnaciously, "But those brass hats are still idiots!"

When we went to our aeroplanes the next day the identification numbers had been painted on and they made everyone stop and stare. We all had the flight and then a number. I was C 1.

Johnny liked his. "Number 2 is my favourite number! Excellent! That is a good luck sign!"

Everyone found something to like about the new numbers. Most of the sergeants and many of the officers were superstitious and they sought some connection with them. It appeared to work for there was a more optimistic and bantering atmosphere as the aeroplanes were checked before we took off.

The down side of giving the major the easiest sector was that we had the toughest. We had to fly to Warlencourt. It was an objective for the advance but it was thought unlikely that any British elements would have reached it. It was not far from Bapaume.

We flew as high as we could once we had all taken off. I wanted to avoid being observed if we had to cross the German lines. Three stray RFC aeroplanes would be a very tempting target for a squadron of German fighters. We saw the advancing British soldiers as they moved through freshly dug trenches to reinforce the new front line and I watched as the Major and his flight peeled off to patrol the small hamlet of Bazentin le Petit.

"Right Sergeant, let's go down and keep your eyes peeled." Warlencourt was just five miles from Bapaume and that was supposed to be the ultimate target for the advancing soldiers. Warlencourt was a tiny hamlet just across from a small stream. I dropped to five hundred feet when we reached the peaceful looking settlement. The peace was shattered by machine guns as the troops in the hamlet and the nearby woods opened fire on us. I banked around.

"Lumpy, give them a burst with your Lewis."

"Waste of bullets sir. Let's try this instead." As we flew over the woods and the gunfire increased he dropped two grenades.

"These have longer fuses, sir. The armourer sorted them out for me. Said as how he was afraid I would blow the arses of the other lads!"

There were two large cracks from below and a pall of smoke began to rise. The gunfire stopped! "Well done. Let's see if we can find the nearest British forces to here."

As we flew down the Albert to Bapuame road we were fired on as we flew over Le Sars, another small hamlet. So far we had only seen Germans. It was at Pozières that we saw the first signs of brown uniforms. There was a hedge and tree lined road and the Germans had blocked the road. We saw advancing soldiers wearing brown. They were moving both down the road and across the fields.

"Any more Mills Bombs?"

"Sorry sir."

"Right then we will have to give them a hand with the Lewis guns." I waved my arm to signal the other two that we were attacking. I hoped my words had sunk in with them. I banked north east and then swung around to come on a north to south line. We would fly along the German defences and machine gun them. I took us as low as I dared and I fired along the line of grey. Hutton sprayed the soldiers to the right. I heard one crack as we zoomed at tree top height and then we had run out of ammunition and I began to climb to enable us to change magazines safely. As I banked to starboard I was relieved to see the other two safely with me but my joy was short lived as Hutton shouted, "Six Fokkers, to the east!"

Had we had altitude I might have been tempted to scrap it out with them but they would have superior speed, numbers and fuel. It was time to run. I headed due west. There was little point in climbing; we would go slower and waste fuel.

"Get on the rear Lewis, Lumpy."

As his cheery face loomed into view I felt happier. He could keep an eye on the two young pilots and the enemy. Of course he had to shout but I could almost lip read now. I kept watching the landmarks below me. I knew that if we could reach

47

the British lines then they might be discouraged from following us but we had some way to go before we reached the secured front.

"They are diving sir! Keep her steady if you can."

Our one advantage was that the German pilot could only fire in the direction of his aeroplane. Our three gunners could converge the fire of their machine guns and follow a moving target. I was not worried when I heard the chatter of Carrick's Lewis; he was the rear Gunbus. The other two would be waiting until the first German came a little closer. The German had one bite of the cherry; we had three. The second Lewis opened up. I heard the double chatter and I saw Hutton cheer. "Got you, you bugger!" He held up one finger to confirm a kill. Then he began to fire. I could feel the sudden heat from the gun. He did it in controlled bursts. I could picture what he was doing. He would fire and the German would shift his aeroplane allowing Hutton to fire again. It conserved ammunition and ensured more hits. Then he held up a second finger. I glanced to the side and saw the British soldiers firing their rifles. We were over our lines. Suddenly, as Hutton stopped firing to change a magazine he held up three fingers. He shouted, "The foot sloggers got the last one!"

I felt happy about that. It would do the morale of the poor infantry the world of good to see such a tangible trophy tumble to the ground. The landing was bumpier than I had expected and as we rolled to a halt the whole aeroplane lurched alarmingly to the right and the tip of the wing crumpled.

I leapt out to see what the damage was. As soon as I saw the branches and leaves stuck in the remains of the wheel I knew what had happened. We had hit the trees when we had been machine gunning the Germans. We were the last flight to land and a crowd gathered around. I could hear Freddie and Johnny regaling them with the story of our attack.

Ted came up to me shaking his head, "You want to watch out, you know some Germans still have the Pickelhaube. That would make a right mess of your undercarriage."

Everyone laughed at our expense. The chief mechanic, Senior Flight Sergeant Mackay shook his head. "You'll no be flying tomorrow sir. That'll take some repairing, all right." We had such huge wings that damage to the ends required much repairing.

It was a high price to pay for alleviating the suffering of those men who were attacking but it was worth it. While I was reporting to Captain Marshall and telling Randolph what we had seen the colonel joined us. "So you won't be flying tomorrow then?"

"No sir. A bit of bad luck that."

He nodded and said, "Perhaps not. I thought we could pop up to the front and see that Colonel of the Liverpool Battalion. Headquarters suggested it might be useful for us to see what it was like on the ground. The experience might inform our reconnaissance a little better."

"Good idea sir, could I bring Hutton?"

"Of course. In fact he can drive eh? It will give us a chance to chat."

Chapter 5

It felt strange to be watching the rest of the squadron take off the next day for a patrol to the front. Hutton was delighted to be driving the colonel's motor car. Before we left Captain Marshall stopped us. "Apparently you need to take your gas masks and steel helmets."

The colonel looked perplexed, "But we don't use them!"

Randolph grinned, "I know. I got some from Quarter Master Doyle." Sergeant Lowery put them in the front seat next to Lumpy.

He winked at him, "You are in charge of these Flight Sergeant Hutton I do not want you coming back with two officers who are gassed or have head injuries. Right?"

"Right, Flight. I'll look after them."

I was not certain of the protocol and so I had my Sam Brown with my service revolver. Lumpy had his Lee Enfield and Mills Bombs. As we drove through an ever more depressing scene of destruction and wounded men in ambulances the colonel began to talk. Ramble would be a better word to describe it because he did not stay on one topic for long.

"If it wasn't for the war you know, Bill, I would be back in Surrey tending my garden and looking after my son." He waved a hand around. "I am too old for all of this. I did my fighting in a different time. Travelled all over the world: India, Afghanistan, West Indies and Sudan. My wife and I travelled the world. Most of it was peace time work. Even when we fought, well, we thought the South African wars were bad but they were a picnic compared with this. This is not a proper war. This is a slaughter." He sounded depressed.

We had been stopped by a military policeman at a bottleneck to allow a field ambulance to pass us. The colonel pointed out of the window at a piece of barbed wire some fifty yards away. There we saw a hand hanging from the wire. "Shocking."

There was nothing for me to say and I sat back in the seat. Like the colonel it depressed me too.

"I hear you have a young lady now? A nurse in London?"

"Er yes sir, Beatrice."

"Are you keen on her?"

"Well, er , yes sir."

"Then do something about it!" There was real passion in his voice." You never know what is around the corner. Life is too damned short! I hate it when you young lads go out each day and I have no idea how many will be coming back. I get more grey hairs every day. You know that Green and his gunner are prisoners of war?"

"No sir, I didn't, but I suppose that is better than lying dead in some foreign field."

"Hmn, I suppose you are right. At least they will survive the war."

He was silent as he stared out of the window. It was sad to see an old warhorse like the colonel so depressed. His words had, however, made me wonder about my life. What would I do when… if, this war ever ended? Would I be like the colonel and keep the uniform? Would I drag Beatrice all over the world? I needed to think about life after the war.

A huge military policeman came over. "This is as far as you go sir. Who are you looking for?"

"The 17th Liverpool Battalion."

He pointed to the north. "They have just been brought off the line. You'll find them in the reserve trenches up there." He leaned in to Hutton and pointed, "Driver, put the car on that patch of land over there. We need to keep the road free for ambulances." He nodded as one drove away from the front. "The Aussies are getting it today."

As Hutton parked the car he walked over with us. The colonel asked, "Where did you say, Sergeant?"

He pointed, "Go down Buckingham Palace Road until you come to Lime Street and ask there." He smiled, "And wear your tin

51

lids too, sirs. The Huns like to lob the odd shell or two over. They are proper sneaky buggers."

We saw the crudely made sign which even had a crown drawn on it and we entered the trench. At this stage of the year it was relatively dry but later they would have duck boards down and the bottoms would become a muddy morass of slippery slime. It was wide enough for two lines of men to pass each other. We saw firing steps but there were no sentries. This had been the front line before the advance and was a measure of the gains that we had made. We met men coming the other way and I couldn't help noticing how dirty they all looked. It made me more aware of our smart, clean uniforms. We received a cursory salute but the look was one of disdain. They thought we were staff. They didn't know that we were warriors just like them.

Hutton said, "Here we are sir, Lime Street." He gave me a quizzical look.

"It is a street in Liverpool. It is the name of the railway station." Enlightenment dawned and he nodded.

We walked down and noticed what looked like caves carved out of the soil along the sides. There was a ragged piece of canvas for a door on each one and we could hear men within. It did not seem prudent to invade their privacy and so we walked on until we saw two soldiers having a cigarette and lounging against the trench wall. They stood to attention.

"Any idea where the 17th are, we are looking for Colonel McCartney?"

One of them took his cigarette out of his mouth and pointed to a trench thirty yards away. His voice marked him as a Liverpudlian as soon as he began to speak, "He's down there sir." He suddenly seemed to see the uniform. He pointed to our flying boots. "Are you the lads who flew those funny looking aeroplanes the other day?"

The colonel nodded, "These two were."

He stuck his head inside the canvas door. "Hey lads it's some of them fly boys we saw the other day!"

Eight men poured out of the hole. They all saluted and stared at the caps. The corporal said, "Can we thank you lads? We were up the creek without a paddle and no mistake."

"You're welcome. It was the least we could do."

"Are you from near Liverpool sir?"

"Burscough, how can you tell?"

"It sounds like home." He pointed to the medals on my uniform. "And, lads, this is a real hero. Look he has the Military Cross."

Some more men came out of nearby trenches and one shouted, "Lumpy? Is that you?"

"It is our kid." He shook the soldier's hand. "It's the wife's cousin sir. Mind if I chat?"

"Go ahead. We'll pick you up when we have finished here."

Just then I saw a group of officers coming down the trench. "Ten, shun!"

"What's going on here, Marsden?" He saw the colonel and smiled, "I am guessing you must be Colonel Pemberton-Smythe."

"Yes Colonel. Headquarters thought it might be useful for us to see the land from the ground, so to speak."

Colonel McCartney shook his head. "Well I can't believe it. They actually have someone at HQ who has an idea! Come on then I'll give you the tour."

I turned to the soldiers we had spoken to. "Good luck lads."

"And to you sir. You have plenty of guts to go up in one of those things!"

As we followed the colonel I thought the same about him. It took plenty of guts to do what they did.

"This is a reserve trench. We will rest here for three days and then go back up the line. I'll take you to the front line so that you can see what it is like." He seemed to see me for the first time. "Were you one of the lads who saved our bacon the other day?"

I nodded, "This is Sergeant Hutton and I am Captain Harsker, sir. We were one of the aeroplanes."

He shook me by the hand. "You were a Godsend. When the Hun opened up we all said our prayers. The Chaplain said God had sent his angels to watch over us."

"We were glad to be of help."

"Do you mind if I am honest with you?"

"Please."

"Until that day we thought you lads were all a bunch of toffs swanning around in the skies. That's all we ever saw of you. High in the sky like little flies having your little fights with the Germans. Now we know that you are on our side. So thank you. Let's get started."

As we followed the Colonel and his Sergeant Major I felt shocked. I could understand how the infantry felt but it wasn't true. We would have to do something about that image when we returned.

It was like a maze. I had no idea how they knew where we were going. We saw increasing evidence of the proximity of the enemy. There were sentries at every junction and they all looked at us warily. At one point the Sergeant Major shouted, "Shell!" He unceremoniously pushed the colonel and me into the side of the trench. There was an enormous crack and crump and after we were hit by a wall of air we were showered in dirt and debris. My ears rang.

The Sergeant Major grinned, "Sorry about that sirs but the Huns like to try to catch us out and fire blind. Of course if the buggers have their spotter aeroplanes up then we have to send for stretcher bearers."

After another twenty minutes we stopped. "This is almost as far as we go. There are Germans two hundred yards away." The colonel pointed to a firing step. "If you stand on there you can see the German lines through the periscope."

I stood on the firing step and peered through the crudely made periscope. I could see barbed wire and then sandbags. That had to be the German lines. I had just stepped down when I heard the sound of Rolls Royce engines. I looked up. "There, it's our squadron."

Colonel McCartney said, "How do you know?"

"The 41 on the tail."

We watched as they dived down to an unseen target. The rattle of the Lewis was the only evidence of action for they were hidden by the sandbags and the trenches. It was infuriating to hear and not to see. After ten minutes or so they hummed into view again.

Colonel McCartney said, "That is the reason we had the opinion of you we did before. They will be back home in a dry billet in half an hour. Our lads live like this." He lifted a canvas door and we peered in to a hole in the ground lit by a candle and with beds cut into the earth walls. "We manage three days and then back to the reserve trenches."

"Look sir! Fokkers!"

I looked to where Hutton pointed. Twelve Fokkers had appeared out of the sky and were diving on the rear of the Gunbuses. I recognised Freddie Carrick's aeroplane at the rear and saw his gunner standing and firing. You could see, from the ground, just how much faster the Fokkers were. The advantage the squadron had was that they were low and it was hard to get in the blind spot but poor Freddie was being targeted by Fokker after Fokker. I saw him suddenly climb. It took the Germans by surprise and allowed Sergeant Laithwaite to bring his gun to bear.

I suddenly saw that you could have three Gunbuses stacked one above the other and they would be able to protect one another. I thought they had escaped unscathed when smoke began to pour from the engines of both of my flight's aeroplanes. Thankfully the ground fire from the British trenches drove the Germans back but I wondered if the two young pilots would make it back in one piece.

Colonel McCartney was an astute man, "I take it you gentlemen will want to get back to your squadron to see how your lads are."

Colonel Pemberton-Smythe said, "Thank you colonel we are a little concerned. Those two aeroplanes are from Captain Harsker's flight."

I nodded, "If my bus wasn't damaged then I would have been up there with them."

"I understand. We aren't that different are we? I won't leave the field until I know all my lads have left." He shook his head, "Its daft I know but they become like family."

"I think, Colonel McCartney, that they are all our family, at least until this nightmare is over!"

"Amen to that Captain Harsker."

All three of us were silent as we drove back to the airfield. It had been a lesson to us all. I could not imagine sleeping in a hole in the ground. We had suffered one shell but to have to endure shelling at night whilst sleeping underground would be the worst kind of nightmare. It made me think of Bert, tunnelling underground. I did not know if he was in this sector but I hoped not.

When we reached the airfield we saw that Freddie and Johnny had both landed successfully but they had been badly shot up. Flight Sergeant McKay stood looking at them. "We no sooner get your bus sorted out than these two need major repairs. These will take a couple of days to repair Captain Harsker. Sorry, sir."

"It can't be helped."

In the adjutant's office I found Archie and Randolph in deep discussion. "There is a pattern to all this." Archie looked up as I entered, "I was just saying there is method in this madness. We tootled up and down for our patrol without seeing anything. We went down to attack a column of Boche coming up the road and they jumped us. Your lads did well, Bill. They kept the Fokkers off our tail."

The colonel had come in during the conversation. "We know, we had a grandstand view from the trenches."

"You were there?"

"Yes and it was a valuable lesson. You might have been attacked, Archie, but it was worth it to help those poor boys in the trenches. They are having it hard. If you had seen the conditions in which they were living it would have broken your heart."

I nodded, "And Sergeant Hutton was talking to his wife's cousin. The ordinary soldiers are really grateful when we shoot up the Germans. It is making a difference."

Randolph held up an order, "And this came in today. We are escorting bombers tomorrow. They are the BE 2s I am afraid."

I groaned, "Why couldn't they be the Martinsyde? They are even faster than we are."

"I know but I think it is a measure of the problems they are finding in the trenches. The artillery simply hasn't the range to hurt them when they are bringing up troops. They have to resort to using Fokker Fodder now. We have to stop their reinforcements reaching the front."

Colonel Pemberton-Smythe put his hand on my shoulder. "Remember Colonel McCartney and his lads. They have to walk across a field of death. At least we are going a little faster than that."

"You are right sir, sorry. As my lads are grounded will I just lead Gordy's flight?"

"You can take up the two new pilots. It will be a baptism of fire but you look after your pilots." I looked at Archie quizzically. He smiled, "Holt and Carrick both grumbled that they would have had no trouble if you had been there, Bill. You are their rabbit's foot."

"Righto sir. I had better see them now and run them through a few things."

I found Lieutenants Swan and Dunston playing darts in the mess. They snapped to attention when I entered. I suddenly felt old for they both looked like schoolboys. We had been so busy lately that I had not even introduced myself to them.

"I'm Captain Harsker and tomorrow you will be flying with me while we escort some bombers."

They seemed not to hear the second part. "I am Roger Swan sir and it is an honour to serve with you."

I saw both of them looking at my medals. I would have to begin wearing overalls to hide them. I found this hero worship a little uncomfortable. "Yes well it will be a difficult operation

57

tomorrow as the BE 2 we will be escorting struggles to fly at more the seventy miles per hour. The Germans have all the time in the world to shoot them down. How many hours have you had in the Gunbus?"

Lieutenant Dunston said, eagerly, "I have ten hours!"

I was impressed, "In a Gunbus?"

He looked crestfallen. "Well no sir, that was in a trainer, an Avro. We both have an hour in a Gunbus."

I tried to keep the fear from my voice. "And have you flown with a gunner in the front before now?"

"Er no, sir. Does it make a difference?"

"Come with me, both of you. Get your flying helmets." It was the middle of the afternoon and no one was flying. I saw Sergeant McKay working on Holt's aeroplane. "Is my bus finished?"

"All fuelled and ready to go."

"Good I'm taking her up." I looked at the two of them. "Right, Swan, get up front in the gunner's cockpit." Once he was there I showed him how to rig our rudimentary speaking tube. "Dunston, when I am aboard, give the propeller a spin."

He looked appalled. "Don't the mechanics do that sir?"

I saw Sergeant McKay suppress a chuckle. "Just do it and stand back when you have done so. One armed pilots aren't much use out here."

I climbed aboard and put on my helmet. "Contact!"

"Contact!"

The freshly serviced engine roared into life and I set her down the grassy runway. As soon as I got high enough I said. "I am going to loop, hang on!"

I did a loop and I noticed that he gripped the cockpit for grim death. When we flew straight and level I heard him give a nervous laugh. "That was fun sir!"

"Good then you will love this. Take off the speaking tube and turn around. I want you to imagine firing the rear Lewis gun."

"You are joking sir!"

"I never joke about flying. Just do it." It was almost comical how long it took him. I could see that he was totally petrified. He gripped the gun as though his life depended on it. I banked a little and he screamed. I shouted, "Shall we try a loop?"

"No sir, please!!!"

"Right, sit down and we will land."

As soon as we landed he jumped out and vomited. "Right Dunston; get aboard. Swan when you have finished examining your lunch, turn the propeller!"

To be fair to Lieutenant Dunston he did not throw up but he looked a little green when we landed. As we walked back to the mess, much to the amusement of the ground crew, I said, "Now then what did you learn up there?"

"That I never want to be a gunner sir! They must be mad."

"Oh we are."

"You were a gunner, sir?"

"Oh yes. I was a sergeant gunner and I was on the rear Lewis when a young officer like you two decided to do a loop!"

Lieutenant Swan looked incredulous, "How did you survive sir?"

"I hung on to the Lewis. Look after your gunner. When he is on the rear Lewis fly as straight as you can. Tell him when you are going to do violent manoeuvres."

"Thank you sir."

"What for? This is just your first lesson. We have to teach you how to change a magazine in the air and how to fly standing up and firing the rear Lewis."

"Really?"

"Really, Lieutenant Dunston." We had reached the mess. I sat them down at a table. "Now tomorrow I want you, Lieutenant Swan, to stick to my tail like glue. You will be fifty feet behind me. I don't want you shredding your gunner on my propeller. Dunston, you will be the same distance behind Swan. We play follow my leader. What I do, you do. Your gunner can fire at any target he sees but you can't fire if I am in the way so don't even think about it. When we come back put both your gunners on the rear Lewis and watch for the Hun in the sun. You will have Lieutenant Hewitt behind you and he was a gunner too. You should be in safe hands. If you survive tomorrow we will work on your other skills."

"Right sir, and thank you." They both looked shaken as they went to their quarters.

Charlie Sharp had been listening and he came over, "A harsh lesson for them, Captain Harsker."

"I know Charlie but better here than with a Fokker trying to kill you."

He nodded, "Yes sir. There is no forgiveness in the skies."

Holt and Carrick spent some time, over dinner, talking to the two young pilots. I saw their hands demonstrating manoeuvres. It would have been better had my two wing men been flying but we had no time for such luxuries.

The four flight commanders went over the maps for the raid. We were heading for the area east of Warlencourt so I knew the location. We were bombing a crossroads. The Germans had stopped bringing trains close to the front. We had wrecked the rails too many times for that. The problem we would have would be that we would be five miles behind enemy lines and the German squadrons would be over us like flies around a dunghill.

"Right Bill, I will fly to the south with Ted and his flight. You take the north. I think five hundred feet above the bombers should give us an edge."

"Yes sir but it is when we try to leave that we will have a problem. They are faster than we are and much faster than the Fokker fodder we will be escorting." Ted had become more confident in the last few months and now voiced his opinion.

"I know."

"Why don't we take them on and let the BE's get a lead?" Ted nodded towards Bill's Bullshit on the wall. We have double the firepower of the Fokker and it eliminates their speed advantage. We fly into them and then head home. The technique Holt and Carrick used might work. Stack the buses one above the other and make it hard for the Germans to get behind us."

"That would normally work, Ted, but I have two Beer Boys with me. They have an hour in a Gunbus I am not sure using such a manoeuvre would be useful for them."

He shrugged and Archie said, "It's the only way, Bill. Have a word with them and explain."

I found the two nervous pilots. I was delighted that they were talking with their gunners. That was progress in itself.

"Listen boys, if we have to attack the Germans and then retreat I want us to stack one above the other to give mutual self protection. I will fly close to the ground; Lieutenant Swan fifty feet above me and Lieutenant Dunston fifty feet above him. The idea is to stop the Germans from getting below me. I will keep as low as I can." I smiled to make it easier, "I know this is a lot to take in on your first day but believe me it is important. There are infantry being slaughtered on the ground. Today we can save some lives."

They both nodded resolutely. It was all that I could ask.

Chapter 6

We circled over our front lines as we awaited the arrival of our bombers. We saw them lumbering along. It took real courage to fly the BE2. They were a stable platform and that was about all that you could say in their favour. The bomb load was not a great deal better than ours. There had been an attempt to make them into a single seat fighter- it had failed.

I ascended slowly to a position north of the bombers. They too began to climb to avoid the inevitable ground fire. "Lumpy, keep checking that the two young lads are keeping station."

He leaned out and looked back. "They are sir. Their gunners are nervous too. They'll be better once they fire on their first Hun and realise they aren't that good." I smiled at Sergeant Hutton's lack of modesty. The Germans were good. Other squadrons were not having the success that we were. It was just that we had a good bus and a good combination of pilots and gunners.

Shells began to burst around us. We had learned not to worry too much about them. The odds on a hit or damage were slim. You risked more danger by jinking around the sky to avoid them. With our huge wingspan we were in great danger of crashing into another Gunbus if we did that. "Better arm your weapon."

"Right sir!"

I glanced down and saw the front line we had visited yesterday. I could see that the Australians had attacked and the stretcher bearers were bringing back the wounded already. Another two days and the Scousers would be back on the line. The nerves would be getting to them already. They would be viewing their comrades and wondering who would buy it this time. We would have to make sure that we did our job and, perhaps, fewer would die.

Having flown the area before I knew where Warlencourt was. "Keep your eyes peeled we are almost there."

I began to climb a little. When the bombers dropped their bombs they would begin to ascend ready to head west. I wanted to give them plenty of room. I saw them begin their bombing run. There was a great deal of ground fire. They only had a rear facing gun and had to endure the gauntlet of steel which was thrown at them. They were brave men. We should have gone in with them and machine gunned the defenders. Hindsight was always perfect!

The bombers were accurate, far more so than the artillery would have been even had we been spotting for them. However there was a cost. One of the bombers was hit and plunged to the ground. It had not dropped its bombs and it must have hit a vehicle loaded with fuel. There was an enormous fireball. I saw two more bombers damaged by shrapnel. The eleven survivors turned to head west. Even as they turned one of them began pouring smoke from its engine and I saw it crash land in a field. Archie and his flight zoomed down to check on the crew. We had heard that some air crews were shot out of hand by angry Germans but it was with some relief that we saw them taken prisoner.

We were to wait until the bombers had crossed the front line before we were to leave but that went by the board as two Jastas buzzed towards us like angry wasps. They must have scrambled and taken off in a hurry for there was none of the usual German efficiency. They were not in any particular order or height. That suited us.

"Right Lumpy, let us go amongst them!"

As we had planned Gordy and his two aeroplanes were on my port side. I hoped that our two aeroplanes could plough a lane through the Germans and send them away from the bombers in disarray. We had the height advantage and we began to dive. It gave us a greater speed and meant that when we turned we might be slightly faster for a few hundred yards. That could make all the difference.

The German aeroplanes opened fire too soon. The bullets zipped around us but were merely an annoyance. I waited until Lumpy had opened fire before I put my fingers on the trigger. His bullets smacked into the engine block of the first Fokker which did give the pilot some protection. How they saw over it I do not know. I banked slightly to the right which allowed Lumpy to stitch a line of bullets along from the engine. He must have hit the pilot for he savagely pulled the nose up and away. He barely missed colliding with a second Fokker. The second German had to swerve and Gordy could not miss. He and his gunner opened up and the aeroplane plunged to the earth. We now had a gap in their lines and we flew on. It would be down to my new pilots now and their gunners.

Sergeant Hutton was enjoying the number of targets he had. I continued with my gentle bank. A Halberstadt came into my sights. They were a faster and a better aeroplane than the Fokker but with just a fixed gun facing forward he had no defence against an oblique attack such as mine. I watched as he tried, in vain, to bring the nose of his aeroplane around to hit me. I waited until the last moment and then I gave him a long burst. My bullets ripped into his engine and then along the cockpit. I saw him slump in his seat and the aeroplane began to spiral down.

We were gradually heading towards Archie and his flights. There were six aeroplanes between us and we hit them with a wicked crossfire. It was hard to see who hit what but four of them were hit. I could not see which ones were actually destroyed but four of them were out of the equation. As our flights converged we began to head west. I signalled for my two rookies to ascend. "Hutton get on the rear Lewis and see if those lads have followed orders."

"Sir."

He did his usual struggle and then, after he had cocked his Lewis he gave me the thumbs up. He frowned and then he shouted, "Lieutenant Steadman isn't there." Lieutenant Steadman was from Gordy's flight. I saw him scanning the ground and then he pointed behind me. I craned my neck and saw the burning Gunbus. A fire like that normally meant no one was walking away. I had thought that we had had a perfect mission but we had lost a good pilot and gunner.

Freddy and Johnny were waiting for us as we landed. I nodded, "The new boys did well. Thanks for giving them the talk."

"You are welcome, sir."

Freddy looked at the others who were just landing. The numbers on the front made it easy to see who was missing. "I see Geoff Steadman bought it. Did he land safely?"

Hutton came up behind me and mimed an explosion, "Boom!"

It brought my pilots up sharply. Geoff had joined the squadron just after they had and they had been friends. Losing friends was always hard but when you lost pilots with less experience it made you question your own mortality.

When I reached Captain Marshall's office Archie and Ted were there already. "Good show out there."

I gave him the figures for the aeroplanes we had damaged and destroyed. He began to tot them up. "How many bombers did we lose?"

"I made it four."

"So with Geoff's aeroplane we lost five in total."

"Not a bad return, Bill."

"But not good enough, sir. Our tactics worked fine. We caught them on the hop and we had them. I know we couldn't do anything about the bombers over the targets; the ones hit by ground fire but we shouldn't be losing any in air combat. The only advantage they have over us now is speed and a head on attacks negates that."

Archie shook his head. "You are looking for perfection, laddie."

"I know sir. I just think it is better than accepting second best."

Gordy came in, "What happened to Geoff?"

"One of the Hun rolled between Steadman and Carstairs. It was a nice manoeuvre. He got Geoff when Carstairs gunner couldn't fire for fear of hitting Steadman."

"But he could have fired!"

Gordy looked at me and shook his head, "Bill, you weren't there how do you know?"

"The same way that you know, Gordy; the gunner can traverse his gun. Lumpy and Sergeant Laithwaite could have done it."

"They are the best gunners in the squadron, Bill."

"Then let us use that expertise to train the others to the same standard." I sighed, "Look sir, it is military economics. Geoff Steadman was a bloody good pilot. We had got him up to the same standard as Carrick and Holt. By having gunners who aren't as well trained as our pilots it means we now have to bring on a new pilot straight from Blighty. I know those two lads today didn't do badly but how long will it take to get them to Steadman's standard?"

I knew my argument had defeated them. "You may be right. Randolph, set up some afternoon training. Bill, tell the two sergeants."

"Right sir."

We began to leave and Captain Marshall said, "One more thing. Headquarters wants to know more details about the Germans we meet; any numbers or identifications. It seems the Hun is reorganising his Jastas. The more we know the better we can defeat them."

"Well those Halberstadts we fought today were painted a sort of buff colour. The handful of aeroplanes we fought last time were a pale blue."

"Good, that is the sort of thing."

Ted looked mystified, "How does that help us?"

"It tells us that were two squadrons."

Gordy nodded, suddenly animated, "And those Fokkers we fought the other day, I noticed that they had their wheels painted in four different colours."

"Why?" asked a still confused Ted.

"No idea," said Captain Marshall, "unless it is like the flight number painted on the front of our buses."

Hutton and Laithwaite were more than happy to share their expertise. When Sergeant Laithwaite left us Lumpy confided in me. "They all come to us in the Sergeant's Mess anyway sir. On our little kills table Jack and me are the top, by a long way. They are all keen to find out how to do it."

"What you tell them is important. Carstairs' gunner didn't fire today because he was afraid of hitting the Gunbus in front of him."

"But you just fire to the side, sir!"

"Exactly and that is what you need to tell them."

We were back on our regular flight patrols the next day. Gordy was given Lieutenant Swan to replace Steadman and I had Lieutenant Dunston. "You fly astern of me. Johnny can watch your rear. Don't try to win the war by yourself. You need time to come to terms with air combat."

"I know sir." He hesitated, "Sir, is it always as terrifying? I mean when the Germans are coming at you so quickly. You have so much to think about. How do you make it look so easy?"

"We have one of the best gun platforms ever invented. You have twice as many guns as the Germans we are fighting. Your sergeant can traverse his gun. If you can hold your nerve until they are close then you will hit them and they will miss."

"Aren't you afraid you will hit your own gunner?"

"The only time that might happen is when they change magazines. Make sure your gunner tells you when he is changing his magazine and you will have no problem."

"And how do you change your magazine?"

"Choose your moment. Wait until you are flying straight and level and there are no enemy aeroplanes close enough to attack. Brace the yoke with your knees and do it quickly." He nodded, "But don't try it for a few days eh? If you empty a magazine then you have fired too many bullets anyway. Short bursts are best."

The front had moved less than hitherto. When we flew over the trenches nearest to the enemy I realised that my friends from Liverpool would be below us. We were too high to wave and

I was more concerned with finding the enemy. But I knew that they were there. The war had become more personal. Hutton's wife's cousin was below us.

I knew that once we had stabilised the front then we would be spotting for the artillery. I decided to see what problems might lay ahead for the artillery and the infantry. We flew south of Warlencourt. This was newer territory to us.

I noticed more woods here. So far they had escaped damage but they would be a deadly battleground once the fighting moved there. Suddenly there came the rapid fire of machine guns and a large calibre of gun. They had guns waiting in the woods. They had made a mistake for had they not fired we would not have seen them. I began to climb as we cleared the woods.

"Sergeant, do you have any of your special eggs with you?"

"Always, sir." I heard the chuckle in his voice.

"Right then we will drop them and then give them the Lewis guns."

I began to spiral up so that I could signal to Holt. I made the sign for him to circle with the others while I dived down. I made sure that all three pilots nodded their understanding and then I began a steep dive. I knew that this would make life difficult for the gunners below. They would have to judge both height and speed. They helped us, again, by opening fire enabling Hutton to get a rough idea of where they were. He pulled the pins and dropped two as we dived and, as I began to climb, he dropped the other two. There were four quick explosions and then a much larger one.

"I think I hit the ammunition, sir."

"Well done. Let's go and pick up the boys and machine gun them on the way home."

After collecting the three Gunbuses we dived down to attack the woods. The explosion had cleared some of the ancient trees and there were fires burning. We came in at a shallower angle. I fired straight ahead while Hutton sprayed to the right. There was no return fire. We had shaken them a little. It was good for the young pilots to have such an easy target. No one was firing back at them. They could concentrate on hitting their targets.

I kept us low as we zoomed over the front line. I risked a waggle of the wings and a wave. I knew that they would have heard the explosions in the woods and I wanted their morale boosting. Our visit had made me realise how important were such tiny victories. We would have no Waterloo in this war!

We landed and awaited the others. Lieutenant Dunston looked a little happier. "I say, sir, that was fun." Sergeant Hutton had just checked over the aeroplane and he nodded as he came by. "Sir, where did your Sergeant get the bombs he dropped?"

I smiled, "I never ask. It seems wiser that way."

Lumpy looked at the young lieutenant, "Why sir? Do you fancy dropping a couple yourself?"

He grinned, "Perhaps my gunner eh?"

"I'll have a word sir."

"Thanks, Sergeant Hutton."

After he had wandered off Dunston said, "When those guns opened up I became worried."

"Why is that?"

"Well they seemed like artillery pieces and I was worried what would happen if they hit us."

"Oh I wouldn't worry about that, Peter."

He brightened, "Why not sir?"

"Because if they hit you then you would know nothing about it for you would be dead." I mimed an explosion, "Boom!"

As I made my way to the headquarters I noticed that there appeared to be a crowd outside and the ambulance we normally used for injured pilots and gunners was parked there. I looked around but could not see any damaged aeroplanes. In fact, even as I looked, I heard the hum of the rest of the squadron returning.

When I reached the office I said to Senior Flight Sergeant Lowery, "What's up Flight?"

He looked distraught, "It's the Colonel, sir, Doc Brennan says he has had a heart attack." I made to go into his office but

Lowery restrained me, "I think he has all the people he needs in there right now, sir."

"You are right."

Archie joined me and I filled him in before he asked. "I thought the old boy wasn't looking too clever lately. He spends too long worrying about us all. It must be hard sending young lads off every day and watching them get killed."

"And it will remind him of his son."

"Aye, I'd forgotten."

"He seemed a little pensive the other day when we went to the trenches. I put it down to the emotion of the place but perhaps he was unwell then."

Randolph came out. "Well he is not at death's door any more but Doctor Brennan wants to send him back to Blighty. I think the Colonel's war just ended. It looks like you will be in charge, Major Leach."

Chapter 7

We were still sat in the colonel's office an hour after he had been taken away in an ambulance. Doc Brennan had spoken to us briefly but he accompanied the colonel to the base hospital. "I am afraid that I am more used to dealing with wounds than heart disease but I think I did enough to give him a chance. I don't think he will be returning, certainly not in the near future."

Archie summed it up best, "He deserves some time in the sun. He owes this country nothing. God Bless him."

We had toasted the colonel with the last of his own whisky. It seemed appropriate somehow. We knew that the rest of the squadron was on tenterhooks. They had only seen the ambulance drive away and knew nothing of the events.

Captain Marshall addressed Major Leach, "Sir, I think, until Headquarters gets in touch that you should assume command."

"Aye, well I suppose that won't be a problem."

"Will you still fly, sir?"

I thought he was going to explode. "Too bloody right I will! You don't think I am past it, too, do you?"

"No," said Captain Marshall, patiently, "but the day to day running of the squadron needs more than just me."

"Sorry, Randolph you are right." He sipped his whisky, "We will need another Flight Commander. Anybody in mind?"

"It's a frightening thought sir but the most experienced are Holt, Sharp and Carrick."

"Good God you are right. Who would you suggest? You know the three of them better than anybody."

I thought back to the conversations I had had recently with Johnny and Freddy. They were still too idealistic. "Charlie Sharp would be the best choice. He knows the Gunbus inside out and he never flaps."

"You are right. Since he has been my wingman I have had no worries about being jumped. What about the other two?"

71

"If you move Johnny Holt to your A Flight he will be a good number two for Charlie and I will keep young Peter."

"Seems a good idea."

Randolph coughed, "Sir, without being too Machiavellian, it strikes me that if we promoted either Ted or Gordy to Captain then it would pre-empt an appointment by Headquarters. The last time they dumped Garrington-Jones on us."

He looked at me and I thought that he was going to ask my opinion again. I would have had to decline had he asked me. They were both good friends of mine. I could not choose. "Gordy, I think and you can have Ted's flight with yours. It will balance things out."

We all nodded and I breathed a sigh of relief. I think it was the correct decision but I was just pleased that I did not have to make it.

"And now sir, you had better tell Headquarters?"

"Quite right, Bill, go and tell the squadron what has happened to the colonel and then bring in Hewitt, Sharp and Thomas. We might as well keep them in the picture."

It was a pleasant late afternoon and most of the pilots and sergeants had eschewed the messes and were lounging on the grass. When I came out most of them stood.

"Can I have your attention please?" They looked at me expectantly. "The Colonel has had a heart attack and Doctor Brennan has taken him to the base hospital. He looks as though he will survive." There was a cheer which I allowed to subside, "However he will not be returning in the near future. We will carry on as normal in his absence."

There was another cheer.

"Major Archibald would like to see Lieutenant Sharp, Thomas and Hewitt in the office now please."

I smiled as I saw the confused looks on their faces. Sharp looked like a naughty boy who has been sent to the Headmaster. I let them all wonder what this was about.

I tapped on the Colonel's door, "Come!" We entered. "Sit, down. Get a chair from Randolph's office if there aren't enough."

I sat down and waited for Archie to begin. "I have just been on the telephone and spoken with Brigadier General Trenchard. He sends his commiserations to Colonel Pemberton-Smythe. He has confirmed me as commander of this squadron."

"Well done, Archie!"

"Thank you, Bill. It seems the reputation of 41 Squadron means that they do not wish to rock the boat. They are also keen to build on our success. The general is sending someone tomorrow to chat to me about operational procedures for the rest of the offensive. We are getting another eight pilots and Gunbuses by the end of the week."

Everyone looked pleased at that. "Now that will mean some reorganisation. Lieutenants Hewitt and Thomas, you have both been promoted to Captain." He must have seen my expression. "It was the general, Bill. He thought we needed more officers of the rank of Captain if we were to have more aeroplanes."

"Don't get me wrong sir, I am delighted."

I could see that Charlie looked confused. Archie soon put him out of his misery. "Lieutenant Sharp you will be the new Flight Commander for A Flight. You are now First Lieutenant. Better get the other pip on your shoulder. Eventually you will be promoted to captain."

"Thank you, sir."

"Don't thank me, it was Captain Harsker's suggestion."

"Thank you, sir."

"You deserve it Charlie."

"I will continue to fly but my second in command will be Bill here. Until we hear from this base wallah tomorrow we will assume we carry on the same as before."

"You realise, Major, that you will not be able to fly tomorrow. You will have to meet this colonel."

"Dammit, Randolph, you are right. Well, Bill, it looks like you lead tomorrow. Well you chaps had better go and tell your men. Oh Charlie, Lieutenant Holt will be joining A Flight. You had better tell him."

73

"Sir."

It was a hectic hour I spent with the Major and Captain Marshall. I had far more to think about than I had when I had taken off that morning. Our mission the next day was another bomb run, escorting the new Martinsyde bomber. It was, at least, faster than the BE 2. This time, however, we would be flying further. Our target was the marshalling yards around Bapuame. It was deemed to be more cost effective than trying to bomb the road crossings.

That evening at dinner, we talked shop. I made sure I was sat with the other Flight Commanders. "It should be easier tomorrow. The Martinsyde can get out of there quicker than a BE 2."

Charlie looked as though he wanted to say something but couldn't. "Come on Charlie, spit it out."

"Well sir, it's just that we will be travelling further over enemy lines. They will jump us and with their increased speed then we might struggle."

"A good point. How about this, we use the stack system. If we keep one aeroplane as low to the ground as the pilot can manage then the Hun can't come from underneath us. Well not without risking a crash."

Ted stubbed out his cigarette and said, "That takes good and steady flying. Who do we get to do that?"

"Why us, of course! If our flights are stacked up in front of us then they will have to take us on first. We are the best four pilots in the squadrons and I know that our gunners are red hot. The advantage we have is that we will be flying over flat ground and most of the trees have gone."

"We still have ground fire to contend with."

"I know Ted but I want every aeroplane to carry a couple of Mills bombs. Make sure they have long fuses for when we drop them over the German lines. If the leading aeroplanes drop them then by the time we four are over the gunners they should be keeping their heads down."

They seemed happy enough but I now began to have serious doubts. In my head it had seemed like a workable plan but when I gave it voice it didn't.

You would have thought that the promotion had been given to Sergeant Hutton from his walk to the aeroplane. He just said to me, "No more'n you deserve, sir. Now we'll show them!"

"Let's just do what we always do Lumpy and try to get through the day."

"You'll see, sir."

I was at the rendezvous early. I needed to make sure that everyone was in position. Charlie had a great deal of responsibility. He had four aeroplanes under his command. I hoped he would not become daunted by the task.

The Martinsyde Elephant was a fine aeroplane but there was no gunner. The pilot had a machine gun just behind his right shoulder. I could see why they needed an escort. They might be faster than we were but they were even more vulnerable to an attack from the rear.

We took up our positions. I was to the south and Gordy took the north. He would have more aeroplanes at his disposal but I would have the more experienced pilots. I knew that Charlie was extremely nervous. I saw him constantly looking around at his new charges. In contrast Lumpy was humming and singing all the time. My elevation to second in command appeared to have had an effect on him.

The Germans had positioned more anti-aircraft guns behind their lines and they put up a fierce barrage. One of the bombers exploded, I suspect the bombs themselves were hit, while a second was forced to turn back when it suffered a major hit to its wing. The closer we got to the railway the worse it was. The Martinsydes were flying as high as they dared but it must have been terrifying for the pilots to endure that wall of steel through which they flew.

The marshalling yards were a bigger target than the crossroads and they went in three lines to maximise their effect and minimise their time over the target. Even so when Lumpy spotted the Fokker biplanes I knew that this time would not be as easy as the first escort duty.

"Arm your weapon. We'll take them on now rather than waiting for them to get here." I signalled to Ted who flew his flight next to mine.

"Sir, it looks like there are two squadrons of them!"

I was going to have a baptism of fire. Young Dunston would have to fend for himself. We would have no time to watch over the combat virgin. This time the Germans had come prepared. They were higher than we were and they were in four arrows. We were outnumbered. What we would not do was flinch. We would meet them head on. I cocked my Lewis. Idly I thought that I might ask the armourer to fit a second Lewis for me. I was not sure how it would affect the weight but the firepower would give us a distinct advantage.

We were approaching each other at a combined speed of over a hundred and ninety miles an hour. They were much faster because we were climbing and they were diving. They also had the sun behind them; so much for 'Bill's Bullshit'.

I intended to go directly at one of the tips of their wings. I would play a game of dare to see who blinked first. "Ready Lumpy!"

"Aye sir, piece of…this won't be a problem. These Fokkers have a bloody big engine in front of them."

Although the huge engine gave them some protection from bullets it also restricted their view. Hutton had perfected a technique of aiming for the propeller. It had worked with the Eindecker and appeared to work with its twin winged bigger brother.

The German opened fire and his bullets were very close. I heard one of the wires on the wings twang as it was severed. We could cope with one or two such blows. Lumpy waited. Which way would the German bank? Would he come straight at us?

As soon as Sergeant Hutton opened fire I knew the pilot was doomed. The bullets smashed into the propeller and the engine. I saw oil pouring from the engine and into the face of the pilot. He lost the game of dare and he banked to the right. Lumpy kept firing and the pilot fell dead.

We continued to climb and Lumpy finished firing the magazine at the next aeroplane. I had no targets and I held my fire. As soon as I was above the Fokkers I banked to my right. I could hear Carrick and Dunston behind me as their gunners fired on both sides. Lumpy had reloaded by the time we finished our turn. The greater speed of the Germans had allowed me to come on their tail. I had height, I had the sun and I had the undefended rear of the Fokker. I waited until I could see the middle of the fuselage and then I let rip. Lumpy was finishing off one of the German Fokkers to the side and when I hit the pilot both aeroplanes began their dive of death.

We were going slower than the Fokkers but they were weaving through the air trying to catch the Martinsydes. The bombers were not making it easy. They were jinking from side to side. I still had plenty of ammunition. We were slowly closing with one of the Fokkers when I felt the thud of bullets to our rear.

"Sergeant, there is someone on our tail!"

He stood and hauled himself to grab the rear Lewis. He wisely said not a word but began firing short bursts. I could feel the bullets hitting us but the Gunbus kept flying. "Got him! Mr Carrick is helping Mr Dunston." He shouted, "There are three Fokkers around him."

"Get back on the front gun." I let the Fokker I was chasing go and, as Hutton sat down again, I banked to the right. I saw the German Hutton had hit. It was heading for the railway line. It would be like a German bomb! I saw smoke coming from Dunston's aeroplane. Carrick was fighting magnificently. He and his gunner were doing all that they could to help the inexperienced pilot.

The three Fokkers were so intent on killing Dunston that they did not notice my stealthy approach from below. As Hutton fired almost vertically I emptied my magazine at a second Fokker. Hutton's target peeled off damaged and I saw the pilot of the one I had struck holding his arm as smoke poured from his engine. The two gunners on Carrick and Dunston's Gunbuses fired simultaneously and the Fokker almost disintegrated in mid air.

I waved and ordered them west. We were low on fuel and ammunition. There was little point in pushing our luck. The skies seemed remarkably empty. I saw dogfights in the distance and, far ahead, the fleeing Elephants. I waved Dunston to the front. He had a damaged aeroplane and Carrick and I flew in tandem. Without being told Lumpy got on the rear Lewis and changed the magazine. He shouted, "Nice flying sir!"

I glanced over the side and saw some of the damaged aeroplanes. I did not see any Gunbuses but I knew that the aerial battle had ranged over a large area. I realised that we had been in the air for longer than usual when I tapped the fuel gauge. We would be flying on fumes once again. I had known the risk I was running when I had elected to bank and then dive on the Germans. It was the best manoeuvre to use but it used fuel at a prodigious rate.

I breathed a sigh of relief as we passed over our front lines. If we ran out of fuel then we would, at least, be able to land. The ambulances, medical staff and mechanics gathered around the aeroplanes which had landed told me that we had suffered damage but it looked as though we had not lost any aeroplanes.

I did not jump out immediately but I sat there with my eyes closed. I held my hands to stop them shaking. This was the first time that I had led the whole squadron and it had been nerve wracking. I had had to trust to men like Charlie and Gordy to follow my orders even when out of sight.

"Having a snooze, Bill?"

I opened my eyes with a start and saw Lord Burscough and Archie staring at me with amusement on their faces. I clambered out. "Er no sir… it's just…"

Colonel Burscough put his arm around my shoulders. "It's just that having the command of a squadron takes it out of one. I know, as does Major Leach here." As we walked towards the Headquarters he waved his arm around the field. "You did well today. They are all down."

"But we lost some of the Martinsyde Elephants and there is damage to our aeroplanes. I nearly lost young Dunston today."

Lord Burscough laughed. "You were always the same Bill; always seeking perfection. Other squadrons are regularly coming back with four and five aeroplanes missing. Another Gunbus squadron had the same job as you yesterday and lost four Gunbuses and had another four badly damaged."

We had reached the office and we entered, "Get us some coffee, Flight."

"Sir."

We sat down and Lord Burscough continued, "It is the main reason I am here. I am sad that the Colonel had a heart attack. He was a fine old warrior." The 'was' sounded ominous. "However the Brass is not as stupid as some people think; at least not General Henderson and General Trenchard. They are trying to build on success. 41 Squadron is successful. There are only a handful of pilots who have more kills to their name than you and you have the lowest turnover of pilots." I began to speak and he held up his hand. "It is not perfect but this squadron has the right idea. That is why we want to increase the size of the squadron. You chaps have wrested control of the skies over the Somme from the Germans. Do not let them take it back!"

"Coffee sir."

The orderly poured the coffee and then backed out of the room. I sipped the hot steaming drink and realised how much I had been waiting for this.

Major Leach went to the cupboard and brought out a bottle of blended whisky. "A freshener sir?"

Lord Burscough nodded. Archie poured a generous slug into each of our cups. "Good coffee." He looked at both of us seriously. "The information you send back is scrutinised back at Headquarters. We do have some fairly bright Intelligence officers. We also have information from Berlin. The Germans lost Max Immelmann recently but they have another star now, Boelke. He seems a clever chap and we know that he is reorganising his squadrons, Jastas they call them. Make no mistake, the Germans do not like to lose and they will come back stronger. I am here to tell you not to get complacent."

Archie shook his head, "With respect sir, I don't think it is in the lads' nature to get complacent. They are a good bunch here."

"I know but don't let up on the Hun. You have your sword in his back. Keep it there!"

Archie laughed, "Aye sir, a nice metaphor!"

Captain Marshall put his head around the door. "Sir, I have the reports in."

Archie looked at Lord Burscough who nodded, "That's fine Archie. I have just about finished. I'll have a chat here to Bill." When he had gone he tapped my medals. "Congratulations on your medals. Lady Burscough told me about it." He sipped his coffee and a mischievous look came into his eyes. "She also told me of the pretty little nurse. She seemed to think that wedding bells would be in the offing."

I shook my head, "Not while the war is on. She deserves a nice wedding not something we do quickly because I happen to have a leave. Besides I want her to meet mum and dad first."

"I can see that but don't wait too long Bill. Grasp happiness while you can. Remember the Marne and Le Cateau; we lost too many friends during the race to the sea." He finished his coffee. "You are very highly thought of, you know, Bill. The General wants to give you your own squadron."

I shook my head, "Not yet sir. Today showed me that I still have much to learn."

He nodded, "That is probably a good thing. Besides we have some new aeroplanes we are just developing. Nippy little single seater fighters. Far faster than the Gunbus."

"I don't know sir. I quite like the old Gunbus."

"This is a fast moving war and we have to move with it. Still they are some months off production yet. Let's get to the end of this offensive and see." He stood and shook my hand. "Lady Mary and I are proud of you, Bill."

"Thank you sir."

"Oh, by the way, your Alice is doing well in London. She has a real future there."

"I was grateful to her ladyship for showing interest."

"Don't be silly. Your family is almost part of our family," He suddenly looked sad, "although by the time this war ends those happy days may never return. The world is changing. There are more men like John and Tom now who want a change in the order of things."

"Not me sir."

"I know, Bill, I know."

Chapter 8

Mine was the last report to come in. Archie took his lordship back to his car and I sat with Randolph who took note while I spoke. I thought back to the days of our dreaded temporary commander, Major Hamilton-Grant. We would have to sit and write out a lengthy report each day. It wasted time and was inefficient. This was a better method.

"Do you know what happened to Dunston then?"

I shook my head. "I was whisked away before I could find out. I'll have a chat later on but he did well just to survive. It was brutal out there."

Randolph held up his report. "It looks like there were two squadrons. The buff coloured ones and a pale blue one. The ones with pale blue apparently had differently coloured wheels. I presume they denoted the flights."

"It would help if we knew where their home fields were."

"You are right. That would give us an idea of their range. Their endurance, according to the Intelligence papers Colonel Burscough brought, is about an hour thirty."

I did the calculation in my head. "That means that they could fly for about seventy miles from their airfield."

"They are hanging around the combats for a long time Bill. I would think that they may be no more than thirty miles from the front."

I stood and went to the map. "We have to assume that these two squadrons will be close together. I would put them somewhere here, east of Bapuame."

"I think you are right. Next time we brief the squadron we will ask them for the direction the Germans take when they head for home."

I stood. "I will go and have a word with Freddy. Find out what happened."

"Good idea. Oh, by the way, your chat with Carstairs must have worked. He bagged his first Fokker today."

"Good, I am pleased." He had been quiet for a few days but Gordy seemed happier with him. Perhaps all he needed was a good talking to.

The ambulances had taken the wounded to the sick bay. Randolph had told me that nothing was serious. We would have enough pilots and gunners. I saw Senior Flight Sergeant Lowery with Sergeant McKay. They both saluted when I walked up to them. "What's the damage then?"

"Three willna be flying tomorrow sir. Just minor damage but it is to the engines. They need nursing a wee bit. We can fix up the wings fairly easily but the engines... well they need ma touch."

I turned to Lowery. "We appear to have credit with Wing; how about getting Mr Doyle on to them. Let's see if we can get more spares. We will be having more aeroplanes and pilots soon. They won't be much good if they are all grounded."

"The lads are doing their best, Captain Harsker."

"I know Mr McKay and that is not a criticism. It's just that every aeroplane we can keep n the air saves lives on the ground. Today we stopped the Germans from using a rail head. When the Tommies attack tomorrow it should be easier."

"Point taken, Captain Harsker. I'll ring Wing myself. As you say they seem to think that 41 Squadron is the best so who are we to disagree?"

I was glad that I had had the coffee for I was flagging. I headed for the mess where I hoped I would find Freddie. Surprisingly it was empty and I went to his quarters. He still shared a room with Johnny Holt despite the fact that they were now in different flights. They were like Gordy and me; they were mates.

They snapped to attention when I entered. "At ease. I just wanted to talk with you about Dunston." Johnny got up to leave but I said, "No, Johnny, I'd like you to stay. Just shut the door will you."

I sat on the chair and began to light my pipe. I had discovered that it encouraged others to talk without peppering them with questions. "It was only a little mistake sir. He wasn't watching you closely enough when you made that right bank and he flew straight on. He was Fokker watching. Two of them pounced on him. That was when his gunner got nicked. Luckily Laithwaite was on the ball and between us we sent them on their way. By the time he had recovered and I had signalled him to take station again you were some way away. Sorry."

"Don't worry. I thought we might have teething troubles. I am just glad that he is surviving."

"Don't worry sir, I will have another word with him."

"I am glad you are both here because we are getting another batch of pilots. The squadron is getting bigger and you two will need to help the new pilots to acclimatise quickly. Dunston will need to be up to speed sooner rather than later."

"Don't worry sir, I won't let you down."

"I know Freddie. You have come a long way since I put you both in the front cockpit."

They laughed and Freddie shook his head. "That put me in my place sir. I thought I knew everything but seeing the world through the eyes of a gunner was a revelation."

"Well it made you a better pilot, both of you for that matter."

The Major led us up the next day and we managed a patrol without too much stress. We saw four Fokkers but they kept well to their side of the lines. From what we could see there appeared to be little ground action, certainly on the German side. Ominously we saw lines of Tommies marching towards the support trenches. That was a sure sign of another push. How long would this battle go on? We had already exceeded the Loos offensive. How many more men would we lose? It seemed to me that we were bleeding the country dry.

There were also new arrivals at the airfield. A dozen lorries disgorged mechanics, sergeants and equipment as we taxied along the grass. As Archie and I entered Captain Marshall's office a harassed Senior Flight Sergeant Lowery hurtled out of the door. He shook his head, "Sorry sirs! They send the men and the equipment but no beds! Headquarters; they have no sense!"

I smiled as he hurtled out of the door, "He is only happy when he is moaning. No sign of the Gunbuses though."

"No, they are due this afternoon. Apparently they are flying all the replacement aeroplanes over together to avoid them getting lost. And we are to stand down until the day after tomorrow. Wing wants us to be able to field all the cover we can muster. I think there is another offensive coming up. They are trying to take Delville Woods and the area around Pozières."

Archie came out of his office and went to the staff car. He shook his head. "Typical, Lord Burscough spends the other day briefing me and now I get summoned to Wing for another briefing. If talk could win a war we would be in Berlin by now. You can greet the new chaps, Bill. God knows when I will be back!"

I went back to my quarters with mixed emotions. I was glad of the rest. The aeroplanes and the crews needed it but an offensive meant that thousands of young men would die. I had seen their faces now and spoken to them. It made it more personal. When I reached my quarters I met Airman Bates for the first time. Major Leach had his own servant, inherited from the colonel, Smith. The rest of us didn't have any. Bates was the first of a number who had just arrived. It was another sign of our status. I had been Lord Burscough's servant in the cavalry and knew what to expect. If I am honest I did not need a servant but Airman Bates stood to attention when I entered my room.

"Airman John Bates sir, your new servant. I took the liberty of tidying up in here sir. I hope it was not presumptuous of me?" He was the most softly spoken man I had ever heard. He had a perpetual smile on his face and everything about him was neat.

"No, Bates that is fine. You carry on."

As he made my bed I examined him. He was a slight man, almost tiny. He looked unreasonably neat. I know he wore the same uniform as the others but he managed to give it some style. His hair was well groomed and I noticed that his hands were manicured. I took off my jacket and he had it brushed, straightened and on a hanger in double quick time.

He turned to me and smiled, "Now then sir, I need to get to know what you like and so on if I am to do my job. What is your routine?"

I sat down and told him the times I rose, what I did, my day and when I went to bed. It felt strange. I had grown up as the son of a servant, I had started my military career as a servant, and now I had my own. It felt unnatural to have a servant.

I noticed that, as I spoke, although he had a serious expression he had twinkling eyes. He looked happy. It was strange. He nodded when I had finished.

"Thank you sir." I noticed he had collected all my dirty laundry and he gathered it up.

"Before you go Bates, sit down and tell me about yourself." He raised a quizzical eyebrow. "I do this with the men I fly with so do not take offence. I believe if you know where a man comes from you can lead him anywhere."

"None taken sir, but it is just unusual for an officer to take any interest in his servant. Well, sir, before the war I worked at Lord Derby's estate. I assisted his Lordship's gentleman's gentleman. I was being trained to become the gentleman's gentleman for his nephew. When his nephew joined up so did I and I became his servant." His face clouded over and I saw sadness for the first time. "He was killed in the first battle of Ypres. I was then allocated to other officers. They were all either wounded or died." He lowered his voice, "To be frank with you Captain Harsker I didn't handle the deaths and the trenches very well. I became... unwell. I was sent to Craiglockhart. When I was cured a nice doctor there asked me if I wanted a discharge. I told him I wanted to serve my country but I couldn't face the trenches. He sent me here."

I nodded and in that moment I had an insight into this neat little man. He coped through order. I would have to treat him as gently as I did my pilots.

"Thank you for your honesty, Bates and I will do my very best not to get killed."

He laughed, "They were right about you sir. You do have a sense of humour."

"Oh and just so you know I grew up on Lord Burscough's estate which is not far from Lord Derby's. I am the son of a groom and if it was not for the war then I too would be a servant on an estate. We are not that different, you and I."

"With respect sir, we are. I was born to be a servant but I know already that you were born to be a warrior."

As he went out I noticed that he didn't so much walk as bounce out; he almost skipped and yet he looked to be almost forty. His voice and his manner were equally lively. Considering I had neither needed nor wanted a servant Bates made a real difference over the coming months. Perhaps it was his experience in the trenches which made him so easy to talk to. He certainly made a difference in my life.

When I had dressed for dinner I heard the sound of approaching aeroplanes. I left the officers' quarters and joined the others as the eight new Gunbuses approached from the west. I looked, with amusement, at the young pilots like Carstairs and Swan, critically analysing the flying of the eight new pilots. The eight would know they were being scrutinised. Sergeant McKay had organised all the new mechanics too. There was a large audience just waiting for them.

Captain Marshal joined me and we lit our pipes. "It seems we have increased our staff generally, Bill. We had two officers who arrived this morning; one is going to supervise Sergeant McKay and the other Sergeant Richardson."

I gave him a wry look, "Well good luck to them! Have they any experience?"

"I think they are both fresh from University." He shrugged, "There were both doing engineering degrees so they might understand the physics."

"I'll stick with the two sergeants. They might know bugger all about physics but they know Lewis guns and Gunbuses."

He laughed, "That's what I like about you northerners. You have a habit of calling a spade a shovel."

"As my dad would say, *'tell the truth and shame the devil'*!"

"And we have half a dozen more sergeants, corporals and privates for the office."

"Do you need them?"

"I think so. Sergeant Lowery and I are rushed off our feet. The trouble is we will have to learn to delegate." He gestured at me with his pipe, "As will you Bill. Get some of the others to do the training. It will be good for them."

"You are probably right."

We watched as the eight aeroplanes landed. At least three of them came down in bounces. I saw Sergeant McKay wince at the potential damage to the undercarriages and frames. None of the landings were particularly good but I suspect the audience didn't help and for most of them this would have been the first time they had landed a Gunbus.

I turned to Sergeant Lowery. "Get them billeted. We will have a briefing at 0800 tomorrow."

"Sir!"

"Sergeant McKay, I want the whole squadron in the air tomorrow at 0900. They won't need ammunition." I pointed to the recently landed aeroplanes. "These only have the two Lewis guns. Better see Percy. I want a pilot's Lewis fitting on each one." He groaned. "I know, Flight Sergeant, it is more weight and it weakens the structure of the bus but at the end of the day that extra Lewis saves lives."

"Sir." He had a resigned tone to his voice.

I gave him a wicked smile. "And ask the armourer if I can have a second pilot's Lewis fitted to my bus."

His jaw dropped and then he mumbled, "Yes sir!"

I knew that the air would be blue as he wandered off and pity the poor mechanic who got the wrong side of him.

Archie did not make it back for dinner. Randolph had assumed he would not and we had spent the afternoon allocating the pilots to the flights. The four who had had the worst landings were divided up so that every flight had one who needed work. The others looked much of a muchness and we just arbitrarily put them in flights. We would be able to move them around later. We put the lists up before dinner. I saw them being scrutinised by the new and the experience pilots.

I had persuaded Randolph to take charge of the speeches at dinner. I was not quite ready for that. I could talk tactics and flying but the social niceties were beyond me. It was inbred into the likes of Archie and Randolph.

There was a healthy buzz of conversation around the table. I sat between Gordy and Charlie. Since he had been made up Charlie had taken to sitting with us. I knew it wasn't snobbery. Charlie was not like that. He just wanted to learn from the three of us. He wanted to be the best Flight Commander he could be. I knew that he felt an affinity for us. We had all been promoted from gunner and he was following in our footsteps.

"Charlie, I want you to take the pilots up one by one tomorrow and put them in the front cockpit. It's the quickest way I know to make a pilot think about his gunner."

He grinned, "Well it worked with Mr Holt and Mr Carrick."

Gordy waved a forkful of Boeuf Bourguignon in the direction of the now crowded mess. "We have an extra twelve officers now! I think you ought to go on another recce and get some more furniture!"

Ted and Charlie laughed. "I don't think so. I got the first lot. It's someone else's turn now."

"We are growing though, Bill. How will we keep track of everyone? Especially in the air."

"The numbers on the nose help a little."

"You can't see them from the side."

"Ted's right. They are only useful on the ground. We need something on the side."

Charlie, who tended to be thoughtful suddenly said, "Sir, you could have a horse painted on the side of yours, being in the

89

cavalry and all. It would mark you out for our lads and we would know where you were."

"What about the rest of us?"

Charlie shrugged, "I could have a Lewis gun. I was a gunner."

"So were we," pointed out Ted.

Charlie grinned, "Yeah but I had the idea first! You have to come up with your own."

In the end it proved to be a diverting idea and we spent the rest of the evening discussing it. We decided that it was only the flight leaders who would need this. Anything else would be confusing.

We were having whisky and enjoying a smoke when Archie returned. His eyes lit up when he spied the whisky bottle. "Give me a double! After a day talking to Wing I need one."

"Bad day skipper?"

"Just as boring as a Presbyterian teetotaller's wedding in Ayr!" We laughed. "You needn't laugh. Next time I send one of you lads. That'll be six hours of your life you'll never have back!"

"And did you learn anything?"

He became serious. "Aye. I am afraid that the day after tomorrow we hit the ground running! They want us to keep the Hun on the ground. Our orders are to patrol their front line and stop their aeroplanes from observing our infantry attack. They really wanted us up tomorrow but they accepted that we would need a day with the new laddies. The attack is in two days time. We have to stop the Boche from seeing what we are about."

"A tall order."

"It gets taller I am afraid, Gordy. We have to patrol five miles of the front."

That shut everyone up. "How?"Charlie's voice came out thin and high pitched. Five miles of the front meant we would not be able to help each other.

"We use flights. That way we can cover a larger area. I'll be with you Charlie." I saw the relief on Charlie's face. He leaned back in his chair. "So what did you do while Father was away?"

Ted stubbed his cigarette out and poured himself another whisky. "We watched half of our new pilots do an impression of a kangaroo."

Archie laughed, "Well that is nothing new. I have yet to see a new pilot land properly. Present company excepted."

"The new buses don't have a pilot Lewis. I got the armourer to fit one to each Gunbus."

"Typical of some official back in England who wants to save a few bob and cut corners."

"And we have decided to paint an emblem on each of our buses, just so that our men know who is who."

"Seems a good idea. Go on."

"I would have a horse because I was in the cavalry. Charlie here would have a gun because he was in the gunners."

Ted grumbled, "I wanted a gun. I had to settle for a hammer."

Archie looked puzzled, "A hammer?"

Ted grinned, "Yes sir, my name is Edward. King Edward was known as the hammer of the Scots."

Even Archie laughed, "Very droll. And you Gordy, what did you come up with?"

"We thought of a Gordian knot and then realised that wasn't very warlike so I decided on a shield."

"I like it. It will give your flights identity: the Cavalry, the Gunners, the Hammers and the Shields. I shall join in and have a thistle on mine!"

At 0800 we gathered for the briefing. We had the gunners with us as well and used the Sergeants' Mess. It was the only place big enough. Archie started the briefing. He was good at this sort of thing.

"Laddies, we have a great opportunity today. Today we begin to write the history of 41 Squadron. We have the best pilots, as rewarded by the King himself. We have the best gunners. Yesterday at Wing I discovered that our gunners have shot down more German aeroplanes than any other observers or gunners in the whole of the RFC. And we have the only aeroplane which can hold its own against the Germans. And you know something? We will need all of that if we are going to help the laddies on the Somme. We have to protect them from above and that isn't going to be easy. Now Captain Harsker will explain what we will do today but tomorrow we will need to be as sharp as tacks because tomorrow we will have to hold off two squadrons of German aeroplanes!"

It was rousing but there were no cheers. It was deadly serious and even the older hands knew that.

"We will be flying in four flights tomorrow. We want the newer pilots to fit in behind the flight commander. Carstairs, McCormack, Holt and Carrick you will all be at the rear. We know that you can cope with that. This morning we are going to take the whole squadron up so that everyone gets to know the signals we will be using and we get used to flying with five or six aeroplanes instead of just three." I paused to let them all take that in.

"We will not be using live ammunition today but I want the new pilots and gunners to practise changing magazines. You change a magazine every ten minutes today. When you get to your aeroplanes you will find some sticky labels. Put a label on each magazine when you change it. This afternoon I want the gunners to come here while Sergeants Hutton and Laithwaite give the new men some tips on aerial gunnery. The new pilots will go to the field where First Lieutenant Sharp will take you on a guided tour of the front." There were titters and giggles from some of the more experienced pilots and confusion from the new ones. "Any questions?" They had been given too much information already and there was silence. "Dismiss."

I was not surprised any more by the youth of the new pilots. Giggs and Fryer looked like young versions of Freddie. I gathered them around me. "Lieutenant Giggs you will be on my tail. Peter behind him. Young Fryer will be behind you and Freddie here will see if you can fly in a straight line. I won't ask how many hours you have in a Gunbus as the men who trained you don't seem to think it is important. It is not the fastest aeroplane in the world but it is a steady platform and it does not come apart when you throw a loop. Hutton!"

Sergeant Hutton snapped forward. I had primed him. "Sir!"

"This is Sergeant Hutton. He is a snug fit in the front of the cockpit, aren't you Sergeant?"

"Yes sir, very snug."

"However if I looped without telling him where would he be?"

The two new lads looking mystified and Hutton answered for them. "I would be splattered all over the ground."

"Now that would not be a good thing would it Lieutenant Giggs?"

"Er, no sir."

"And why not, Lieutenant Fryer?"

"Because he would be dead, sir."

"Yes he would and that would be a great loss to the RFC as Sergeant Hutton here has shot and damaged ten German aeroplanes. He has shot down more enemy planes than Lieutenant Carrick. Isn't that correct, Lieutenant?"

Having been pre warned he said cheerily, "Yes sir."

"And Lieutenant Carrick is a very good pilot who has, himself, shot down a number of German aeroplanes." I paused and watched the terror on the faces of the new pilots and gunners. "What I am saying is if my senior pilots and sergeant give you advice then please take it. They do know what they are talking about. Now I hope that you read the sheet I sent to you last night with my signals. Today, gentlemen, we give you a test!"

I gave them a hard test. I took them towards the enemy front but stopped over the British lines. We dived down to tree top level. We peeled left and right. I took them through every manoeuvre including our famous circle. I hoped to God that we would not need to use that in the near future. I needed my young pilots bedding in easily.

When we landed I smiled, "Well done, lads. Now get some lunch. Giggs and Fryer, report here after lunch and your sergeants join the others in the Mess Hall."

Peter joined them while Freddie lit a cigarette and waited with me next to my aeroplane. "What do you think Freddie?"

"They seem like they know what they are doing but it's like me and Johnny, until you put them in a dogfight you don't know how they will react. After I lost... well you know... I never thought I would get in an aeroplane again."

"I know but you did and I, for one, am glad."

The mechanic came over. "Everything all right sir?"

"Yes Green, she is sweet as a nut. Now I have a little favour to ask."

He smiled, "Ask away sir."

"I need a horse painting here on the side of the cockpit."

"A horse?"

I sighed. Green was a good mechanic but he lacked imagination. "Yes, Green, the four flight commanders are going to have an insignia painted on the side. I chose a horse because I was in the cavalry."

"I'm not very good at painting sir."

"Look it doesn't have to look like a Stubbs. It just has to look like a horse."

"I can do it sir." We both looked at Carrick; me with surprise and Green with gratitude. "I was going to study art if I hadn't joined up. I could give it a go."

"I'll sort you some paints out sir." Grateful that he no longer had a job to do Green scurried off.

"I would be delighted if you could give it a go."

"Actually, sir it might do me some good, you know, to do something creative. How big do you want it to be?"

"So that the flight can recognise my aeroplane."

"Righto, I'll grab a quick lunch and make a start." When he went off whistling I knew he was doing something he wanted to do. I had no idea he was an artist. I wondered what hidden depths the others had.

When the new pilots returned after the Charlie Sharp show, as it became to be known, they were both green and chastened. I knew that it would have the desired effect and the gunners would be safer. It still did not guarantee that they would return alive on the morrow but they had a better chance now. I left the mess as soon as dinner was over. I had still to receive a letter from Beatrice and I was worrying that perhaps she was having second thoughts about us. I rationalised by telling myself that none of us had had mail in some time and the Somme Offensive was causing the problems. However, as I was now more aware of my own mortality I wrote another letter explaining how I felt. If I was to die then I wanted her to know how much she had meant to me in the short space of time we had had together. I slept easier with the letter written.

Chapter 9

Bates was in my room when I woke up. He had my uniform laid out with a freshly laundered and ironed shirt. "Good morning, sir. A few clouds about today but I don't think it will rain." He began to tidy the room. He picked up the letter, "Shall I post this for you Captain Harsker?"

"No, thank you Bates, I have to go to Captain Marshall's office to collect the maps."

I dropped off the letter in the admin office before I left. Senior Flight Sergeant Lowery grinned as I dropped it off. "That is one job I don't have to do any more sir. I have a clerk who just deals with letters!"

As I walked to the aeroplane I reflected that Lowery was much happier with the influx of the new men now that he realised his job was easier. In contrast, mine was harder. I would need eyes in the back of my head if I was to watch over my two new charges.

I was stunned by Freddie's artwork. He had had a limited palette of paint but he had done a good job. No not just a good job but a work of art. It was a rearing steed. It was not the same colour as Caesar but that was my fault as I had not specified the colour. Even more amazing was the fact that he had painted an identical one on the other side. It was all that I could have hoped for and more.

Hutton was fiddling on in the cockpit. He looked up when he heard me, "Lovely isn't it sir? Mr Carrick has some real talent there. I wish I could do one thing half as well as he paints."

"How about being a gunner?"

He shook his head. "That doesn't even come close. He has made something beautiful there, sir. All I am good at is destroying things."

It was the most reflective I had ever seen Sergeant Hutton to be. His veneer of good humour was just a means to cope with what he did. I was learning about the men I led.

My flight was the first one to be ready and, as we did not need the whole squadron to accompany us, I took off. We had heard the guns from the moment we woke but we were so familiar with the sound by now that it did not register. The dust and debris flying in the air on the horizon was not unusual. Mindful of my new charges I took us up higher, to 10,000 feet. It was safer. The air was definitely chilly at that height and I was grateful for my thick leather flying coat. Although it was the middle of July we all knew that the nights would soon become longer and the air colder. Summer was brief when you were high in the sky. It was, however, a beautiful morning. The sun's rays fought the dust and destruction thrown up by the artillery and a myriad of colours could be seen. It was as though nature was making something ugly as beautiful as it could.

"German lines ahead, sir."

"Right Sergeant Hutton, eyes peeled and try to watch behind whenever you can eh?"

"Look at this sir." He held up a stick to which he had attached a mirror. "I can watch behind without getting a crick in my neck."

"Well done!" It was such a simple thing. Flight Sergeant Hutton was remarkably inventive. I would have one fitted to my cockpit. It would give me the comfort of seeing what the new boys were up to.

"They look to be on station, sir."

The guns ceased. While talking to Colonel McCartney I learned the silence of the guns was the signal for an attack. He had told me that the French had mastered the art of the rolling barrage which enabled the artillery to fire ahead of the advancing infantry for longer and kept the German heads down. He had told me philosophically that a creeping barrage would save hundreds of men in an attack and he prayed for the day that the British Artillery would learn that skill.

I looked down and saw the thin brown line as it left the British trenches. "Let's go down and buzz the machine gunners, sergeant. We can help those lads down there."

The enthusiasm was back in his voice as he said, "Good idea." It might not be the Liverpool Pals down there but Lumpy and I had a picture in our heads of the men we had visited. To us every Tommy in the trenches was a friend.

I banked to the left and we seemed to accelerate faster than we had before. It must have been my imagination but it felt like the days when I charged with Caesar. I think it was the Rolls Royce engines performing better at that altitude. It was a rapid descent and, I hoped, it would catch the Germans unawares. We were close enough now to see the grey uniforms emerged from their holes like so many ants and flock to their guns. As Hutton fired obliquely at those on the right I fired ahead. We were flying at two hundred feet above the trenches but directly along them towards the north east. As we had seen there was protection from front and rear in the trenches but nothing along the sides. The short bursts threw German soldiers into the bottom of the trenches. Hutton was moving his gun from side to side to maximise casualties. The Germans had nowhere to run. When we had passed there were more Gunbuses dealing death and destruction. When my Lewis clicked empty I began to climb.

I hoped, as we banked right, that we had made life a little easier for the advancing Tommies. After Hutton had changed magazines he held up his mirror and said, "All your little chicks are there, Captain Harsker."

"Thank you." It remained to be seen if they could reload their magazines. They had all done so in the training exercise the previous day but this was a different scenario. When I levelled out I changed mine and we headed south down the German lines.

"Fokkers sir, to the east."

I looked to where Hutton was pointing. Eight biplanes were heading our way. Hutton was guessing at the make; the Halberstadt looked identical to the Fokker from a distance. "Right, let's go and meet them eh?" I waggled my wings to tell the flight that we were attacking. I banked east and I was glad that we had climbed. The Germans must have been close to their base for they were much lower than we were. From the angle of their craft I could see that they were climbing to meet us.

They would expect us to go for the middle of their line. It had been what we had done every time so far. I decided to vary this. It was easier to do this with a flight rather than a squadron. "Lumpy, I am going to aim for the aeroplane on the far right of their line and then swing around behind them. I will edge that way gradually."

"Righto sir!"

The Huns were too concerned with gaining height and keeping their formation and they did not appear to notice that we were not following our normal pattern. They were still a couple of hundred feet below us. The rising sun would not come into play yet and so I dived at the first biplane. Hutton had been correct, they were Fokkers. This was the blue squadron. It was important to take out the first aeroplane and Hutton and I fired at the same time. The climbing Fokker's parabellums zipped over our heads but our converging fire ripped into him. He had been climbing and had not adjusted enough for our descent. He wasted his bullets.

I banked right as the line of Fokkers tried to bank to meet us. We had the advantage of gunners who could fire to the side. I had no targets but Hutton fired short bursts as we flew south. There were no bullets coming back at us as the Germans were still turning. By the time we had reached the end of the line Sergeant Hutton had emptied the magazine.

I banked and climbed as we headed back north. It was a glorious sight to behold as I turned. The eight Germans had been riddled with bullets from our gunners. I saw five of them heading east with smoke and damage. Two were spiralling to the earth and the last was climbing in a desperate attempt to avoid Freddie and Sergeant Laithwaite who were both pouring .303s into it. When it began to drop to earth I headed west. We had enough fuel to get home and we had done our duty.

Although we had left first we had strayed further into enemy territory than the others and we were the last to land. They were just lining up their buses when we landed. The fact that there were no ambulances nor huddles of mechanics told me that the day had gone better than we might have expected. I knew we had been in the air for a long time when the wound in my shoulder began to ache. I suspected that, once we came into wet weather, it would ache even more. As I clambered out of the cockpit I was just glad to be alive.

"Well done, Lumpy. That was fine shooting."

"Do you reckon that is half a kill each then sir?"

I waved an airy hand, "You can have it all." I patted the horse's head, "After all you were upholding the honour of Harsker's Cavalry."

He grinned and a cheeky look came over his face, "You are right sir. We are the cavalry. I do like that."

We waited for the others to join us. I was anxious to see the reaction of Giggs and Fryer. I could see their animation as they came towards me with hands soaring, banking and diving. "Nice shooting, Sergeant Laithwaite and you Lieutenant Carrick. Whose kill was that?"

Freddie nodded to his gunner. "I am certain that Sergeant Laithwaite would have been the one to make the killing shot. Mine was just reactive."

"And how about you Peter?"

He had genuine relief on his face. "That was much easier sir. I think I actually hit something up there and I changed a magazine."

I adopted an amazed look, "A hit and a changed magazine? Is there a pilot lurking beneath that youthful exterior?"

"I hope so sir. Thanks for giving me a chance."

"Don't worry you deserved it." I glanced at the other pair, "And you two."

"It was more frightening than we thought but we felt more confident when you hit that first German."

"Good. Now check your buses and then see you in the mess for a little tiffin eh?"

"Right sir."

Gordy and Carstairs were waiting for me. From the look on Carstairs' face he had something important to tell me. I saw Gordy wink and had it confirmed.

"Sir, I shot down one Fokker and my gunner and I damaged a second. I am off the mark!"

I shook his hand, "Well done. That is excellent news. I am genuinely delighted."

"I know sir and I want you to know I won't let you down and…" he hesitated and looked at the ground, "and I am thoroughly ashamed of being such an absolute fool when I first arrived. I don't know why you didn't send me packing right away."

Gordy laughed, "If we did that with every Second Lieutenant who behaved that way we would only have five pilots in the squadron! That's the Captain's job, Jamie. He turns public school boys into pilots." He tapped my chest, "He didn't get the Military Cross for fighting Germans. It was for working wonders with the pride of Eton and Harrow!"

Archie, too, was delighted. "Today went well, Bill. Very little damage to us and half a dozen Germans either shot down or damaged."

I gave a word of caution, "We caught them napping today sir. It might not be as easy in the future. We know what quick learners they are. Let's wait a week or so, until the end of July before we start congratulating ourselves."

Captain Marshall laughed, "Are you turning into Doom and Gloom Thomas? You sound just like him."

"Let's just say I have lost my naïveté since I was wounded. Just when you think you have it all under control, bam! Something smacks you one."

Bates was waiting for me when I reached my quarters. "Really Captain Harsker, you need to look after yourself more. You work harder than anyone. I have drawn you a nice hot bath. What would you like to drink?"

"Er, a cup of tea?"

"An excellent idea sir. Now come along, get undressed I have your robe ready!"

He was a fussy little man but his heart was in the right place and, to be fair, the bath was the perfect temperature. He came into the bathroom, seemingly oblivious to my naked form. He handed me a cup of tea. Cocking his head to one side he said, "I asked the mess orderlies how you liked your tea. I shall soon get to know your little ways, sir."

As I drank my tea I hoped he had not been looking in the bath when he said that.

Dinner was a boisterous affair with much good humour in evidence. I commented to Gordy that it was in direct contrast to the atmosphere when Major Hamilton-Grant had been running it. After dinner we crowded into the seating area of the mess. The young officers all deferred to the older ones and allowed us the seats.

Ted said, "Captain Marshall, can't you get the engineers to enlarge our quarters? We are a bigger squadron after all."

"You are right but it still won't help the seating arrangements. Quarter Master Doyle was playing darts. He had his usual cigarette dangling precariously from his lip. It seemed to be an art form. "Sir, if you give me a few bob of Mess funds I should be able to wangle something."

"Really, Quarter Master? How?"

He tapped his nose, "Let's just say I have been getting to know the locals and I think I know where to lay my hands on some nice furniture."

Randolph smiled, "I shall ask no questions Mr Doyle and then any legal ramifications will be your preserve."

Interestingly enough Ted, Gordy and I found ourselves the subject of a barrage of questions. The main focus appeared to be how we had acquired our skills as pilots without having either gone to University or flying school. We answered them as best we could. Jamie seemed almost disappointed by the answers. I think he thought that there was a blue blooded skeleton in our closets. He seemed convinced that my family came from a liaison between some noble and an obliging servant. He had a vivid imagination. I found out that he came from a long line of noblemen. Noblesse Oblige coursed through his veins. He was desperate for the old days of knights on chargers. He told me that he would have joined the cavalry but he had heard that they no longer charged into battle. When I told him of my experiences it confirmed his decision.

"This is better. We are knights of the skies. That is why I wish that I was in your flight. You are the cavalry and you shall do noble deeds. I will have to find a way to find my own Holy Grail!"

I thought Ted was going to choke on his beer.

"I don't know about noble deeds, Jamie, but we can make a difference to the troops on the ground."

When I returned to my room I found my night attire laid out ready for me and a glass of whisky next to the bed. Bates was a very thoughtful man and a most efficient servant. I had not been anywhere near as good when I had served Lord Burscough.

Archie had decided that, as we had been so successful the previous day, we would use the same model. I was not sure. The Germans might be expecting us. I gathered my pilots around me. "We need to be flexible today. I have a feeling that the Hun will try something different. If our normal method is going awry then Hutton will fire a Very Flare. As soon as he does then I want Carrick to fly next to me. Make it two aeroplanes width and Fryer will be his wingman."

They nodded but Freddie asked, "Do you mind me asking why sir?"

"The last four patrols we have undertaken we have flown in line astern and gone directly for the leader. Then we have either flown across their rear or their front. If I was their squadron leader then I would be laying a trap. I would try to draw the leading aeroplane in and then attack the rear. My plan is just a way out of that trap. By leaving the gap for two aeroplanes between us we might get at least one in crossfire from the two gunners and we could plough the field ahead." They seemed relieved and all nodded. "Of course this puts a great deal on your new gunners." I looked at my new men. "Are they and you up to it?"

Giggs set his jaw resolutely, "We are sir!"

"Good man!"

As we headed for our sector I saw the brown lines wavering forward. To the north and the south I saw the other flights on the squadron looking like so many dragonflies. I checked my altitude. We were flying at four thousand feet. "I think we shall climb a little more, Sergeant."

"Righto sir but it does use a lot of juice up."

"We can always leave early. I want to be above any trouble."

There was silence for a while and then Hutton said. "We ought to carry a couple of bombs, you know sir. It wouldn't add too much to the fuel consumption and we could do more damage to ground troops than with the just the Lewis Guns."

"You are right. We will try that tomorrow."

"Sir, look in the east."

I saw five Fokker biplanes. They were flying in a V formation and heading for us. They were slightly below us. If I had not taken us up we would have been flying at their altitude. Something did not smell right. "I'm going up a little more Hutton."

"But sir, there are just five of them. We took on eight yesterday; this is probably all that they have left."

That decided me, "No, Lumpy, if they only had five left they would not have sent them out. This is a trap."

I was about to swing the flight around and abort the mission when Sergeant Hutton said, "Sir! Above us! Another ten Fokkers!"

They had the advantage of height and there was no point in fleeing. Their superior speed would enable them to catch us. We had to break them up and then try to get home. "Hutton, fire the Very Pistol."

"Sir!"

As the rocket soared aloft I could see that they had worked out our Modus Operandi. If we had attacked the five Fokkers then the others would have swooped down on our unprotected rears. We would have been picked off one by one. I eased back on the throttle to allow Freddie to join me. I pointed to the twelve Fokkers and he nodded. These were flying in four Vs of three aeroplanes each. The nearest flight to me was Gordy's to the north. I pointed to the second V and Freddie nodded. We would try to isolate the end six aeroplanes. The five which had been bait had a long way to climb to reach us. I was also acutely aware that we were nearing our ceiling height. At least that would give us an extra five miles an hour.

"Hutton, I want you and Laithwaite to take out the aeroplanes between us. Lieutenant Carrick and I will fire at the Fokkers either side of the leader."

"Right sir. By the way do you see he has a red propeller!"

"You are right. If we get back we will tell the adjutant about that. Here we go!"

It must have looked, to the Germans, as though we were walking into their trap. The six aeroplanes on the left of their formation would be able to sweep around and harry the end of our line. They would not know that we intended to blow a hole in the middle of their squadron.

The leader was a cool customer and he held his fire as long as we did. When he did fire he aimed at me which meant he aimed his aeroplane at me and that, in turn, swung the whole of the line. It was his first mistake. I turned my bus slightly and the bullets thudded into the fuselage just behind me. I opened fire at the second aeroplane and caught him moving so that he could not fire at me. I hit his engine with one burst and then fired a shorter five bullet burst. I saw his head disappear in a red mist and his aeroplane continued its turn. I had time to watch the next aeroplane have to swing out of line to evade a crash.

Meanwhile Hutton and Laithwaite had concentrated their fire on the leader. One of the rounds must have struck the fuel tank for it exploded in the air. Freddie had damaged his enemy and, as he glanced at me I waved north. He nodded and we both began to swing our aeroplanes towards the three, now isolated Fokkers. As they came around Fryer and his gunner both struck one aeroplane. Hutton and Laithwaite struck the second and, as the third tried to head east Dunston and Giggs hit him. Suddenly there was clear air before us. Two Fokkers were heading east while a third fell to its death.

I dipped my nose, desperately trying to use the altitude and extra speed to put air between us and the Germans. "Rear Lewis, Hutton."

He had a fearful expression for manning the rear Lewis when diving gave you the feeling that you were about to fall backwards out of the aeroplane. When he was secure he shouted, "They have reorganised. There are nine of them and they are diving." I looked at the altimeter. We were now down to five thousand feet but, more importantly, we could see Gordy ahead. It looked like they were strafing ground troops. I pulled my Very Pistol out and fired a flare. I hoped he would see it and know that we were in trouble.

"They are gaining, sir. Mr Dunston is taking hits. They are too far away for me to hit." Suddenly he shouted, "Reload the Very sir and hand it to me!" I did as asked, my curiosity piqued. He seemed to aim it, firing at a very shallow angle. He watched, his tongue peeping between his lips. Then he shouted, "Yee Haw!"

I would have to wait until we landed to find out the reason for the shout. Perhaps it was the second flare which Gordy saw for his five aeroplanes began to ascend in a ragged line. I saw Freddie look over and I signalled for a turn to port. We would sweep around and climb with Gordy. The Fokkers would have to face ten Gunbuses and twenty Lewis guns.

Hutton shouted, "Mr Dunston is hit. He is heading north."

Those were my standing orders. If you were damaged then you headed for home. Our turn helped him as we swept around and Giggs and his gunner hit the pursuing Fokker who thought he had an easy kill. He proved to be the easier kill. The Germans were not expecting reinforcements and a wall of bullets made them decide that they had done enough for their dead leader and they turned. One pilot, with a red jagged line running the length of the fuselage bravely tried to take on Gordy but D flight converged on him and his brightly painted Fokker was riddled with bullets.

Amazingly it did not fall from the air. He was a good pilot and he dived below us and out of the range of our guns.

It was time for us to head home too. We followed the smoking Gunbus of Lieutenant Dunston and I thanked whatever premonition had warned me of danger. It had saved all of us.

"While you are there Lumpy, check the damage to the other buses."

"Righto sir." I saw him scanning both sides. "They are all pretty badly shot up, sir. We'll be lucky to take a full flight up tomorrow. How are we?"

The controls felt a little sluggish and the yoke was not as responsive as it normally was. We too had been damaged. I prayed that the undercarriage had not been hit. That often killed crews which had survived fierce fire fights. The problem with dogfights such as the one we had just experienced was that they happened so quickly and you were so busy firing that you shut out the hits to your own craft. The windsock in the distance made me feel a little better. Dunston fired his Very pistol and I saw the ambulances race to the field. He landed, safely enough, and I saw him jump down and run around to the front cockpit. The injury was to his gunner.

I let the others land first. They managed it successfully except for Giggs. His undercarriage had been damaged and as it collapsed he caught the tip of his wing and the whole bus slewed to the side. Both of the crew climbed out safely.

When we rolled to a halt I leaned forward and kissed the instrument panel, "Well done Caesar! Well done!"

I climbed out and Lumpy Hutton patted the horse insignia. Although there were many holes in the cockpit, the horse had not suffered at all. "This is a lucky horse sir."

"What did you hit with the flare?"

"Nothing sir but it exploded just in front of the leading aeroplane and he swerved away. It took him five minutes to get back in a firing position."

I shook my head in admiration, "My God, man, you have a fearful imagination!"

Chapter 10

I took my pipe from my pocket. I could feel myself slowing down. It was always the same after action. I had found that filling and smoking my pipe brought me back to earth easily. Gordy and Ted walked towards me as I left Sergeant Hutton to complete his examination of the aeroplane. "It looks like you ran into trouble."

I began to fill my pipe, "We did, Ted." I told him of the ambush. By the time the pipe was going we had reached the headquarters. "The trouble is I think they have a higher ceiling than we do. We were pretty much at our limit when we engaged them. It means that they can always have the height advantage and, with the speed advantage, that puts us on the defensive."

Captain Marshall and Major Leach were in the office and heard the end of our conversation. "Your buses look pretty badly shot up, Bill."

I nodded, "And I think we took some casualties. Dunston's gunner was hit. The boys did well and it could have been much worse."

"It is not going so well on the ground either. It looks like the advance is going slower."

Ted asked, "Slower?"

"In the first week the offensive gained some miles. In the second week it has been in yards. We have made a bump in the front line."

"Is the offensive over then?" A large part of me wanted it to be. I was not afraid to face the Germans but it seemed such a waste of brave infantry to bleed so much and to gain so little.

"No, the generals will continue to push and hope that the enemy breaks first."

"The good news is that the Engineers will be over tomorrow to build a couple of new buildings and to make some emplacements for guns. We are getting some anti-aircraft guns. It seems the Germans have been bombing airfields in other sectors. Wing wants us be prepared."

Bates must have been watching for me. As I entered the building he tut-tutted me. "Captain Harsker, I have seen that aeroplane of yours! I have seen moth eaten suits with fewer holes in it. You need to take more care of yourself, sir."

I chuckled. Bates had no concept of aerial warfare. Perhaps I ought to take him up for a spin. Then I looked at the neat little man. He would go but it would break him. "I am afraid, Bates, that the Germans were out to get us today. They had twice as many aeroplanes as we did. We were lucky to get out unscathed."

He looked incredulous, "You call that unscathed sir? Dear me. Well let's get you in the bath and cleaned up. You will feel much better."

He was like my mother when I had been a young boy. But he was right. When I re-entered the bathroom in my robe he was waiting for me with a drink. "Here you are sir." As I sipped it he looked at me critically. "Sir, do you mind an impertinence?"

"That depends how impertinent Bates. Go on."

"Your moustache, sir, it just seems to grow."

"That's what hair does Bates."

"Yes sir, I know," he added patiently, "but with a little judicious trimming it could have more style."

I stood and looked in the mirror. He was right. It looked like a ragged hairy caterpillar crawling across my top lip. I had grown it to emulate Lord Burscough but it looked nothing like his. I contemplated shaving it off. "Perhaps I will remove it."

"No sir, just sit down and let me go to work." He beavered away with the scissors for ten minutes or so and then said, "There you are, sir, look at it now."

I looked in the mirror and it was neat and looked like Lord Burscough's. "Excellent Bates."

He looked crestfallen, "Sir, it is not finished!" He took a small bottle with an aromatic liquid in it and put a tiny amount on his fingers. He began to work it into the moustache and then spread his arms at the mirror.

I looked and saw that it now had style. "That is a good job Bates but how will I get it to look as good as this on my own?"

"You do not need to, sir. You have, Bates!"

He spun, almost like a ballet dancer and left triumphantly. It was at that moment that I saw that I was part of his rehabilitation. He could not have done this for his gentlemen in the trenches but he could here and each time I returned he would have more confidence that I would survive. He was like one of my young pilots. I needed to nurture and care for him too. I had thought it was the other way around.

When I was dressed and feeling human again I went to find Senior Flight Sergeant McKay. "Well, Flight, what is the damage?"

"I reckon we can have you and Mr Giggs in the air tomorrow and that will be it. Sorry sir."

"Not your fault. Get your lads to rig the bomb racks to the two aeroplanes."

He frowned, "I didna see that on the schedule for tomorrow."

"You didn't I will go and see Major Leach now."

Archie was in his office, apparently drowning in paperwork. "I can see why the Colonel never flew! This stuff seems to have a mind of its own and just grow and grow."

I laughed and began to fill my pipe. "How is he by the way?"

"Much improved. He is back in Blighty now in a civilian hospital specialising in heart cases. Headquarters confirmed he won't be back. If he doesn't want to retire they will give him a desk job."

"Good. Listen, Major I want to try something tomorrow."

He leaned back and put his arms behind his head. "Go ahead, any distraction is welcome!"

"I only have two aeroplanes fit to fly tomorrow."

"We have nothing major on. The offensive is going nowhere and the brass is planning what to do next. You could just stand your flight down. They have had a tough time of late. I know that the others are going to stand down. Their buses need some maintenance."

"I know but Giggs and I both have new buses and Hutton came up with an idea. He suggested taking four bombs up with us when we fly. If we don't meet aeroplanes we can do more damage with bombs than guns alone. I was going to take Giggs up today. He hasn't used bombs yet and I will be able to gauge how viable a proposition it is."

He leaned forward and picked up his pen again, "You are second in command laddie, if you think it is a good idea then just do it."

"Thank you sir."

After dinner I took young Giggs to one side. "Tomorrow, Rupert, there will be just you and me flying."

His face broke into a grin, "Good show sir!"

"Get excited after I tell you what we are about. You are having bombs fitted to your bus. If we don't see the Hun we will find some Germans to bomb and strafe. Hutton is telling your gunner all that he needs to know about bombing."

He looked disappointed, "Bombing sir?"

"It is a valuable mission, Rupert. We are not here to garner glory by shooting down Hun planes. We are here to support our infantry and win the war! Never forget that."

"Sorry sir, right sir. I will go and have a word with Reg now."

Word soon got out and I was inundated with young pilots keen to join me. The exception was Lieutenant Carstairs. I could see from his expression, when Rupert told him what we were going to do, that he thought it beneath a noble knight. Bombing was like being a delivery man and not a knight.

As I was eating a light breakfast the next day I heard guns to the west. It sounded like there was an attack going on after all. The front was still quite fluid in places and battalions tried to

112

eliminate those strong points which might be used to launch sneak attacks or use as artillery observation points. Perhaps a colonel had elected to take matters into his own hands.

As Rupert and I made our way to our buses I saw the vehicles arrive with the Engineers. A few moments couldn't hurt and I waited as they drove up to the Mess Halls. I was delighted when Bert, now a sergeant, jumped down. He saluted me and I pulled his cap down over his eyes and then shook his hand, "It's still me you daft bugger. How are you doing, Bert?"

He tapped his stripes, "I thought I was doing well until I saw the MC. Well done our kid." I shrugged. "And our Alice says you have got a young lady. Very pretty and nice by all accounts. I shall have to get myself wounded and find one for me."

"Don't you dare. Listen I have a mission to go on. I'll see you when I get back."

"Oh we'll be here. We have enough work for two days."

There was a spring in my step as I strode to my Gunbus. Bert looked well and he had filled out. I had begun the war with three brothers and Bert was the only one left. It made him more special somehow.

Rupert was waiting with the two sergeants by the aeroplanes. "Now you will have to just follow me today. When and if we go in for a bombing run give me a couple of hundred feet." I looked at his gunner. "It's Reg isn't it?"

"Yes sir."

"Sergeant Hutton here is a good bomb aimer. Look to where he drops his and try to drop them close. No one is judging you today so don't freeze. We just want to see how you both cope with this. Right?"

"Right sir."

"And you are my wingman today so Reg you will be on the rear Lewis all the way home!"

Once we were in the air Lumpy said, "He'll be fine sir. He has his head screwed on. They are a funny pair. Mr Giggs is as posh as they come and Reg comes from a tiny house in Leeds. They get on though."

113

"Good."

As we headed towards the front I noticed some explosions to the north east of the front. "We'll head towards the action today. Better arm the Lewis."

I glanced down at the map and saw that it looked like an attack in the Delville Wood area. It was not far from Pozières; a place we knew well.

"Keep your eyes peeled for fighters and balloons."

"The sky looks empty, sir."

It did but that could be deceptive. There was little point in gaining altitude. A bombing and strafing run were better at a lower altitude but I was acutely aware of the potential for a Hun in the sun. As we neared the woods I saw brown uniforms, not marching in lines but darting forward close to the village of Longueval. I later found out they were South Africans and Rhodesians. They were trying to use whatever cover they could. The Germans had mortars and machine guns and it was a killing ground.

"Sergeant we will fly over the woods and see if we can spot anyone."

"Righto sir."

I lifted the nose and climbed a little so that when I dived I would have a few extra knots of airspeed. I wanted to make us a difficult target to hit. I aimed the aeroplane towards the centre of the woods. As we screamed down the air was filled with small arms fire. Most of it seemed to fly through the empty fuselage. As we climbed on the other side Hutton said, "I think I saw them sir. If you fly the reverse of this course but two hundred feet further west we should be able to get them."

"Good man. One bomb run or two?"

"Two and I have a couple of Mills Bombs so we might manage three." He was irrepressible.

This time the Germans would be ready. I cocked the Lewis gun and, as we zoomed down, I began to fire short bursts. I could see nothing but trees. I just assumed that there would be Germans beneath the green canopy. I saw Hutton holding one bomb in his left hand while his right was held over the side. He didn't drop the bomb, he threw it and then deftly switched the other bomb from his left to right and threw that. He then grabbed his Lewis and began to fire down at the ground. I lifted the nose and he continued to fire until his magazine was empty.

I began to bank. I saw the explosions throw branches and trees into the air. Giggs had done as I said and as he flew across the woods the debris was falling to the ground. There was a longer gap between Reg's throws but it was a good attempt to hit the target. I swung the nose around for a second run. The four bombs had made a hole in the middle of Delville Wood and Sergeant Hutton and I could see the damage we had caused already.

I opened fire again. Hutton did not make quick throws this time he actually aimed. He threw the first one and there was a gap before he hurled the second. As he began to fire his gun there was an almighty explosion. We began to climb and he said, as he changed his magazine. "Ammunition sir!"

Banking around I saw that Giggs and his gunner were flying lower. They had more confidence this time. The two bombs threw trees into the air and the sky over the woods was filled with smoke and debris. "Time to go home, sergeant. If you get the opportunity drop your grenades."

"Righto sir."

I did not fire my Lewis. We were heading for the advancing South African soldiers. I didn't want any of them struck by a stray bullet. I kept us low and Hutton suddenly hurled one of the Mills Bombs and then a few seconds later the other. He quickly fired the machine down the length of the trench. We had noticed that these were not the deep tranches we had explored. The ones they were using were hastily constructed and Sergeant Hutton could not miss. As we passed over the South African Division we heard their cheers. I waggled the wings and Hutton waved cheerily. It had been a good mission.

As we neared the airfield I could see the work which Bert and his men had done. There were pits in which the artillery was setting up guns. They were not huge pieces but they would deter any German bombers. The extensions to the buildings were clearly visible and it looked like another barracks was being erected. We would be snug for winter. Now we just needed Mr Doyle to make good on his promise of furniture.

"A proper home from home now, eh sir?"

"It is indeed, Sergeant Hutton. It is indeed."

Chapter 11

Lieutenant Giggs and his gunner were animated when they joined me. "What did Sergeant Hutton hit with his second bomb sir?"

"Ammunition I think."

Giggs nodded, "You were right sir. I can see how that makes a difference to the troops on the ground. We could hear their cheers as we flew over them. Why don't we carry bombs more often, sir?"

"It slows us down and if they are hit by German machine guns the crew tend to be spread all over France!"

"Ah. Still, it might be handy to carry a couple of grenades like Sergeant Hutton."

"Now that is a good idea."

I wandered over to the Engineers. I saw Bert straight away. He was stripped to the waist and handling a sledgehammer as though it was a child's toy. He had put on a great deal of muscle since he had joined up. His officer who was watching snapped to attention when he saw me approaching.

"Carry on, I just want a word with my brother if that is all right with you, lieutenant?"

"Of course sir. Hargreaves, take over from Harsker."

Bert pulled a cigarette from behind his ear and lit it. "You got back safe then?"

"Aye, I did."

"Your two chums, Gordy and Ted, were chatting to me about you. You are quite the hero aren't you?"

"Don't you start, as well."

He shook his head, "No I just wanted to say that I always looked up to you and you were a bit of a hero to me but I am so proud of you now because you are a genuine hero. It makes what we do seem like nothing."

I turned to face him. "Now don't think that way. We are all part of one big team. I happen to know that what you do, digging mines and laying explosives under the enemy's lines is far braver and more courageous than anything I do. I know that the newspapers don't see it that way but what do they know? The journalists are safely sitting in Fleet Street while other poor sods are getting killed."

He laughed, "Watch out, you sound just like our Tom and John."

"Maybe I am it's just that I don't see the upper classes as the enemy. I see incompetent generals and newspaper men who make all of this sound glorious. It is not glorious to fall in a ball of flame. It is not noble to spiral five thousand feet and hit the ground. It is a tragedy that the finest young men in Great Britain are being slaughtered. The fat cats at home are reaping the reward of their sacrifice."

"Do want a hand to get down our kid?"

"What?"

"From your soapbox! We can't change things. Dad taught us that. We just make the best of what we have."

"Well, perhaps, when this madness is over we can change the world a little."

"Mebbe. Anyway I'll get back to work. I'll see you later."

Just then Bates approached, "Sir, your bath is getting cold!"

"I'll be right there Bates."

Bert began to laugh, "Why you two faced bugger! You have a servant and you want to change things! That's rich."

I smiled, "Perhaps, later, I will tell you what I do want to change."

In the end I did not get much chance to chat with Bert. After dinner, just as I was making my way to the Engineers' camp I heard the drone of an approaching aeroplane. I recognised the sound. It was a Fokker! The duty sergeant had heard it too and he rang the bell for air raid. Everyone flooded out of the messes. Archie said, "How many?"

"I can just hear one, sir. It is German and it is coming from the east. I would guess a Fokker D11."

"You have heard more than most I will take your word for it."

The sentries had their rifles aimed at the sky. Twenty four hours later and we would have had guns in place to fire at them but tonight we were helpless. It was hard to see the Fokker against the cloudless sky. I heard the crack of rifles as the sentries saw the shape. I didn't have the heart to tell them it was a waste of bullets. They needed to be doing something. I heard Sergeant Lowery shout, "He's dropped something!"

All of us hit the ground. A bomb thrown at a crowd of men could be devastating. All we heard was a thud and then the sound of the Fokker began to recede. It was going east. What was all that about? The sentries continued to waste ammunition and take pot shots as it droned towards the east. We had had a lucky let off. If there had been more of them or if he had had a bomb then our milling around would have enabled him to wipe out most of the pilots of our squadron in one fell swoop.

One of the sentries ran to the object and brought it to Archie. Someone shouted, "Watch out sir! It could be a bomb!"

"Don't be daft laddie! It would have gone off. Let's get it inside the mess and have a wee look at this."

The officers headed for our mess. The disappointed sergeants and engineers excluded from the examination stood around, a murmur of conversation and glowing cigarettes marking their position.

As we walked into the light I saw that it was a white flying scarf around a rock. It seemed a strange weapon. Inside the mess Archie slowly undid the scarf. There was an air of anticipation as he revealed the rock. He held it and began to examine it. He held it to his ear and he shook it. "Perhaps they are running out of bullets?" Everyone laughed.

Randolph looked at the white scarf and laid it out. It was a silk scarf and looked expensive. He said, "Sir, there is a letter." He slowly unfolded it and laid it on the table before us. He opened it and began to read,

To the commander of Squadron 41

Sir,

I send this to the pilot who flies the aeroplane with the rearing horse. You are the best pilot in the RFC. Yesterday you killed my squadron leader, Otto. I challenge you to a duel in the skies above the front. I will meet you over No-Man's Land south of Delville Wood. I shall be there at dawn.

Oblt. Stephan Kirmaier

Jasta 2

Everyone turned and looked at me. "Fine English," said Captain Marshall.

Archie turned to me, "Your fame is spreading. You have got under the Oberlieuteant's skin."

Ted lit a cigarette, "What a maroon; as though anyone would be daft enough to meet him at dawn. They will probably have the whole squadron waiting."

Jamie Carstairs said, quite passionately, "Oh no, sir. He sounds like an honourable man. He mentions a duel. You must meet him sir. Honour demands it."

Gordy laughed, "Honour my arse! Captain Harsker is not going are you, Bill?"

"Of course not. Just because this German pilot is deranged is no reason to join in the madness."

Freddie said, "That must have been the chap with the red propeller you shot down the other day."

"He wasn't anything special."

Freddie continued, no sir but do you remember that madman with the red jagged line who tried to take us all on? I bet this chap was him."

120

"You may be right. Do you mind, sir, if I have this for a souvenir?"

"Of course but first we send it to Headquarters. This is valuable intelligence. It gives us the name of a senior pilot and the name of the squadron."

I nodded, "Righto."

Jamie spent the rest of the evening trying to persuade me to fight. Eventually Gordy sent him to bed. "God, it's like being the parent of a naughty child. This is good practice for when Mary and I have children."

"Steady on, old man, you aren't even married yet."

He put his arm around my shoulders. "Don't forget, Captain Harsker, I am not the only one in the situation. I'll tell you what, I'll be your best man if you'll be mine!"

Ted said, indignantly, "What about me? Am I invisible?"

"When we are certain that you know what a woman is we will include you!"

We bantered and joked through half a bottle of whisky and I went to bed quite happily. I had been quite taken with the thought that the Germans thought I was the best pilot. I didn't but I had been noticed and that was no mean feat. Bates had turned down my covers and placed a glass of water and whisky next to my bed. I saw my clean uniform laid out for the morning. I realised I was getting used to being pampered and I liked it.

I had a dream. I normally dreamed but could not remember them. This one I could. I was young and we had gone on a day trip to Blackpool. I was on the ride called "The River Caves of the World." We were underground and the ride was buffeting against the sides of the water. I saw our Bert fall into the water but I couldn't help him. I tried to shout but now words came out. I suddenly sat bolt upright in bed. I was sweating. I took the glass of whisky and drank it down in one. It burned as it went down. Suddenly I thought I heard a noise. I shook my head and looked out of the window. It was not even dawn. Then I heard the unmistakeable sound of a Gunbus being started. Someone was flying… and it was not even dawn.

I downed the water in one and began to dress. I had a bad feeling about all of this. By the time I was dressed I could hear the sound of a Gunbus taking off and there were shouts too. What on earth was going on?

I was the first one out of the officers' quarters. I ran directly towards the parked aeroplanes. Sergeant Gillespie was the duty sergeant. "Sorry sir. It was Mr Carstairs and his gunner. They said they had permission to take off and the lad," he glared at a young private, "let him."

"It is not your fault, either of you. You," I pointed to the private, "go and wake Sergeant Hutton tell him I need him."

"Sir!" He raced off, happy to be away from the sergeant's baleful stare.

"Sergeant, get my bus turned around."

"You're going after him sir?"

"If I don't we will be one pilot short in the morning."

I ran back to my quarters and grabbed my flying helmet and flying coat. It was cold at four a.m.

By the time I reached the FE 2 it had been turned around and there was a gaggle of officers there, Gordy and Archie included. I smiled when I saw that they were all in their robes. I saw Hutton rushing to me, hurriedly dressing.

"Who was it, Bill?"

I looked at Gordy, "It was Carstairs. I should have known from the way he was going on about honour."

"He's in my flight, Bill. I'll go."

I shook my head, "By the time you and your gunner are dressed he will be dead meat. Every second I waste talking to you means that your young pilot has less time to live." I hated being so brutal to my friend but time was wasting.

"Hutton, get her started."

I clambered aboard and heard, "Contact!"

"Contact!" Despite the early morning cold the Rolls Royce Engine started first time.

As we soared into the dark I heard Hutton say, "A bit bloody parky at this time of the day!"

122

"Thank you for this Lumpy. I just don't want Mr Carstairs to do anything stupid."

"That's not a problem, Captain Harsker. The young have a habit of making mistakes." There was a pause. "Did I hear right, there was a challenge from some Hun?"

"Aye, some spike headed stiff necked German with more schooling than sense!"

He laughed, "Where are we heading then sir?"

"Delville Wood."

I wondered if the woods were cursed or something. We were certainly being drawn to them. I saw dawn break on the horizon. Below me I heard the bugles as reveille was called in the trenches. We were passing the front lines. I wondered what they thought was happening above them. I was trying to get every ounce I could out of the bus but she was not the fastest aeroplane on the front.

"Better arm your gun, Hutton, we shall have to get in and out quickly."

"Righto sir."

I armed mine at the same time and I also checked my Luger. I could not let Carstairs down. He was doing this for me. I knew I had not asked him to but he had a distorted sense of right and wrong. When I got him back I would sit him down and give him a serious talking to.

When Germans began to fire at us I knew that we were over their lines and then I heard the chatter of the Spandau followed by the double chatter of the two Lewis guns. I was too late. They had met. I had counted on the German being late. I should have known that the Teutonic need for efficiency would have brought him there early.

They could just be seen twisting and turning in the brightening sky. In theory, the two guns of the Gunbus should have given Carstairs the edge but the faster Fokker and the experience of the German would more than make up for that.

"Come on Caesar, a little bit more please!"

It might have been my imagination but I felt the aeroplane move a little faster. The two fighters, seemingly intertwined, now seemed to be just a mile or so away. Carstairs was doing his best but he was wasting bullets. He was firing when he should have allowed his gunner to do so. He could have side slipped out of the German's sight but he seemed intent on making the hit himself.

Suddenly I saw the Gunbus judder. We were closing rapidly and I saw the gunner slump in the front cockpit. The German then did the Immelmann Turn. Carstairs had never seen it. He would be confused. He had no rear gunner and was on his own. I had to watch helpless as Oberlieutenant Kirmaier dropped down to the rear of the Gunbus and emptied a magazine at the engine. The Rolls Royce is a fine engine but it was demolished by the steel jacketed parabellums. It went into a vertical dive and smashed into the ground. The only saving grace was that Carstairs would have felt nothing. He had his noble death!

"Right Lumpy, let's get this bastard!"

"I'm with you, sir!"

The German had not seen us and began to head east. I was not thinking about honour and fair play. I was going to shoot this arrogant German aristocrat; even if we were shot down. I owed that to a young man who might have become a great pilot.

I climbed to get above him. He had superior speed and appeared to be getting away from us. I just needed patience. When I reached eight thousand feet I put the stick down. We began to pick up speed and gained on him.

"Sir, I don't want to worry you but I see a German airfield ahead."

"What's the matter Hutton? Do you want to live forever?"

"No sir, but my mum has promised me socks for my next birthday!"

We were now less than five hundred feet behind him and I dipped the nose a little more. He was slowing, preparing for a landing. Suddenly he was less than a hundred feet ahead.

"Now sir?"

"Now Lumpy!"

The chatter of the Lewis shredded his tail. I saw him look around in horror. He could not move left or right as he had no rudder and he showed what a good pilot he was by trying to climb. Hutton kept on firing and then shouted, "Jam!"

I side slipped and anticipated his next move which was a dive. My bullets hit his undercarriage and then he flew the engine into the line of .303 bullets. I saw the propeller stop. I raised the nose and emptied the magazine. I saw the bullets strike him but the magazine ran out before he was dead. We were overtaking him and I drew my Luger. Drawing level I looked directly at him and aimed the Luger. I began to fire. My first bullet struck his shoulder and he fell forward. The Fokker began an even steeper dive.

Suddenly the air was filled with lead as the Germans fired at us. "Sir, he is finished, can we go home now?"

I felt weary, "Yes Lumpy." A thought struck me. "Any grenades?"

"Always!"

"Then let us leave them a little present."

I changed my magazine and banked. We had been heading east. As we zoomed down the airfield I fired at the line of Fokkers and Halberstadts. I saw the two steel eggs get thrown over the side and then Hutton fired his Lewis. I heard the crump as the grenades went off and, as we soared west I glanced over and saw that we had hit four aeroplanes and there were soldiers gathered around the men we had hit. Carstairs had been avenged.

It was a glorious dawn which broke behind us but I was not in a celebratory mood. I felt that I had failed young Jamie. I had started to understand him but the German intervention had sent him on this self destructive course.

I heard Hutton's voice in my ear. "Sir, we have company." He held up his mirror. I could see four or five biplanes pursuing us. I checked my fuel gauge. I had just enough fuel to reach home. If I had flown more conservatively on my way east I might have had a reserve.

"We can't climb. Let's see how low we can go."

"Righto, sir. I'll see if I can collect some eggs on the way back!"

I smiled. Hutton was irrepressible. The sound of his voice always cheered me up.

I dipped the nose just as we came over the German trenches. They were standing to but we took them by surprise. I suspect they thought that we were one of their own. They just stared as we zoomed across their lines. Hutton kept the mirror held out so that he could follow the enemy's progress. We went slower when he stood on the rear Lewis and he knew, as well as any, that we needed to gain speed and conserve fuel.

"Here they come, sir."

I saw him struggling to turn around and man the rear Lewis. The leading German fired a few bullets just to get the range. As he did so the ground in front of us erupted in small arms fire as the Tommies fired at the Fokkers trying to catch us. As Sergeant Hutton cocked the Lewis he shouted, "Good lad!" He looked at me. "They have hit one and the others are heading home."

We were so low that I could see the faces and waving arms of the South Africans. I waggled my wings and waved at them. Hutton was waving as though he was George the Fifth at a royal parade. As we touched down we were almost flying on fumes but we were alive and we were back.

Chapter 12

There was no question of my leading a patrol that day. My Gunbus needed attention. Senior Flight Sergeant McKay gave me a shake of his head as he walked around the bullet ridden front. "One of these days Captain Harsker, there will be too many holes in you never mind yon aeroplane."

Archie and Gordy strode over to me. The fact that we had returned alone spoke volumes. Gordy cocked his head to one side. I shook mine, "He did his best but he was outfoxed. That was a good pilot he was facing."

"Did you get him?"

"I chased him back to his lines and shot him down but I don't know if I killed the bastard. It was the one with the red zig zag stripe running down the side."

"You found their airfield then?"

"Yes sir. It looks, from the number of aeroplanes, as though there are two squadrons there. Hutton damaged a couple with Mills bombs and the Tommies shot down one that was chasing us home."

"Right. We will strike while the iron is hot." He shouted, "Sergeant Richardson, I want all of the aeroplanes fitting with bombs."

"You will need me to lead you there sir."

"Are you sure? You have no aeroplane."

I pointed to the Avro we used for training; it was regularly serviced and the sergeants who wanted to be pilots had lessons in it. Charlie Sharp had been the last one to do so but I knew it was a good, if slow and ponderous, aeroplane. "So long as you don't mind going there slowly I think I can lead you."

"Good show. Get yourselves something to eat. It will take time to arm the Gunbuses."

"Sergeant Hutton, get some food. We are going up in the Avro. You better rig a Lewis up when you have eaten."

"Right sir."

I was alone in the Officer's Mess. Bates rushed along. "Captain Harsker. It doesn't do to go flying on an empty stomach." He wagged an admonishing finger at me. Turning around he saw the orderlies cleaning up. "I'll get you something." He pointed to one of them. "You, whatever your name is, get the Captain a cup of tea, two sugars and milk in second. Chop, chop!"

The surprised orderly nodded and raced off. "You can't get the staff you know. Now you sit here and I won't be two ticks!"

I lit my pipe as I waited. The two German squadrons would be going nowhere. The crashed and damaged Fokkers meant they would have an airfield to clear. I had plenty of time for a late breakfast.

The orderly brought my tea and said, sotto voce, "He's a bit of a whirlwind is your Mr Bates, sir. Even Sergeant Cole is polite to him."

"Yes he is a force of nature. I am glad he is on our side."

Bates did not suffer fools gladly. The tea was just as I liked it and all the more welcome for my having waited for it. I was on my second cup when the miraculous Mr Bates arrived with a tray. He deposited a plate with a mountain of food: ham, three eggs, Cumberland sausage, Black Pudding and devilled kidneys. He then placed another plate with a mountain of toast. "I'll go and get the butter. What would you prefer Captain; marmalade or jam?"

To be honest I normally took the nearest, "Er, marmalade."

"Right sir." He reappeared and flourished the butter and the marmalade. "I shall have to get some decent marmalade, sir. This has barely any peel in it. It is more like an orange jam." He stood back. "Enjoy sir and I will lay out a fresh uniform for you."

I paused with a forkful of Cumberland sausage and ham. "That won't be necessary, Bates, Sergeant Hutton and I are going up again after this."

He shook his head, "Dear me, sir. You are put upon are you not?" He toddled off shaking his head. It is funny but Bates and Hutton between them induced a state of equilibrium in me. I felt refreshed already and I realised that I had put the death of Carstairs to the back of my mind.

It was some time since I had flown the Avro. It felt strange to be in an aeroplane with a propeller in front of me. The riggers had put the Lewis so that, by leaning, Hutton could fire to the front, the rear and to the right. It was more restricted than the Gunbus but I hoped we would not be needed to fight.

McKay had a mechanic to turn the propeller. The engine sounded noisier and less smooth than the Rolls Royce but it was a good aeroplane. I waited until Archie waved and then we rolled down the airfield. It felt nose heavy as I pulled back on the yoke. I began to climb. It seemed to take forever but at least the Avro had a greater ceiling. If we had to we could climb above the Fokkers.

There appeared to be little action on the ground. As we passed Delville Woods I saw the South Africans digging in. Beyond them we saw the Germans creating trenches in, as yet, unsullied soil. We had the same endurance as the Gunbus and I was not worried about fuel. Our slow speed meant that the squadron could even take their time over the target. Major Leach was leading my flight. I wondered how they would view the change in leadership.

I saw the German field ahead and I waggled my wings. I turned and shouted, "Lumpy wave to show the major where the field is."

A moment later he shouted, "He has seen the signal sir. They are attacking now."

Of course Lieutenant Giggs had bombed before but the others might be finding it a strange experience. I spiralled up to get out of the way. I could have headed for home but that was not my way and I wanted to see my flight and my squadron in action.

The guns placed by the Germans began to open fire. They had heavy machine guns mounted in sand bagged emplacements on either side of the field. These were the 7.92mm guns. They also had some ancient 15cm artillery pieces and these, while they made a great deal of noise did little damage. You would have to be extremely unlucky to be shot down by one of those. Especially at the low altitude the major was using. The machine guns, on the other hand had converging fire. The later Gunbuses would face a fierce fire.

My flight had the easiest of bombing runs. The Germans were still manning their weapons and I saw all of the bombs strike aeroplanes and emplacements. Then it was Charlie Sharp and his flight. Their bombs compounded the damage done by C flight. When Ted and B Flight zoomed down they were able to target the headquarters and other buildings. His flight also suffered the first casualties. Lieutenant Carrick was hit. I saw the smoke pouring from his engine. He banked and began to limp west. He would not make our lines. I just hoped he could get close to Delville Woods. Perhaps the South Africans might be able to help.

When Gordy and his flight dropped down to finish the work of the squadron he flew into a maelstrom of metal. I saw his gunner slump forward after he had thrown two of his bombs. He had the smallest flight now and that meant the Germans could concentrate their fire.

Major Leach saw the danger and he led my flight to strafe the gun emplacements. Perhaps he should have done so earlier for the anti aircraft fire ceased but I saw Lieutenant Charlton holding his shoulder and Lieutenant Swan's gunner looked to have been hit. The squadron began to head west. I stayed high to watch them. Some of them were leaking oil while others appeared to have suffered engine damage.

Lieutenant Morley fell further and further back. I could see him looking for somewhere to land. I saw, ahead, Lieutenant McCormack's crashed bus beyond Delville Woods and was relieved that he had made the South African lines. Lieutenant Morley would have no such luck. "Lumpy, get ready on the Lewis; we are going down to help them."

"Righto sir."

I thought Morley and his damaged Gunbus was going to make the woods but the engine finally cut out and he slammed into the ground just forty yards from the German trenches. We were diving now and I banked to come across the trenches and allow

130

Hutton to fire to the right. I drew my Luger. Our crashed compatriots were firing with their service revolvers but the Germans were using rifles and machine guns. The Rolls Royce engine afforded some protection but soon the infantry would swarm over the Gunbus to capture the crew.

Hutton fired as soon as he could. I was flying at thirty feet. I was not even sure how much clearance I had beneath my wheels. I aimed the Luger at an officer who was directing fire. I hit his helmet and he fell to the floor not injured but shocked. I kept firing. We needed their heads down. Hutton's withering fire had bought Morley and his gunner time. They sprinted for the woods and the safety of the South African lines.

I began to bank. "Do you have a Mills bomb?"

"Of course, sir."

"Then when I fly over destroy the Gunbus."

The Germans were already swarming out of their trenches to pursue the two fleeing crew. The two young men were fit and had a start. The Germans failed to notice us for we were no longer firing. Lumpy could not miss the crashed bus and, as we soared and banked west, the grenade exploded. The fuel tank erupted and the eager Germans were all destroyed. Morley and his gunner waved as they trotted into the protection of the wood.

"Let's go home, Sergeant."

"Aye sir," he shouted. "I reckon we have earned our rum ration today!"

The Avro had served us well but I would not trade it for my Gunbus. Gordy was waiting for me. "Are they safe?"

I nodded, "They made it to the South African lines. How about the wounded?"

He shook his head. "Two of the gunners died. There are three with wounds. Doc Brennan thinks he can fix them up here. Archie is standing us down tomorrow. I can't see those two squadrons being able to do anything." He hesitated, "Thanks for going after Jamie. I appreciate it. He had potential. If he had gone to an ordinary school which didn't fill his head with heroic nonsense he would have survived."

"It was quick but you know, Gordy, the one I feel sorry for is his gunner. The poor sod hero worshipped Jamie and he died needlessly."

"We'll make sure it doesn't happen again."

I nodded, "I had to have a serious talk with Freddie and Johnny some time ago. They seem to have taken it to heart. Their heads are screwed on now."

For once I did not have a report to make and I headed for my quarters. Bates was bouncing around like a spinning top. "I have run your bath sir and there is a large whisky but I have the most wonderful news, sir! You have letters from home and from the perfume all three are from ladies!"

He was even more delighted than I was, "Thank you Bates." I put my hand on his shoulder. "And thank you for the breakfast this morning it was delicious and thoughtful of you."

He seemed embarrassed, "Sir, that is my job and I am just pleased to serve you. Now get into the bath while it is still hot."

I laid the three letters out in the order I would read them. I had known who they were from as soon as he had said three. I would read mum's first, then Sarah's and finally, save the best until last, Beatrice's. I forced myself to luxuriate in the bath and sip my whisky slowly. I knew we might not get more mail for weeks. I would be able to read and re-read them to my heart's content. I washed the war away. After I had dried myself Bates helped me to dress.

"Would it be impertinent of me to ask who they are from sir?"

"Of course not, Bates. This one is from my mother. I am the eldest boy now and I know she frets about me. This one is from my sister, Sarah; from her I will get the truth no matter what little white lies my mother tells me. And this one is from my young lady, a nurse who cared for me when I was wounded."

He clapped his hands together and giggled, "I just knew it! Now I shall get your laundry done and I will make sure you have no interruptions until dinner."

I lay on the bed and opened my mother's letter.

Burscough July 1st 1916

My Dearest Son,

I hope God continues to watch over you. When our Alice told me you had been wounded I thought the worst. I was more than relieved when Lady Burscough said how well you looked.

Your father was proud as Punch when the King himself gave you your medal. We cut the photograph from the newspaper and put it in a nice frame. You look so handsome in your uniform.

Alice also told us that you have met a nice girl, a nurse. I hope she is nice, Bill because there are some hussies down there. Alice seems to think she is a good girl but I will hold judgement until I have seen her. I am still not happy about our Alice living in London. It is a sinful place. I only let her go because her ladyship persuaded me.

Your father should be retired but they need him with the horses. Most of them men have joined up, there is just Cedric left at the Big House and he is getting fed up with the comments of some of the people in the village. It is a shame. I wish you were all home. These Germans are evil using gas and killing civilians. We have heard that they have been bombing London! I have Alice to worry about now.

Well I shall go now. Little Billy has just woken up. Please, our Bill, continue to write. Just because you have a young lady is no reason to forget your own family.

Your loving mother

xxx

When I had read it I folded it and returned it to its envelope. Kissing the envelope I said, "Dearest mother; as though I could ever forget you."

I sipped some of my whisky and opened Sarah's.

June 28th

Burscough Hall

Dear Bill,

I was relieved when our Alice told me that she had spoken to you and you were not badly wounded. We all think the world of you up here. It is not just the family that think highly of you. Her ladyship is always singing your praises. You probably didn't know it but many of the girls on the estate had their heart set on you. I think their hearts were broken when we told them about your new young lady. You dark horse, you! I am pleased for you. Her ladyship and Alice told me what a nice girl she is. Ignore Mother's comments. You were always her favourite. Beatrice will have to be special to match up to her expectations!

Mother might be a little happier soon. Her ladyship has a surprise. She has contacts in London and has arranged to have a proper copy of the photograph of you with the King. We are going to give it to her on her 60th birthday. (That is September the 1st in case you have forgotten!)

We now notice the war at home. It is lucky that we produce so much food for ourselves. The shelves in the shops are empty now. It is those U-Boats! They are strangling this country!

Cedric is the only man left on the estate and dad still has to work. Some of the snide comments people make about Cedric upset him. They know better than to make them while I am around or they would get the sharp edge of my tongue. Our family has done enough. I have lost two brothers already and my other two brothers are both heroes.

Your nephew grows bigger day by day. Mother swears she can see you in him. I am not so certain but it pleases her.

You take care, brother. You know we love you. I know we rarely say it but that is how we feel. Dad, in particular, misses you. He said to me that with you and Bert away there is an ache in his heart. It almost brings me to tears. Try not to be the hero all the time. I want to be at your wedding!

Your sister,

Sarah,

xxx

I found myself becoming emotional as I read that. I realised just how much I missed my family. I folded the letter, returned it to the envelope and kissed it.

I held Beatrice's letter. I was afraid to open it. I had poured my heart out to her. Suppose she had had second thoughts? Suppose she had met someone else? There must be far better looking young officers with better prospects coming through the doors of the hospital all the time. I finished the whisky off and poured a second one. It was just to delay opening the letter.

"Stop being a bloody fool and open it! Better to know one way or the other!"

My fellow officers would think that I had finally cracked hearing me talking to myself. I lay down on the bed and opened the envelope with a knife. Bates was correct, this letter was perfumed. I held the folded letter in my hand. I had to force myself to open it.

Hyde Park,

June 30th 1916

Dearest Bill,

This is the first chance I have had to write to you since you left so quickly. I have come to the chestnut tree under which we sat on those blissful afternoons. I like to come here as it makes me seem closer to you.

I know you said many things before you left and I hope that you meant them. However if you were just playing with my affections then I would like to thank you for the lovely times we had. I will be waiting for a letter to let me know how you feel now that you are back in the war.

Whatever you decide I will understand.

I have had tea with your sister and I think she is lovely. She thinks the world of you. I am an only child and I miss what you have, a loving family who are close to you.

I hope and pray that you are keeping safe. We read in the newspapers about the terrible casualties and I see many of the results of the war. I could not bear to think of you dying over there or anywhere for that matter.

I decided I would keep this letter bright and breezy but I cannot. I have to tell you that I love you deeply and dearly. I cannot imagine life without you. I know that we have only known each other a short time but I knew the instant you looked at me that you were the man I wanted to spend my life with. I hope that you feel the same way too.

I shall go now because people are looking at me beneath this tree bawling my eyes out.

Your loving Beatrice,

xxx

xx

x

I found my own eyes filling up. I hoped she had received my letter. I resolved to write another one. I could not bear the thought or her being so upset over me. I was not worth it.

I re-read the letter four or five times. There was a knock at my door and Bates stood there. He was beaming; was he a clairvoyant?

"There you are sir. Now you look happier. Let's get you dressed for dinner!"

He hummed as he dressed me. "Will there be anything else sir?"

I said, sincerely, "No, Bates, you have done more than enough for me for today."

He flicked a piece of fluff from my jacket. "My pleasure, sir. My pleasure."

Our lost little chicks had returned and they all came to see me. Lieutenant Morley said, "We owe our lives to you and Sergeant Hutton. Thank you, sir. How on earth did you manage in that ancient aeroplane?"

"So long as you have a gun and some skill you can work wonders you know. And the Avro is not a bad aeroplane. I learned to fly in that very one."

I had an early night and wrote a long and heartfelt letter to Beatrice. I had a future to plan.

Chapter 13

As my bus was ready to fly I sought out Percy Richardson the armourer. "Sergeant Richardson, I would like a second Lewis fitting on my aeroplane."

"You have three already on your bus sir!"

"I know Senior Flight Sergeant but I sometimes do not have time to change the magazines. Two guns for me to use would make life easier. It won't add too much weight and we have spares surely?"

He leaned into me and spoke confidentially. "The trouble is, Captain Harsker, that what you do one day they all want the next."

"And what is the problem with that?"

He seemed flummoxed, "Well, where will it end?"

I grinned, "I have no idea so just do it Senior Flight Sergeant."

I wandered over to the office. Captain Marshall's smile met me at the door. "Morley and McCormack reported that the South Africans were singing our praises. It seems your timely attack broke the back to the enemy and they took it with fewer losses than they expected."

"The case for arming at least one aeroplane in each flight with bombs is now proven. We are always finding targets and bombing is less risky than a strafing run."

"I'll put it to Archie but it seems like a good idea." I filled my pipe. "Your brother said to say goodbye to you yesterday." I jumped up as though he would still be there for me to speak with. "Don't worry. He fully understood. He knew what you were doing was important. He really admires you, Bill."

"I know. It is why he joined up and it makes me feel guilty. What if something happens to him? How could I live with myself?"

"You can't live other people's lives for them. It is fate. You just have to live your life the best that you can. And you do Bill. Believe me."

"You are becoming quite the philosopher, Randolph."

"I think it is the job. I am never in danger here and so I can think about the danger you boys are in. I can look at the war from a detached perspective. Believe me I wish I was up in the air with you chaps. I envy you your success. You seem to have a knack for this sort of thing."

"I have no idea why. I just loved horses and joined the cavalry."

I finished off the flight's paperwork and checked on the upcoming missions. I had the luxury of a morning free of any duties. I wandered down to the bus. I was not surprised to see Lumpy fiddling on with the engine.

"Problem Sergeant Hutton?"

"No sir. It was just when we were in the Avro yesterday I realised that it had a worse engine and yet there was only five knots between them. There must be potential in this beast that we are not harnessing. The Avro has a hundred and thirty horsepower but the Rolls Royce has a hundred and sixty." He spread his arms. "We are going wrong somewhere."

I took off my tunic and rolled up my sleeves. "You are right. Let's see if we can beef this fine engine up. A few more knots would come in handy. These Fokkers are fast. When they develop them a little more then we will be in trouble."

We worked all afternoon on the timing and the carburettor. We looked at the filters and the fuel supply. We would not know if we had succeeded until we flew but I was certain that it would have made some improvements.

"Another good day's work, sir."

It was the second time he had said that. "That is important to you isn't it sergeant?"

He became serious. "Yes sir. It was drilled into us as kids by my dad. You had to do the best and producing a good day's work regardless of others was important. It's what I try to do

139

every day. When I worked in that factory I always did my best. Some of the other lads didn't but I went home every night feeling like a man. You feel better, don't you sir; when you know you have done your best?"

He was right and it struck me that my father had said the same thing. They came from different backgrounds but they were both hard working English working class men and I was proud to come from that stock. They had been the stalwart bowmen who had faced the might of armoured horsemen at Crecy and Agincourt. They had stood in red lines at Waterloo and Balaclava and held off the greatest of armies. A hundred of them had stood at Isandlwana and fought off four thousand Zulus. It was that which would see us through this war and not the rhetoric of the politicians and newspapers.

When we did patrol, a day later, we were depleted in numbers. Archie flew with Gordy and his flight. I think Charlie Sharp had come to realise that he could command a flight as well as any. His flight had had the least casualties and damage; he led them well.

There was a stubborn streak in me and I asked for the Delville Wood sector again. The Hun knew who I was and I was not going to let them think they had won and frightened me away. Dunston and Giggs both had bomb racks fitted. We had devised a signal to use when I needed them to drop them. We would not land with bombs aboard. If we found no juicy targets we would drop them on the roads leading to the front.

We crossed the front at five thousand feet. "Arm your Lewis, Hutton."

"Righto sir."

I looked at the two Lewis guns before me and I armed them. Percy had done a good job and rigged them on the same frame. I could, if I wished fire both at once but that would necessitate me using my knees to fly. I did not expect to have to do that but it was an option. It just meant I did not need to reload and, in a pinch, that might be vital.

As I cocked the second one I heard Lumpy chuckle, "Nice bit of firepower there, sir. Perhaps I should ask for another one."

"I think it would make the front a little too heavy, Hutton. Besides Senior Flight Sergeant Richardson might have a heart attack!"

"That's not very nice sir, calling me heavy!" I heard the self deprecating tone and smiled. Lumpy could handle himself.

As we crossed the German lines I saw a line of vehicles ahead heading along the road towards the front. Closer to the front they used horses but, here, we were a mile or so from the German trenches. The vehicles were a good target. I signalled for Giggs and Dunston to attack while we watched for fighters. The two pilots were two hundred feet apart and they strafed the column as they flew down the road. The gunners had spoken with Hutton and the first four bombs were hurled to the ground in quick succession. One made a direct hit on a German lorry. The others shredded the soft sides of the vehicles and threw shrapnel to scythe through the men cowering in the ditches. As they began their second run Hutton shouted, "Sir, up ahead, German fighters!"

Giggs and Dunston would have to join us when they had finished. I would have to take the Germans on with just Carrick and Fryer. As I looked ahead I frowned. They were not in their normal formation. They appeared to have copied us. There were six, what looked like Halberstadts, and they were in a single line. I immediately scanned the skies above for other fighters. The sky was cloud and fighter free. It was not an ambush. They say that imitation is the sincerest form of flattery but I was still wary.

"Sergeant, this looks odd. Be on your toes."

"Righto sir."

Behind me I heard the explosions as the bombs struck and the stuttering fire of the Lewis guns. My other two pilots would soon be joining us but we would have to fight at odds of two to one until they did so. I edged the nose up slightly to gain as much altitude as I could. Surprisingly the Germans appeared to be flying straight and level. As they closed with us I could see that they were identical to us; they were in single file. Once they flew beyond us the gunners behind me would have the chance to down them and they would not be able to fire back at us. It looked as though they had made a mistake.

The first Hun held his fire. Hutton gave a burst with his Lewis. It was a good shot for I saw it strike the engine. When the German did fire it was obvious he was aiming at Hutton. As the German dived below us I heard Hutton shout, "Sir, they have hit it, the Lewis is buggered!"

"Take out your Lee Enfield!"

The second fighter was aiming at Hutton and I fired a long burst from the right hand Lewis. This time I managed to hit the propeller before it too dived below us. I heard the pop of the rifle as Hutton tried to hit the pilot. When the third German used the same tactic I could see that they had worked out that a head on attack might work if you took out the gunner. I almost emptied the first Lewis firing at the third Halberstadt. Behind me I could hear Laithwaite's gun as he fired on the diving Halberstadts. I had no time to worry if they were attempting the Immelmann Turn. I had to stop them from killing my gunner.

I could almost see the exultation on the face of the pilot of the fourth Halberstadt. He must have thought we were defenceless. I gripped the left hand Lewis and held my fire. His bullets zipped around my head. As he dipped his nose to correct his line of fire I gave him a burst with the Lewis. His manoeuvre had taken away the protection of his engine and my burst struck him in the chest. This time it did not dive but continued in its death glide to Delville Woods.

The next aeroplane fired from further away; the pilot was obviously shaken by our ability to continue firing. I fired a very short burst but his early dive meant I hit nothing. The last German had a yellow painted propeller and seemed determined. I did not know where his companions had gone but the sound of gun fire behind me was a good indication that my flight was engaging them. As he began to fire I dipped my nose slightly and fired at the same time. My bullets struck the engine and propeller. The Halberstadt's engine began to scream and Hutton took the opportunity to fire at the pilot. We both saw the pilot clutch his left arm and, as he began to bank away, the pilot saluted us. I had neither the time nor the inclination to return the salute and I banked to head west again. I was anxious to see my flight.

I was relieved to see them all intact. The downed German was burning on the ground and I could see the others limping east. Their attempt had been clever but my extra gun and the resolute crews behind me had seen them off. I headed west over the road which was still covered with burning vehicles and dying men. It had been another successful mission.

When we landed, everyone crowded around the front of our bus. The Lewis gun had taken all of the German's bullets and was damaged beyond repair. It had, however, saved Hutton's life. In its shredded and mangled state it had protected my sergeant as he had used his rifle to fire at the fighters.

He smiled at me, "Well sir, I think I owe you and Mr Lewis here. That's as close as I want to come to joining the angels!"

Archie and Randolph were equally concerned about the German tactics. Archie shook his head. "Tomorrow we give you a different sector. First we had that German wanting to fight a duel with you and then we have an ambush for your flight. Your luck will run out one day, Bill."

"The second Lewis works a treat though, sir. It doesn't detract from the performance and the extra firepower gives us an edge. I fired at six Huns and I did not need to change a magazine."

Captain Marshall chuckled, "Senior Flight Sergeant Richardson has already been in here warning me that we might need some more Lewis guns. I have passed a requisition on to Mr Doyle who, by the way, has made good his promise. He had some carts this morning bringing in more furniture. It isn't new but we will all get to sit in comfort in the mess."

It was more comfortable to be able to sit with a little space between us. I sat with Ted and Gordy. I did not see much of Charlie Sharp these days. He had taken to his role as Flight Commander like a duck to water. He would sit with his pilots and I

143

noticed that he listened more than he spoke. He would know his men inside out and that could make all the difference in a pinch. It was obviously working for this was another day where they had suffered minimal damage and no casualties.

Gordy folded his letter and put it in his tunic pocket. "How is Mary?"

He frowned, "The Germans have been bombing London. She is quite worried." He tapped the pocket containing the letter. "She doesn't say so but I can read between the lines." He smiled, "She says she had arranged to meet your young lady. They were going somewhere up west for tea."

I nodded, "Beatrice went for tea with my sister Alice. They will probably go to the same place."

Ted snorted, "All very cosy, this happy families!"

Gordy playfully cuffed him about the ears, "Listen you miserable old scroat, when you get someone who can stand to look at your ugly mug then you will understand!"

"I can get plenty of women."

Gordy shook his head. "I have served with this chap since 1914 and I have never seen him with a woman yet."

"Just because I am discreet there is no need to be offensive!" He waved his arm, "Orderly, another beer!"

My pipe was pulling nicely. "Have you and Mary named a day yet?"

"That depends upon leave. I can't see us getting a leave until this offensive is over."

"I know what you mean. We have been pushing for almost twenty days now. I thought the French fought for a long time at Verdun but this doesn't look to have an end in sight."

Gordy shook his head, "They can't keep bleeding for a few yards of mud. Germany and Britain don't have enough men."

I agreed with Gordy. I would be surprised if it lasted until August. "Well we are due some more pilots this week. It will mean six aeroplanes in each flight. That might make life easier."

Gordy's face clouded over, "I'll have to make a better fist of training them this time. I don't want another Jamie Carstairs."

144

"I don't think you can change a person's nature. He had the streak in him. I flew with him, remember? He knew his own mind and he had great self belief. We are lucky in 41 squadron. We have fewer casualties than anyone else. That is down to the likes of you, Ted and Charlie. You are good leaders."

Ted laughed, "Is this the same shy lad we first met, Gordy? By gum, but he has grown. He'll be ready for long trousers soon!"

It was good to talk with my two oldest friends. They could bring me down to earth when I got above myself.

Chapter 14

The following week was uneventful in that we lost no aeroplanes neither did we shoot down any of the enemy. They seemed wary of us and, now that the offensive had stalled, the front line was becoming a little more permanent. We fitted all of the aeroplanes with two Lewis guns. As Captain Marshall told us Wing would give us anything we asked for. Our replacements arrived and the lull enabled us to give them air time in the Gunbus.

There were just five of them and that made life easier. Gordy now had the most inexperienced flight and we flew in tandem with his flight until they were bedded in. The loss of Jamie Carstairs had badly affected the rest of the flight and we knew it would take some time to get them back to full confidence.

It was Bates who gave me the key to it. When I came back from a training session he saw my furrowed brow. "What is the problem sir?"

I was about to tell him it was nothing when I saw that he really wanted to help. He had a concerned expression on his face. "Oh it is just Captain Hewitt's flight. They are all still thinking of Lieutenant Carstairs."

He stopped his tidying and said, "I know what they are going through sir. When my officers died I was close by and watched them. You feel a range of emotions. You are sad at the thought of their death but relieved that you have survived and that makes you feel guilty. Then you have the worry that death is just waiting to take you. He is the first officer killed since I have been here and so you are all lucky; luckier than you can possibly know. You do not see as many deaths. When it does happen it knocks you for six. The officers who survive in the trenches become hardened to death. They hide their feelings deep inside."

He went back to his tidying. "I couldn't do that sir. It broke me." There was a catch in his voice and his words hung in the air. You could have cut the silence with a knife. Then I saw him shake his shoulders. "But you have helped me here sir and I am grateful. I don't wake in the middle of the night screaming like I did in the trenches and Craiglockhart." He turned and I saw that the smile had reappeared. "I get a good night's sleep here. So you see sir, it is good that they are upset. It shows that they still feel and haven't been damaged. They will come around soon, you mark my words."

Once again my servant had given me an insight not only in to my men but also myself.

The last week in July saw us, once again, helping our colonial colleagues. We were back over our old stomping ground of Pozières. The Australians had been given the task of taking the ridge to give us a strong point. The artillery barrage went on all day and all night and when the squadron took off the next day to see just how far the Australians had advanced there were still shells being lobbed from the Germans lines.

The day was overcast and I worried about German aeroplanes lurking in the low clouds. Mercifully they were not. We flew in four lines with half a mile between each flight. The scene below us was distressing beyond belief. The ground was strewn with bodies. You could see the sites of the fiercest fighting from the huddles of grey and brown uniforms twisted together in death. It looked to me as though the Australians were holding on by the skin of their teeth. My flight was to the north and I could see that the German artillery was dug in around the village of Thiepval. I took it upon myself to lead my flight and investigate the village.

This time they were not hidden in the woods but they were sheltered by the village over which they fired. They looked to me like the twenty five cm guns. They were perfect for firing over the village. Each gun was sandbagged and there were the inevitable machine guns ringing them.

I signalled to Giggs and Dunston to begin a bombing run. I led the rest of the flight to take out the machine guns. This was the first time we had used our new firepower. I was keen to see the effect. We climbed to the east and dived down to less than a hundred feet. Hutton and I fired at the same time. I did not worry

147

about conserving ammunition and as soon as one Lewis was empty I fired the second. The cone of bullets ripped through the machine gunners. Their sand bags protected them against blast and infantry but not against bullets from the skies. I aimed the Gunbus at their faces. I could not miss.

Hutton took the opportunity to spray the artillery positions. The gunners dived for cover. As I climbed, I banked north to make another run, this time from west to east. As I climbed I saw my two bombers wreaking havoc with the artillery. We only had eight bombs but they caused devastation for the gunners had taken cover wherever they could and the shrapnel ripped into them. Levelling out I changed the magazines.

We zoomed in again. We flew down the other set of machine gun nests. I was just firing my second Lewis when I saw Hutton lob two hand grenades in swift succession. My other pilots knew what to expect when Lumpy did that and I heard the sound of their engines as they screamed to a higher altitude. There was a small explosion and then a larger one. Lumpy said, "Petrol sir!"

We rose to a safer height and circled the village. The guns had stopped which was a mercy for the Australians but we had not destroyed the guns. Two of them had been knocked from their carriages and others were damage but they looked like they could be repaired. More devastating would be the loss of trained gunners. We had bought the Aussies some time.

Archie had the rest of the squadron circling to await our return. We now had the numbers to intimidate the German Jastas. Our modifications had given us a knot or two more but they were still faster. They could overtake us and they could fly higher but we still ruled the skies.

At the start of August we began to sense a build up on the German side of the lines. It was unbearably hot and had been for some time. It meant that there was a slight heat haze as the temperature approached ninety. Charlie and his flight were doing a reconnaissance one day and reported large numbers of horse drawn guns being brought close to the front and columns of infantry. The presence of a couple of Jastas prevented him from disrupting their advance or inspecting closer. The heat haze also prevented the perfect report which I know Charlie wanted to deliver. Archie and Randolph took the news themselves to Wing. Charlie and his maps accompanied them. He had always had an eye for maps and detail when he had been my gunner and now it proved to be an invaluable ability.

They returned just before dinner and Archie called in the Flight Commanders. "It seems that Charlie has spotted something which might be useful. The Hun has fortified a line from Maurepas to Longueval. There is a fortified quarry and many new trenches. More importantly the Hun has observation posts on the ridge. We have driven the fighters away, temporarily I feel, and so he is resorting to old fashioned methods. An attack by French colonial troops was badly handled by the Germans. Tomorrow we will be bombing the ridge."

Ted stubbed his cigarette out, "Sir, how come they can't use the Martinsyde Elephants for this? They can carry a bigger bomb load."

"I am afraid we are a victim of our own success. They are using DH 2s to escort the Elephants in other sectors. They think we can handle this on our own."

I began raking out the ash from my pipe. "The thing is, sir, the German squadrons have been quiet for a couple of weeks. I can't see that lasting. It normally means they are planning something. If they have observation posts and spotters for the artillery on the ridge then you can bet that they have telephones and radios there. When they see us coming they will call in air support. It won't be like the last time when we surprised them at Thiepval. There, we jumped their artillery without warning. We can't do that here."

Archie stood up and walked to the map. "You are right." He circled the ridge with his finger. "This is the only place we have made a serious advance and we have to hang on to it. We will be bombing tomorrow, Bill. But you are correct, the Germans will be waiting and there is nothing we can do about it."

I slowly filled my pipe as I spoke. It gave me time to think. I smiled as I looked at the picture on the tobacco tin. It was a baby. The tobacco had been sent by my dad and was called 'Baby's Bottom' it made me smile.

"Something funny Bill?"

"No sir." I held up the tin lid and they all smiled. I now had my thoughts marshalled. I got my pipe going. "There is something we could do sir. We now have more aeroplanes than we did. Why not have two flights flying as high as we can and watching for the Germans while the other two flights have their bombing run. When the first flights have bombed they climb and take over Fokker watch. The next two flights begin their bombing run."

"That might work sir." Charlie sounded quite animated. "We haven't bombed as a squadron since we raided the German airfield. We usually just use a couple of buses to bomb. The Germans will start to clear up after the first bombing run and we might catch them with their trousers down."

Randolph nodded and said, in an absent minded fashion, "Lederhosen."

"What, sir?"

"German trousers, Charlie. We will catch them with their Lederhosen down!"

We all laughed and Archie said, "We'll try that then. You are right Bill and it can't hurt. I'll try a fill of that baccy myself. It seems to stimulate the mind!"

"Help yourself sir!"

We were elected to be the first Angels along with D Flight. We were at eight thousand feet when Charlie and Ted led their Gunbuses down the ridge. They flew from the north west to a point close to Guillemont. We circled watching to the east. Ted's flight had just finished their first bombing run when we saw the unmistakable shape of the Fokkers in the east. "Right Sergeant here we go!"

"Righto sir." To my amazement he took out a bugle and played the cavalry charge.

150

"What was that Lumpy?"

"I learned to play the bugle in the Boys Brigade. Me mam sent it to me. Me and the lads thought that if we are the cavalry flight we ought to use the charge."

"Well it works for me."

We had the height advantage for the German airfield was just a few miles east of us. Gordy flew to my left and I saw that they were in their usual formation of four aeroplanes in a V. There looked to be about eight aeroplanes in total. For once we outnumbered them. Then Lumpy shouted. "Sir, look to the south. Another Jasta; looks like Eindeckers and Fokker D1s."

I was wrong. They would outnumber us.

There was little point in worrying about the odds. Archie would bring the rest of the squadron to our aid as soon as he could. Until then we would have to do our best. The first Jasta began to climb towards us. Gordy and I had flown together so many times that we almost knew what the other was thinking. We would isolate the central flight of four and try to destroy that. The risk would be to Gordy and me. Sergeant Hutton had reinstated his bully beef and cardboard bullet proofing. It made his seat difficult but it did afford him some protection.

I saw him arm his Lewis and I did the same with mine. Behind me I could hear the machine guns of the rest of the squadron and the explosions as the bombs struck. They had not seen our danger yet. The wisdom of our plan could now be plainly seen.

Once again a combined speed of almost two hundred miles an hour did not allow for measured and calculated shooting. This was where our extra firepower came into its own. I fired at the same time as Hutton and, as the leading German began to smoke, Hutton changed his aim to the Fokker on the right. The other gunners behind me were preparing to attack the same aeroplane which had no one to attack. As we swooped through their lines I banked to the right and Sergeant Hutton combined with the other gunners of my flight to destroy the second German.

The second German Jasta was almost upon us. I had a choice: I could continue my turn and come upon the rear of the first formation or take on the second one. I chose the latter. It enabled my gunners to fire at the first formation which would be turning to try to take us on.

"What is it like behind, Sergeant Hutton?"

He held out his mirror. "The flight is still intact and Mr Hewitt is engaging the others." He glanced to the right. "It looks like Major Leach is coming to help us."

"Right. When we engage these next Germans I intend to bank right and climb."

"Righto."

It was some time since we had fought the monoplane and they must have been desperate for them to enlist them. Their only advantage was the ability to fire through the propeller but their speed was as bad as ours and their rate of climb even worse. We dived and Sergeant Hutton managed to empty his magazine into the engine of the first Fokker. It seemed to hang in the air before it plunged vertically to earth. The others converged on us and hit us with a cone of fire. I had no target and Hutton was changing his magazine. I began my bank. A black cross on a fuselage came into view and I fired a quick burst. I hit it but it continued to fly. Sergeant Hutton had reloaded and he began to fire at the same Fokker. It was his day for his bullets stitched a line along the body of the aeroplane and it too, fell towards earth.

We appeared to be a bullet magnet. Although many went through the empty fuselage some were hitting the engine. I was suddenly smacked in the face as a sliver of wood flew from the edge of the cockpit and embedded itself below my goggles. I felt a smack on my goggles as another piece of my own aeroplane struck me. I could feel the blood dripping slowly down my cheek.

And then we were through their lines and heading west. I saw Archie and the rest of the squadron coming to our rescue. Sergeant Hutton turned around and manned the rear Lewis which began chattering death and destruction behind me. He stopped firing and grinned at me. His expression suddenly and dramatically changed, "Bloody hell sir! You've been hit."

"It's nothing. Get back into position and we'll get rid of these bombs."

I ignored the sound of machine guns behind me. Archie and the others would have to deal with them. I headed for the smoking ridge. Ironically it was as we had planned; the Germans were busy rescuing the wounded and repairing the damage. I did nothing fancy I just dropped us to two hundred feet and, while Lumpy held the bombs ready I emptied one of the Lewis guns. I had just armed the second when the first of Lumpy's bombs exploded. It was a long ridge and we managed to drop all four bombs. I climbed to a safer height and watched the others as they dropped their bombs. To my horror I only counted four aeroplanes. Lieutenant Fryer was heading for the ground with his engine on fire. He struck the ground close to a machine gun emplacement and it exploded in a fireball as his fuel ignited the ammunition. We had survived the dogfight against superior odds only to lose a pilot to ground fire. I banked and headed west and home.

By the time we had landed the blood on my face had begun to congeal but my flying coat was covered in blood. I had seen where the bullets had struck the edge of the cockpit. I had been lucky; a long splinter to the throat could have ended my life and Sergeant Hutton's!

I was the first to land. Hutton had wanted to fire a flare but I told him to save it. I was not dying and who knew what other injuries there were. Sergeant Hutton leapt out quicker than I had ever seen him and he tried to help me down.

"Flight Sergeant Hutton; this is a scratch!"

"Wait until you see it sir then you can say."

The others landed and I waited for them. Sergeant Hutton's opinion was confirmed when Freddie saw me. "My God sir! What the hell happened?"

"It was a splinter and it looks worse than it is. Look I'll go and wash it off and then people will stop bothering me." I turned,

"Sergeant Hutton check the…" He was not there! "Now where has he gone?"

I was answered a moment or two later when Doc Brennan and one of his orderlies ran towards me. "Look Doctor. It's just as I told you."

"It is fine, doc."

Doc Brennan put his hands on his hips. "When I presume to give you flying lessons then you can advise me on medical procedures. Your young lady may be a nurse but she isn't here. Now get to sick bay, chop, chop."

As the orderly took off my flying coat, Bates burst in. "Dear oh, dear. Here sir, give me your coat. I'll have a nice drink waiting for you," he stared at Doc Brennan, "look after him Doctor. He never takes enough care!"

When he had left us I said, "It's like having my mother on the base."

"You should be grateful he cares so deeply for you." He examined my goggles which were still on my head. He pointed to the left lens which was badly cracked. "It is a good job you were wearing these or you could have lost your eye." He took my helmet off and I stared at the goggles. I could not remember the blow as being that hard and yet it had cracked the lens. I had been lucky.

He went to wash up while the orderly cleaned away the blood and then pressed some clean gauze to the wound.

"Right then, Captain Harsker, if you lay down here the doctor will stitch you."

I started, "Stitch me!"

The orderly laughed, "Well if we don't you will be bleeding all the way through dinner sir. Now come along and lie down, there's a good officer. I have to keep pressure on this gauze."

I saw Doc Brennan tapping a syringe. The orderly wiped some alcohol on my cheek and then the doctor injected me. I had felt little pain before but now I felt nothing. It was strange lying there and watching the doctor stitch me up. It was as though I was detached for he just focussed on his hands and the needle.

He stood back. "There. That is as neat as I can make it. I am afraid you will have a scar. It will be one the Germans seem to like; a sort of duelling scar. The ladies love them apparently. Here."

He handed me a mirror and I could see that the wound was three inches long. It was no wonder that they had all been shocked. I thought it had been much smaller.

I went to the adjutant's office. My face still felt numb. The doc had said the anaesthetic would take hours to wear off. Archie had a sombre look on his face. When he saw my wound he shook his head. "The plan worked but at what a cost. You were lucky but we lost Fryer, Watson, Parr and Sutton. I hope that the brass appreciate the sacrifice."

I too was shocked but I was also a realist. "Sir, when you lose a thousand officers and twenty thousand men in the first day of a battle then eight fliers doesn't even rate a raised eyebrow."

Archie slammed his hand into the desk making Flight Sergeant Lowery jump a little. "Well it damn well matters to me!"

He slumped into a chair. Randolph said, "We lost all of them on the way back. The Germans have better anti-aircraft fire now. Lieutenant Sharp has good eyes and he noticed they are using twin machine guns which, of course, have twice the chance of success as a single gun."

We had mastered the Fokkers but now they had developed another weapon. I left the office in a depressed state. Four pilots gone in a heartbeat and I had nearly lost an eye.

Chapter 15

Our losses were put into perspective when Archie attended the next meeting at Wing. The Australians had suffered more than five thousand casualties in their attack. We had no time to recover either for the Germans were trying to counterattack. Although we had lost four aeroplanes we had destroyed nine of the enemy. Archie was convinced that we would be able to fly with impunity. Ted was back to his morose self at the briefing.

"You can't keep expecting these young lads to fly over the Germans lines. We have the beating of the aeroplanes but it is the ground fire we have to worry about."

"Tomorrow we just have to observe. We are directing the artillery fire. Your observers are being issued with mirrors. Our squadron will be spread across the whole of the front and each of us will be directing the fire of a four gun battery. Our job is to knock out the enemy artillery and then the strong points. If the Germans are attacking then direct the fire at them. We stay in the air as long as possible." He looked at the four of us in turn and punctuated each word as he said it, "We do not engage enemy aeroplanes. We can fire at them but no pursuit. We keep station until this job is done!"

As we taxied I was reminded of the old days of no engagement but Hamilton-Grant had done that for a different reason. I had been in the trenches and I could understand this particular order.

As we climbed to our correct altitude I checked in with Sergeant Hutton, "Are you happy about the signals, Sergeant?"

"Oh yes sir. I learned Morse Code in the Boys Brigade. We just start each signal with C, that is our call sign and let the guns know if they are long, short or on target."

"What happens when the target is destroyed?"

"Then I flash them hit, hit, hit and give them new coordinates." He chuckled. "To be honest sir I am quite looking forward to that. It will be like I am an officer giving orders."

He always saw the positives.

"Here we are sir. This is it. If you would hold her steady I will tell them we are here."

While he flashed I studied the ground below us. I could see the German gun emplacements. They were camouflaged but I could make them out. They had no anti-aircraft protection which was a good thing. Further west I could see trenches lined with machine guns. Their gunners were ready and braced for an attack. I could see their white faces as they looked up at us. One or two of the infantrymen tried to take pot shots at us. They missed!

"Ready sir."

I flew in a small loop as we waited for the shells to strike. They fired just four. I noticed that, when the shells screamed over, the machine gunners dived into their trenches. I could see that the shells landed long by about four hundred yards. The Germans returned fire but it had to be blind. Hutton flashed his signal. This time the shells landed just short but they managed to hit some barbed wire.

Hutton flashed again we waited in eager anticipation for the next four shells. Three of them converged on one gun which was destroyed. A fourth shell landed well short.

Hutton said, "One of the gunners is a dozy bugger, sir! Just keep her steady while I pass this on."

There seemed to be a longer gap. I didn't know but I imagined that the senior officer would be checking all the guns to ensure they had the same settings. The lull seemed to fool the Germans for some of the gunners came out of their trenches. The next four shells took out a whole gun and damaged a second as well as killing some of the gunners. Hutton flashed his message back and the guns rolled for fifteen minutes until there was no German artillery left intact. Unlike the ones we had bombed these were now just so much scrap metal.

"Right sir, steady again. This will be a longer message."
Once again the lull after the guns stopped fooled the German gunners in the trenches. They began to emerge. They were

expecting an attack. They did not know that there were no infantry coming now that the guns had stopped.

"Right sir, this should be interesting."

Whether the guns had warmed up or the gods of the guns were with us I do not know but the first four shells were bang on target. The machine guns and the bodies of the gunners were flown high into the air like so many rag dolls. This time, when the Germans fled into the trenches, there was no relief. The guns kept pounding and they destroyed the limited protection afforded by the sandbags and corrugated iron. I saw Germans running from the trenches; they looked like rats fleeing a sinking ship. The guns were firing so rapidly now that they were simply disintegrated when the shells exploded amongst them.

Hutton said, "Poor buggers." Soon there was nothing left to hit and Hutton ordered the cease fire. Any more shooting would have merely wasted ammunition. As we headed home I realised that we had not seen a single German aeroplane during the entire patrol. This was not like the days of 1915 and the Fokker Scourge. Now it was the RFC which ruled the air.

The others had had equal success. The Germans were cowed. They would not be advancing west any time soon and, more importantly, when the brass decided then we could move east to claim a few more bloody miles of France.

For the next four days we continued to spot for the artillery. We liaised with different batteries as the German artillery was gradually silenced. I was still worried that the Germans would return stronger than ever and swat us from the skies but, so far, my fears had been groundless. On the tenth of August we had a day off; it rained and was misty. There would be no flying that day. The mechanics were delighted for it meant that they could service the aeroplanes which had been suffering wear and tear with the constant hours they spent in the air.

We took the opportunity to have a run out in the squadron car. We took Charlie with us. He had been my gunner and we had been especially close but he and Ted had become firm friends and it would have been rude to leave him alone.

We intended to drive to Abbeville which we had been told was a pretty little town but the rain made driving unpleasant and we opted for Amiens. Amiens was bigger and busier than the small town would have been. It was the hub through which the majority of supplies and men were sent. Consequently it felt like an army camp.

Charlie came into his own when we became depressed at the sea of khaki which greeted us. "Why don't we just drive down a few side streets until we find a bar or something?"

We left the main road and found ourselves close to the canal with the floating gardens. There was no khaki in sight at all. We parked the car and dodged into a small bar filled with the thick smoke of pungent French cigarettes. There were eight or nine old men either seated around the tables or standing at the bar. There was just one table left and we pounced on it.

The owner trudged over and we ordered four beers. Our French was adequate and no more. I lit my pipe and leaned back on the rickety wooden chair. When the beers came we toasted each other. I looked outside of the window and saw the rain hammering against the glass. The streets were glossy with water and it felt chilly. Yet despite all of that I felt happy. I was with my friends and I was alive. I did not have the smell of gun oil or engine fumes in my nostrils and I was not craning my neck to see the Hun in the sun. The rain had some admirable qualities.

We tried to avoid talking about the war although that was difficult.

"Do you reckon we will get leave soon, sir?"

"Charlie, we are off duty now. It's Bill."

"Sorry, I was your gunner for so long it is hard to get used to the pips on my shoulder."

"Well you are one of us now. To answer your question I would need to get into the mind of the Generals who are making such a mess of this war. If I was a General I would hold what we have. We have shown that, with our air superiority we can rule the skies. I would send bombers over to destroy their supplies getting to the front. We destroyed so many of their guns the other day that they will struggle to replace them. If we could stop them resupplying then we could launch an offensive and drive them back."

Gordy nodded as he held four fingers up for four more beers, "Aye, it was easy directing the fire of the guns and we could easily bomb and strafe their machine guns after the artillery has stopped."

"Then why don't we do that?"

Ted nodded to me, "He's the one who fought with those kinds of Generals."

I shrugged, "They are trying to fight battles the way that they used to fight them. The aeroplane is new. We are finding new ways of using them. Look at the advances the Germans have made. They can fire through their propeller. They can fly faster than we can. Someone told me they can fly at more than a hundred miles an hour. They are smaller and nippier than ours. All of this in less than two years."

"Then how come we are still winning?"

Ted answered, "The Gunbus is huge, we know and it is slow but it can take a lot of damage and with four machine guns it is like a hedgehog. The fox likes a tasty bit of hedgehog but its prickly spines make it hard to get to the soft meat so it scavenges instead. When they find out how to get inside our guns then we will be in trouble."

We drank and smoked in silence for a while. "I'm getting hungry. Bill, ask him if they do food."

I asked and he shook his head. "I guess not."

"Come on, it has eased off, let's find somewhere to eat."

We paid the bill and, leaving the car on the street we wandered the old town. There were more wooden buildings than we were used to but it looked to be untouched by war. That in itself was amazing, as we had fought in this town two years ago and the front was less than twenty miles away. Charlie spied the chalked menu outside the restaurant. The rain had made it unreadable but it would serve food and that would do.

We were actually welcomed by the owner. He was a rotund little man who looked like Lumpy Hutton with a moustache. The place was almost empty which explained his welcome. He spoke to us in English which was far better than my abysmal French.

"Welcome gentlemen. I have a lovely table for you." He guided us to a table which looked out on a small garden at the back. He flourished four menus and then disappeared. He returned with a bottle of red wine. We had not ordered it but none of us complained. He poured us a glass each and then stood with pencil poised over his note pad. The menu, of course, was in French. Ted put the menu down and said, "I tell you what, pal, why don't you bring us a stew or something like that eh?"

"Stew?"

I searched my memory, "Er fricassee?"

His face split into a grin. He scooped up the menus. "Of course, I have lapin!"

He disappeared. Charlie asked, "Lapin?"

"Rabbit!"

Charlie looked disappointed.

"You didn't expect roast beef did you?" scoffed Gordy.

"Well I am fed up of bully beef."

I smiled, "I think you might be pleasantly surprised."

The owner brought us some bread and it filled a gap until four steaming dishes were brought in. There was a thick sauce on the rabbit. "What is the sauce?"

"Er moutarde, mustard. Enjoy!"

Even Charlie enjoyed it. It was rich, it was unctuous and it didn't taste as though it had come from a can. We felt like kings and the wine, although rough, went well with the game."

We raced back to the car through the rain which had reappeared. The beer and the wine had made us quite jolly and we sang all the way back to the airfield. We were ready for the war again. It had just taken a five hour break and a little peace.

Chapter 16

A few days after we returned from our day trip the replacement pilots arrived. They came when the weather broke. The summer weather turned wet, cloudy and, at times, stormy. We ended up with three days without flying. The day after our trip to Amiens we had a storm of Biblical proportions.

When we found a brief window when we could fly we took the boot boys up for a circuit of the field to evaluate them. The four of them were keen and enthusiastic, but hopeless. They had not been trained on a Gunbus and had not even been taught how to fire a Lewis while flying or change a magazine. They tried their best but they were the worst trained fliers we had received from Blighty.

The depression was in my voice as I reported to Archie and Randolph. "They can't go up sir. They would be a liability to all of us/'"

We were in Archie's office deciding what to do about the new pilots. "You are right but we need to rotate our pilots. I wanted to give one pilot in each flight a day off every week. The difference in morale and efficiency after the rainy days was amazing."

"You are right sir but why are they coming to us like this?"

"The brass in Blighty is trying to take advantage of our air superiority and they are rushing the pilots through training. The generals in England thinks that so long as they can fly they will be all right."

We sat in silence trying to come up with a solution. Eventually Archie sighed and said, "I will form E flight. While the rest of you patrol I will take these four up and make them combat pilots. It won't help us to relieve our other pilots but at least these four will have a better chance of survival."

In the end it was not until the eighteenth that we were able to fly. We spent the rainy days in the middle of August showing them how to change a magazine and, sitting on the ground, how to find the Hun in the sun. The problem was the aeroplane was on the ground and the Germans were not trying to kill them. We drilled them until they could do it blindfolded. We knew that the problem would come when they tried to handle the huge Gunbus in aerial combat. It was far bigger than the aeroplanes they had trained in. The wingspan was enormous and it was a pusher. They could not believe that we still used what was, to them, an antiquated aeroplane. They did not know that the guns at the front and our gunners were our advantage.

We led our flights on our first patrol for many days on the twenty first of August. The scene below us, as we flew over No-Man's Land was depressing. The rains and the storm had turned the crater filled pieces of disputed land into a muddy morass of sucking and cloying clay. There were still puddles in the deeper craters. Some looked like small ponds. It would make any meaningful advance by either side almost impossible. We were even more depressed when we ventured over the German lines. They had used the rain as an opportunity to bring up more guns and to make their defences even more formidable. All the work we had done in the first week in August had been wasted. It was as though we had not even shelled their lines. We would have to start all over again. Their artillery was surrounded by machine guns and they had used sandbags to make them into small forts. The only good news was that there appeared to be no German aeroplanes. We still ruled the skies.

Sergeant Hutton hated the thought of a flight over the German lines without expending some ammunition. "Sir, how about strafing those batteries?"

"If you notice, Flight Sergeant Hutton, they are now protected by machine guns. I don't see the point in risking the few pilots we have left just so that you can fire your gun."

His silence was eloquent. He was however right. We were wasting fuel by just observing; we were a combat aeroplane. I decided that I would bring more bombs on the next patrol and we would try a higher level bombing run. We would not cause as much damage but we would not risk losing valuable pilots. As we headed home I was acutely aware that the four pilots I had left were worth their weight in gold. They were trained and experienced. You could not buy that!

The others were equally despondent when they landed. Archie, on the other hand, was quite cheerful having managed to teach the four young pilots how to fire in the air and change a magazine. "It can't be that bad, surely?"

I shook my head, "It's as though we didn't damage their artillery at all and they have reinforced their batteries with machine guns and anti-aircraft pits. We will have to try high level bombing. If we try a low level run, it will be suicide."

Captain Marshall said, "We are still trying to secure Delville Wood. I envisage another attack in the next few days, sir. It might be better to try and disrupt the guns. I will send a report to Wing about this."

Archie nodded, "Very well then. We will try high level bombing runs tomorrow. Was there any sign of the Fokkers?"

Gordy shook his head, "Nary a one. I don't know why though. If we had those Fokkers and Halberstadts we would have a field day! They are fast, small and can turn better than our lumbering beasts."

"You want a new aeroplane for Christmas, Gordy?"

"I just want to have a chance to survive this war. We are such a big target I am amazed that they miss us. Our only saving grace is our gunners. If the Hun ever realises that all they have to do is kill the gunner then we will really be in trouble."

Gordy was turning into Ted but he was right. Our weakness was the front of the aeroplane. The German engine protected the pilot. It gave him the chance to land and walk away from his aeroplane. We were operating over German lines. Even if we managed to land we would be behind enemy lines and that meant a prisoner of war camp. The front went from Switzerland to the sea near Ostend.

I gathered my pilots and gunners around me as we prepared to launch our attack. "Today we try high level bombing. This will be harder." I turned to the sergeants, "You gunners, I want you to throw one bomb at a time and watch its flight. We will fly in a circle until all the bombs have been dropped. Pilots, watch for the Hun in the sun. They can fly higher than we can and this time we will be over the target for a longer period." I looked at their young faces. They were like family to me now. "Any questions?"

As they clambered aboard Hutton sounded the bugle and they all gave a cheer. It was a silly and frivolous gesture but it worked. I know the other flights were jealous but I knew that it made my flight a closer band of brothers. That had helped me when I had been in the cavalry and I was sure it would help us here.

When we reached the batteries, some two miles or so from Delville Woods, we began to circle. Each gunner would drop his bombs when he was ready. I scanned the skies and flew over the target. Sergeant Hutton was in charge of this part of the flight.

Hutton shouted, "Bomb gone!" I glanced over the side and watched it plummet to the earth. It exploded between a machine gun pit and a large artillery piece. "Bugger! I'll try again the next time around."

As we flew in a circle I saw that some of the other bombs, dropped by the others in the flight, had been more successful. One machine gun was destroyed and one artillery piece was lying on its side.

"Steady sir. Bomb gone!"

I glanced over and saw that Hutton had corrected his aim. This time he hit the gun he had aimed at on the side and I watched in fascination as the huge piece rose into the air and then fell back to earth, shattered.

"That's better!"

He carried on with his other runs successfully hitting one machine gun and damaging another large gun. I looked up and saw black dots in the eastern sky. "Germans! Get on your gun!"

I saw that the others were still circling and dropping their bombs. I began to climb to meet them. There were just six of them but they had the advantage of height. "Hutton take the one to your right and I will go for the one directly ahead."

"Righto!"

It was a tried and tested technique. By blasting a hole in the middle of their formation it made them manoeuvre out of the way. We had heard of Germans flying into each other in the confusion. Germans like order. If you upset their order then you had an edge.

As we climbed I was acutely aware of how much smaller their aeroplanes were compared with the huge Gunbus I was flying. Our wingspan was almost twenty feet longer than the Fokkers we were fighting. That said, our longer wingspan meant we could take more damage. It was hard to knock down a Gunbus- unless you hit the pilot! The new wood around my cockpit was testament to the fact that the Hun had worked that one out!

It seemed a painfully slow climb and the Fokkers were approaching us at a much faster rate. I made sure my right Lewis was ready and held the trigger. The Fokker fired early. He used short bursts and I could see that he was aiming for Lumpy and me. His angle of attack meant that his bullets were going below the cockpit and I saw him begin to lift his nose. I fired when he was a hundred feet away. It was further than I would have liked but I wanted to put him off. The Gunbus was very stable and I had no propeller obscuring my view. I saw the sparks as my bullets struck his engine. They did not penetrate but a ricochet could cause damage to a wing or a cable.

Hutton began to fire at the second Fokker which had no target as yet. Lumpy emptied the magazine for he had struck the engine with his first burst. The Fokker peeled away; too badly damaged to continue. My Fokker tried to soar above me but I finished off my first magazine as he climbed into the sky. I could not miss and I saw his tail as it shredded. He began to spiral down to earth. He was behind his own lines and he would probably land and walk away. It meant we had punched our hole through their line.

"Banking left!"

I knew the other four would be desperately trying to get on my tail. They would not know if I was going left or right and that slight hesitation might just save us. As I banked I saw my flight climbing to come to my rescue. We outnumbered the enemy now but it would be some time before they reached me.

As I banked I caught a glimpse of a black cross and I took a snap shot with my left hand Lewis. I hit his tail but did no serious damage. However, the bullets striking him made him bank to the right. As I came around I saw the last Fokker on this side of the formation heading for me. Hutton opened fire and I fired the rest of my magazine. He was struck by a wall of bullets. I suspect we hit his propeller for he veered off course and began to drop slowly below us.

"Get on the rear Lewis!"

Hutton stood and manned the gun as quickly as he could. I knew there was a Fokker on our tail for he began to fire straight away. I heard the parabellums hitting the engine and I winced. I kept looking ahead and flying as straight as I dared for I did not want Lumpy to fall nor did I wish to fly into one of my flight who were climbing to our rescue.

Freddie was leading the other three in a line abreast to maximise their fire power. As soon as their gunners fired I breathed a sigh of relief. I saw Sergeant Hutton grin and he shouted, "Mr Carrick nailed him, sir. The other one has buggered off home!"

The tuning we had performed on the engine had helped us to fly faster when we were attacking but the bullets striking our engine had caused some damage. We were losing power. I saw Delville Woods ahead and knew that, even if we crash landed we would be behind our lines. I coaxed and eased the damaged engines all the way home. The bus struggled to stay in the air and I worried that the engine would cut out. When the wheels touched the grass I patted the instrument panel, "Well done, Caesar!"

We checked the damage to the bus. There were numerous holes in the engine. Senior Flight Sergeant McKay shook his head.

"It's a new engine for you Mr Harsker. It will take at least two days for us to replace it and test it."

Lumpy and I trudged away from the field feeling both deflated, we would not be flying for a couple of days and pleased that we had fought off so many Fokkers.

Archie was happier. "Excellent! You can take the Avro up and train these new pilots and I will lead your lads."

I made my way back to my quarters. I didn't mind training the young pilots but I always preferred leading my flight. Bates was positively bouncing when I reached my room.

"I have your bath ready sir." He nodded to the side cabinet. On it was perched a letter. "I took the liberty of fetching your mail sir. I believe it is from your young lady, from the perfume."

My day suddenly brightened up and I too felt as happy as Bates. I did not luxuriate in my bath as long as normal. I just wanted to read the unexpected letter. As I dried myself I deduced that this must be in response to my first letter. I wondered if our letters would ever become synchronised.

Bates closed the door, "I'll see that you are not disturbed for a while, sir. Enjoy you whisky and your letter."

I lay on the bed and slowly opened it with my knife.

Hyde Park
July 21st 1916

Dearest Bill,

My joy was unbounded when I opened your letter. By now you will have received mine and wondered what this scatterbrained young girl was thinking! Simply put, I was not!

I am so happy that we both feel the same way about each other. We can begin to plan for a future after this madness is over. I have spoken to Captain Hewitt's young lady, Mary, and I know that you soldiers do not like to plan; your existence is so parlous. Let me do the planning for both of us. You just need to know that I

168

will be here for you when you need me and I shall plan on finding somewhere for us when the war is over.

I know that you are a brave officer and care for your men but please, my love, care for yourself too. I am happy that we have found each other. I would hate to lose you. You are more valuable to me than life itself.

I now see your sister Alice and Mary once each week. It makes it seem like I am closer to you. Your sister tells me the stories of you growing up and Mary tells me of the esteem in which you are held by your men. It is not the same as holding you in my arms and listening to your voice but, until you come home again, it will have to do.

Your loving and devoted,
Beatrice
xxxx
xxx

I read and re read it. I folded it and placed it in the tin my mother had given me with some fruit cake on my last leave. The cake had been a godsend; the letters were better, they were my treasure.

Chapter 17

The four pilots had all had their session in the gunner's cockpit and I did not need to cover that. I decided to teach them air combat. I chose one at random, "Lieutenant Griffiths I want you to be flight leader for today. The rest of you follow him as though he were. The best of you can be flight leader this afternoon."

I looked up at the sky. The day was cloudier than it had been in the last couple of days and there was enough cover for me to find somewhere to hide. "Lieutenant Griffiths in thirty minutes I want you to take off and climb to five thousand feet. You will patrol the perimeter of the airfield."

They all looked at me expectantly. Lieutenant Griffiths said, "And where will you be Captain Harsker?"

I grinned, "Why I will be with Flight Sergeant Hutton and we will be attacking you!"

The sergeant was up for this and after we had taken off we flew high into the clouds. "Do I get to use the gun sir?"

"Yes but for God's sake don't hit them!"

He snorted indignantly, his professional pride punctured, "Sir, as if I would!"

I headed east and then turned. I looked at my watch and estimated when they would be in position. When we were at eight thousand feet I began to scan the sky beneath me. I glimpsed the tail of one of the Gunbuses and I began to descend. I did not use full power as I wanted to be as quiet as I could. The clouds ahead of me parted and I saw them in a straight line. They had no one on the rear Lewis and all eyes appeared to be fixed forward or looking up; no one was watching behind. Despite the lack of cloud cover in this part of the sky I was coming from the east and the sun was behind me. I dived at full throttle towards the rear FE 2. It was Lieutenant Gerard.

Hutton asked, "Now sir?"

"Whenever you are ready."

As we zoomed beneath the tail of Lieutenant Gerard Hutton fired a burst behind us towards the east. I then flew underneath the four aeroplanes and Hutton continued to fire at the side. When I reached Lieutenant Griffiths I flew next to him and signalled for them to land.

We circled while they landed. I wanted to see if the experience had daunted them. They managed to land quite well and then I joined them on the ground.

"Well gentlemen. If I had been a Fokker D111 then you would have all been dead. Lieutenant Gerard, why did you not have your gunner on the rear Lewis?"

He looked shamefaced, "I forgot sir."

"Well you are honest at any rate. If you are the last aeroplane in a flight you must keep a gunner watching the rear once you cross the enemy lines. To be honest we have been attacked on our side of the lines. These are a good bus but they have a weakness. They can be attacked in the rear and they are not quick. The Avro is almost ten miles an hour slower than you and twenty miles an hour slower than a Fokker. You are bright lads, you do the sums. Now after we have refuelled we will go up again. Lieutenant Chapel you are flight leader."

We went through the exercise six times until I had them drilled into what to expect. I led them in loops and banks. I showed them how to fly so low that you risked clipping the tree tops and finally I demonstrated the Lufbery Circle. After we had landed, Sergeant Hutton took the gunners away to explain how to be a better gunner while I went to the mess to find out more about the young pilots and their background.

When the rest of the squadron returned I felt exhausted. Teaching was more strenuous than fighting in the air! That first drink of the day was looking more and more attractive.

The day had been frustrating for Archie and the squadron. The clouds had obscured their view of the ground and they had had to be wary of German fighters pouncing on them. They returned without having engaged anyone. I did not feel so bad about having spent the day teaching.

We sat with Archie after dinner. Ted grumbled, "This is bloody August! I thought it was supposed to be nice here on the Continent?"

Gordy nodded his agreement, "Back home we would expect this."

"You are right, on the estate they would have harvested by now." I tapped my pipe out and began to clean it. "Major Leach when do you think there will be a leave?"

He laughed, "You know, Bill, before you met that young lady I can't remember you ever using the word 'leave'. Ah to be young and in love."

I felt myself colouring as they all laughed but I caught Gordy's eye, "It isn't really me I was thinking of, sir. I had time off when I was recuperating but you and the others have gone since Christmas without a leave." I gestured at the skies, hidden beyond the mess walls. "It was Ted's comment about the weather. If we get an October or November like last year we won't need all the crews here will we?"

He smiled and patted my knee. "You are right Bill and I was only joking. I don't think we will get the chance to grant leave until this Somme Offensive has run its course."

Charlie swallowed the last of his beer and waved his glass for the mess orderly to bring a refill. "Surely it has stalled sir. There has been little movement for a week or so."

Captain Marshall tended to listen more than he spoke but he was Intelligence officer as well as adjutant. "You are right Charlie but the Somme offensive has produced a sort of bubble sticking into the Germans lines. The French did not take their objectives and so the generals want to get the line as straight as we can before winter sets in." He sipped his whisky. "Realistically I can't see us being granted leave before the middle or end of November."

Ted groaned and Gordy said, "The thing is, sir, I plan to get married on my next leave and Mary, well Mary will need a little time to plan it."

"I see."

172

Archie looked at Randolph who said, "We could grant a special leave to get married."

Gordy shook his head, "No sir, I want Ted and Bill to be there too." He looked apologetically at Charlie. "I would have you too Charlie but I know that we will need to leave a Flight Commander here."

Charlie grinned, "I am honoured that you would even think of inviting me. No sir, the three of you have always been the Three Musketeers."

Gordy nodded his thanks, "So you see, sir, if you are telling me that the first week in December might be the time when we can get leave that is fine. I will make the arrangements with Mary."

Archie looked at Randolph. "Well if you three had the first two weeks in December then the adjutant, Charlie and I could have the last two weeks." Gordy's face lit up. "A word of warning though; that means you three will be here over Christmas and New Year."

Ted and I nodded our agreement, "That is fine, sir. We will live with that."

And so Gordy wrote to Mary to ask her to make the arrangements. I wrote to Beatrice too although I knew that Mary would tell her. It was strange to think that an offensive in France determined the date of a wedding in London. Such was the world of 1916. No one's life, at home or at the front could avoid the icy grip of the war.

The last days of August meant that we did not fly at all. It rained. There were localised floods although we were spared that horror. I dreaded to think what it would be like in the trenches. The rain we had had earlier had made small lakes and large ponds. The trenches would be inundated. I guessed that the plans to consolidate the front would be put on hold.

It did mean, however, that we had a full squadron with Gunbuses which had been well serviced and repaired. We had not lost a pilot for a couple of weeks. Sergeant Hutton and Senior Flight Sergeant McKay had consulted on the adjustments we had made and implemented them on the entire squadron. We would have a mile or two more an hour at our fingertips. With these faster Fokkers that was vital. We were also issued Buckingham tracer ammunition which would help us to see where our bullets were going. It was an innovation and we were all keen to try it out.

We were ordered up on the last day of August. The Tommies had been fighting close to Delville Woods and had finally secured the Flers Road. We were to ascertain what the Germans were up to.

This was the first time we had taken up our new boys and I put Lieutenant Gerard in front of Freddie. I could not ask for a better rear pilot than Carrick. He never panicked and he was as reliable as Charlie, Gordy or Ted.

My flight was allocated the area around Longueval. As soon as we reached the front we saw German aeroplanes. For the first time in my experience they were not flying high they were low and obviously identifying our weak spots. They had taken a leaf out of our book and were machine gunning and bombing the ground. I pointed down and began to dive into the attack.

We flew west to east so that we would fly over the whole flight of four aeroplanes. Sergeant Hutton opened fired and I watched, almost mesmerised as the tracer arced towards the German. The sergeant was able to adjust his aim and the first aeroplane began to flame and fall. As we came up to the next aeroplane I fired a burst. I saw that my bullets were going to miss and so I took my finger off the trigger and lifted the nose a little. This time when I fired the bullets struck the engine and, as we flew over the German, they stitched a line along the middle of the aeroplane. The pilot died.

We were beyond the last aeroplane and I lifted the nose. I saw that only one of the Fokkers had survived intact while a second was smoking so badly it would not survive. As I banked around Hutton shouted, "Sir, there are large numbers of Germans waiting in the lanes near to the village. They are going to attack!" He pointed to the north east and I could see the grey uniforms.

"Let's go!" I banked to the left and swooped down. The Germans popped at us with their small arms but we were moving too swiftly. They hit the wings but their bullets did little damage. I pulled the trigger when I saw the columns of Germans. Even though the range was further than I would have liked they were so densely packed that I could not miss. The tracer meant I could watch my bullets actually killing men.

Sergeant Hutton fired to the side. When I glanced in that direction, I saw that he was firing at German cavalry. To my horror I saw not only men but also horses being scythed down. I felt my heart sink to my boots. It was like killing Caesar all over again! I forced myself to concentrate on the infantry and I continued to fire. As we reached the end of the column I began to climb. I looked back and saw that the survivors had taken shelter in the few buildings which still stood. I could barely bring myself to look as Giggs and Dunston dropped their bombs. The cavalry regiment ceased to exist!

I led the flight over the German artillery positions. We had used our bombs but I had Hutton mark them on the map. As we were running out of fuel we would head back and report to Captain Marshall and Wing. This was a major German attack. The use of their aeroplanes at a low altitude was testament to that.

When we landed I could not join in the elation and celebration of the others. At heart I was still a cavalryman and the slaughter of the horses broke my heart. The adjutant did not notice my demeanour when I entered the office.

"Bill, get your flight refuelled. You are going up again this afternoon. Your attack this morning slowed up the German advance but Wing need you to see where the Germans are and, if possible slow them down."

I nodded, "We saw their artillery. I'll get the armourer to fit the bomb racks."

I ran to the mess. My pilots were just getting food. "No time for that! Sergeant, make sandwiches and bring them to the field. We are going up again as soon as we have refuelled." As they ran after me I said to Freddie, "Get to the Sergeant's Mess and tell them the same."

Flight Sergeant Richardson was just heading to the mess. "Percy! Get the bombs fitted to my flight's buses. We are going up again this afternoon."

Senior Flight Sergeant McKay was enjoying a cigarette in the anticipation of a leisurely afternoon. My shout ended that hope. "I want them rearmed and refuelled Sergeant McKay. Chop, chop!"

The pilots and confused sergeants gathered around me. "Right lads. We have to go back and bomb those German guns. I don't want to risk their machine guns so we will try bombing from two thousand feet. We should still be reasonably accurate and they would have to be bloody lucky to hit us with machine guns. Then we have to see where the advance has got to. Sergeants, make sure you have your signalling mirrors." Half a dozen orderlies arrived with sandwiches and a huge teapot. "We eat and drink on the hoof today. As soon as we are refuelled we are off again."

The other flights arrived. Archie ran over when he saw the unusual sight of aircrew eating next to their craft. "What's up Bill?"

"We stumbled upon a German attack. Randolph is sending us up to see how far the Germans have got."

He nodded. "Mr McKay, when you have finished with Captain Harsker's flight, refuel and rearm the rest. Orderly, we'll have the same!" The orderlies put their trays on the ground and ran back to the mess. "How bad does it look?"

"Pretty bad. The Germans even had Fokkers flying at low level. They mean business. It is close to the Flers Road and Longueval."

"We will come in high in case they send fighters after you. When you have finished then you can give air cover for us."

"All done, Captain Harsker."

"Thanks Flight. Right boys. Get on board." I saw my flight grabbing handfuls of corned dog sandwiches and throwing the last of the tea down their throats.

We had the benefit, on our return flight of knowing exactly where we were going and we made much better time. I could see that our earlier attack had merely slowed down the grey flood. They were moving resolutely forward and the German creeping barrage was driving the defenders back to the woods. We were in danger of losing the gains and sacrifices of the past months.

"Right Sergeant Hutton, whenever you are ready. I will fly north west to south east. Let me know if you need a second bombing run."

"Righto sir." I could hear that he was still chewing. Flight Sergeant Hutton liked his food; even if it was just sandwiches. The new anti-aircraft guns puffed smoke around us. I saw a hole appear in the lower starboard wing. It was annoying rather than worrying.

"Right sir. Hold her steady."

Lumpy Hutton was an efficient bomber and he did not waste any time. He watched the flight of his first bomb which told him the effect of the wind and the altitude and then he threw his other three bombs in quick succession.

"Bombs gone!"

We continued on the line I had chosen. "Watch for fighters!"

"Sir."

I could hear the bombs of the others as we continued through the puffs of anti-aircraft fire. I saw Lumpy hold out his mirror. "That's it sir. Mr Carrick has waggled his wings. All bombs are gone."

I banked to starboard and saw the destruction we had wrought. There were fires and the damage to the artillery was obvious. More importantly there were no more shells falling in front of the advancing Germans. We now had to stop the advance.

"Here we go, Sergeant. You take the right and I will fire ahead!

We screamed down to a hundred feet above the ground. The noise of their own small arms fire hid the sound of our Rolls Royce engines and the first that the German infantry knew of our presence was when I opened fire with my right hand Lewis. The tracer showed me the corrections I needed to make and the Germans flung themselves into the pooled craters to seek shelter. Hutton's gun and those of the other gunners scythed down the advancing Germans. When my first Lewis clocked on an empty chamber I fired my second. Once I reached the Bapaume Road I pulled up the nose and banked to port.

I levelled out so that we could reload our guns. I could see the smoke coming from them. The three Lewis guns had given good service this day. The armourers would have to give them a good clean when we returned.

I glanced up and saw the soldiers waving in the woods. "Sergeant, signal them and tell them we have destroyed the artillery."

"Sir. If you could slow down a bit it will make life easier."

"Will do."

He began to flash. It took some time for a reply then he flashed the longer message. I turned and flew back down. "Incoming message sir." I saw the flashing light. I could read Morse but not as quickly as Hutton. "Thanks for bombs. Could you hang around? Will try to retake trenches."

"Tell them, yes."

After he had sent the signal I began to climb. "Tell the other aeroplanes what we are about."

"Sir!" He began to flash with his mirror.

I checked our fuel. We had forty five minutes left before we needed to head back to base. It took fifteen minutes for the infantry to begin to move forward. Hutton suddenly shouted, "Sir, they have some flame throwers!"

I saw, to my horror, the dreaded Storm troopers with their flame throwers moving forward. No soldier will advance into such fire and, almost before it had begun, the attack began to stall. We zoomed down and opened fired. The mud had helped us for the Storm troopers could not move swiftly and Hutton killed six of them before they began to flee back. As we climbed Hutton shouted. "There sir, to the west and high. The rest of the squadron."

We climbed to meet them. We would have to turn back soon but I wanted Archie to know the situation. "Signal the Major and tell him what the infantry want."

The message was soon flashed back and Lumpy said, "Righto sir. It is acknowledged."

"Then let's go home."

I took us back by the northern route. That was determined by the prevailing wind which made life easier. We had to pass the Ypres road. Close to Beaulencourt Hutton shouted, "Sir, German reinforcements."

"Damn!" We were low on fuel and ammunition but an attack on the flank of Delville Woods could be disastrous. "Right Sergeant we'll attack. If you have any grenades then drop them, if you please."

"It will be a pleasure sir."

We zoomed down with two Lewis guns chattering death. While firing with his right hand Hutton casually lobbed first one and then a second grenade over the side. The two waves of concussion threw us up a little. The sergeant said, "That's it sir. Out of ammo; no more bullets and no more bombs."

I finished off the magazine in my second Lewis and I too was out of bullets. "That's it sergeant. Let's go home."

If it had not been for the following wind we would have been forced to crash land. As it was we barely made it to the field before we had used every precious drop of fuel. The aeroplanes were a mess. The wings were riddled with bullet holes and shrapnel damage. Poor Sergeant McKay shook his head as we trudged back to the mess. It had been our longest day.

Chapter 18

We had but one day respite before we were ordered into the air again. The German attack had been repulsed but the lost ground had to be regained. Once more we were spotting for the artillery. This time we were to fly to the south of Delville Woods and the village of Guillemont. The artillery had been brought closer so that they could see our signals.

It was Randolph who briefed us at five a.m. on September 3rd. "The artillery has been taking lessons from the French and we want to minimise friendly casualties. Consequently the ground troops will, when you fly over them, lay out white sheets to mark the forward positions. You will direct your battery's fire to any Germans ahead of them. You will then signal, by mirrors, to let the infantry know when the area is cleared in front of them."

"That is a lot of signalling for our gunners isn't it?"

Captain Marshall spread his arms, "It is but Wing and the brass seem to think it will work. The infantry will keep moving their white sheets forward as they progress."

"We will only be able to be over the front for an hour."

"I know and so we will use A and C flight first. They will be relieved by B and D. We will continue to do so until the attack is finished."

I saw the look of disbelief on Ted's face. "The pilots and the buses will be wrecked!"

Archie's tone was not conciliatory in the least. "The men in the trenches do not have the luxuries that we do Lieutenant Thomas. Don't whinge to me about having to fly for eight hours a day. Those poor sods on the ground could well be fighting for twenty four hours."

Ted's face tightened, "He is right Ted. When the colonel and I visited the trenches it made me realise how well off we are. We might be tired but we get to sleep in clean sheets and eat hot food every day. And we don't have Germans dropping shells on our heads and threatening to bury us alive in our own trenches."

He nodded his agreement. He would not admit he had been defeated but we all knew what we had to do.

When we were in position, high above the ground, Hutton signalled to the ground troops. After a few moments the sheets could be clearly seen. Hutton flashed an acknowledgement and we turned to inspect the German positions. There were hurriedly dug trenches with some sandbags. The rapid advances of the other day had meant they had not had time to consolidate their defences.

"Right sir."

We turned and flew back to signal to our battery. I could see, as Sergeant Hutton flashed out his instructions, that the rest of the flight were spread out in a line and doing the same as we were. Below us the Tommies were waiting behind their white sheets.

"All done sir."

We turned to watch the fall of shells. The four guns we were directing were straddling the German defences. Even so they were causing damage. Sergeant Hutton said, "I reckon that will do sir. Look."

As I watched I saw a machine gun and crew blown into the air. A handful of Germans tried to run back and were hit by a shell which was long. The guns kept firing and soon there were no German defences; there were just the dead and the fled. Sergeant Hutton signalled the cease fire and then signalled the soldiers below us. The battalion rolled up their sheets and moved forward. When they reached the dead Germans they laid out their sheets again. We repeated this for forty minutes until I heard the drone of Rolls Royce engines and our relief arrived.

We waved cheerily to the Tommies below. It looked to me as though it was working. It was slow going but it was progress. The Germans were being forced back. However, as we headed west we heard the German 10cm K14 guns. They were firing blind but they were hitting the positions that their troops had occupied. The infantry had suffered no casualties when they had advanced but, as they dug in they were. I hoped that Gordy and his flight would be able to direct our artillery to target these deadly German guns.

When Major Leach heard our news he was troubled. "We need those guns silencing. You will need to take off straight away. We can't guarantee that the two relief flights will understand the ramifications of the shelling. I will fly with Lieutenant Sharp's Flight and that way I can make more informed decisions."

"Right sir."

This time the food was waiting for us and I grabbed a handful of sandwiches and a mug of tea. I had half eaten my sandwich when the mechanic waved to tell me that we were refuelled. I swallowed down the hot tea and threw the tin mug to the surprised mechanic.

As we began to climb Hutton grumbled, "We'll get indigestion if we keep doing this!"

When we reached the front I was surprised to see that Gordy and his flight were not there. Hutton shouted, "There sir, to the south!"

I could see what looked like insects in the distance. It was Gordy and his flight. They were engaging German aeroplanes. The Tommies below us were sheltering where ever they could. Even as we watched I saw a handful begin to run back to their own lines.

"Sergeant Hutton, signal the guns we have a new target."

"Yes sir, but we can't see them yet."

"We will do soon."

I climbed higher and I could see, beyond the ridge, the ten guns which were causing all the damage. "Signal their position, sergeant."

"You will have to get higher sir. I can't see our forward observation post."

It took a frustratingly long time to reach a position where we could see both our observers and the guns but when we did so Sergeant Hutton wasted no time in sending out the coordinates. This time we needed to be accurate. It took three salvoes for our four guns to strike gold. As soon as they were on target they pounded the 10cm guns into submission. Hutton signalled to the infantry first and they began to move forward once more. Once we

182

saw that they were heading for the small ridge we signalled the artillery and they stopped firing.

"Keep your eye on Mr Hewitt, sergeant."

Out of the corner of my eye I caught sight of a Gunbus approaching. It was Major Leach. His gunner began signalling. "Sergeant Hutton, we have a signal coming."

The mirrors flashed between the two sergeants. "Sir, we are to go and help Lieutenant Hewitt. The Major will stay here with A flight."

"Acknowledge and we will pick up the others."

The rest of the Flight had anticipated the move and we were soon in line astern and heading south. I could see that there were just five Gunbuses. Either one had returned home or was down.

There looked to be eight or nine Germans. They were zipping around Gordy and his flight. I could see that he was attempting to form a circle but one of his aeroplanes suddenly began to descend and I watched in horror as the smoke poured from the engine. It seemed to scream as it headed towards earth and destruction. The debris thrown up and the explosion told me that no one would survive that impact. The sun was just behind us and we still had the height we had gained to observe the German artillery. I led my flight directly into the heart of the unsuspecting Germans. With no rear gunner they were as vulnerable to an attack from the rear as we were.

I had time, as we sped towards them, to see that Gordy's aeroplane had many holes in its wing and cockpit. We needed to strike quickly or it might be too late for the remaining four aeroplanes. Hutton opened fire first and he caught a Halberstadt just behind the propeller. The aeroplane juddered and then began to slowly spiral towards the earth. I took a snap shot at a black cross which zoomed in front of me. The tracer showed that I had hit it but it continued to fire at Lieutenant Charlton. As it left my sights Hutton fired at it and he hit the tail. He must have damaged the rudder for the aeroplane began to swing towards a Fokker

183

which was heading for me. The two Germans hit each other and both aircraft tumbled from the sky.

My flight's machine guns now beat a deadly tattoo. We brought twelve Lewis guns to the party and the Germans, having lost three aeroplanes and numerical advantage, fled the field. I waved to Gordy and was relieved when he waved back. We formed an umbrella in the skies above their heads as the four damaged aeroplanes limped westward.

When we landed Gordy looked gaunt. "Thanks Bill. We lost Hedges and Griffiths." Our new pilot had lasted less than a week. "It would have been worse if you had not arrived."

We trudged up to the adjutant's office. "What happened?"

"They jumped Griffiths. He was at the southern end of the line. Charlton and Williams went to his aid and they were surrounded. By the time we got there we were just trying to limit the damage. They were too slow to get in the circle." He shrugged, "Not their fault and those nippy little Germans fighters were inside us. It could have been worse."

As we entered the office I knew what he meant. Had we not noticed them then they would have all been picked off one by one.

After we had given our reports Randolph said, "I know that you are both upset at losing pilots but it was a small price to pay. We have held the Germans. Today was a victory. We captured Guillemot. That was the object of the exercise."

"It doesn't feel that way to me, Randolph."

"I know Gordy. I know."

I flashed a cold stare at Randolph. He was cocooned in his office and he did not have to brave the terrors of the front with young pilots barely out of school. We knew what they were going through Randolph did not.

We were lucky in that the next day was so wet and overcast that no flights were possible. It did little for morale, however as the young pilots brooded about their dead comrades. Griffiths was new but Hedges had been here for some time and that disturbed the newcomers who regarded the old ones as invincible.

Johnny Charlton had also been wounded which left Gordy with just a flight of three until he recovered.

The weather was not kind to us for the next few days. It enabled Lieutenant Charlton to be returned to limited duty but it was felt unwise to send him over the enemy lines. When the next push started, less than a mile from the village of Guillemot, we were required again. The generals wanted us to spot for the artillery but Archie told them that the cloud cover made that impossible. He was on the telephone for half an hour and when he had finished he slammed the phone down so hard that Senior Flight Sergeant Lowery had to check that it had not been damaged.

"Bloody fools. I told them we can't spot and so they want us to harass the German artillery. We are flying this afternoon!"

We used Gordy as air cover and Archie flew with them. They had to lurk in the thin cloud just above us. The overcast conditions meant that we were flying lower than we would have liked. We were a big target at low altitude. We saw the Tommies charging towards the little village. They were running from shell hole to shell hole and the German artillery was making life very difficult for them.

I led my flight to find the artillery; that would be our first priority; destroy or harass the gunners and allow the infantry to get into the village. Charlie and Ted would have to deal with the village and the machine guns. As we flew over the village I saw that it was ringed by machine guns. It would be a death trap to the advancing infantry.

We found the German guns a mile or so to the east. They, too, were ringed by machine guns. Lieutenants Giggs and Dunston dived in to drop their bombs. The rest of us flew parallel to them and machine gunned the defending machine guns. Peter had just pulled up when Rupert bought it. He seemed to be hit by a 10cm shell intended for the infantry. It must have struck a bomb on the aeroplane for the whole Gunbus disintegrated. As it fell the fuel tank must have struck some burning material for there was a second explosion which threw all of us into the air.

185

Peter had guts and he began to descend again to run the gauntlet of the guns and drop his last two bombs. "Hutton, use your grenades when we descend this time."

There was grim determination in his voice when he said, "Yes sir, it will be a pleasure." Rupert and his gunner had been a popular pair.

Lieutenant Harrington followed Freddie and Lieutenant Gerard followed me. I was as low as I could without actually landing. I hoped that Gerard was as low. The German machine guns found it hard to depress and Hutton and I cleared the first three posts. When Hutton's magazine ran out I saw him lob first one and then a second grenade at the artillery emplacements. I emptied my gun at the crew of a Kanone 14 artillery piece. The explosion of the last two bombs and the grenades went off one after another and, as we rose, I saw that half of the batteries had been destroyed and many of the crews of the rest had been killed or wounded.

As we headed back towards Ginchy I saw a British flare soar into the sky. We had a foothold in the village.

Hutton flashed a message to our lines that our infantry had entered the village. There was no signal in reply. "Too far away sir, you'll have to get closer. It's these poxy clouds! Sorry."

"Not your fault." I left the other flights to continue to machine gun the village and I headed west.

"Here will do sir."

Hutton began to flash his message. I saw the flash of a mirror in reply and after Hutton had signalled back he said, "They say thank you sir."

I heard the drone of engines and saw the rest of the squadron heading west. As I glanced at my fuel gauge I saw why.

The day had been one of the worst for some time. We were three pilots down and the atmosphere in the mess was sombre. Bates had tried to jolly me along when I had landed. He knew exactly what I was going through. "You have to convince yourself, sir, that they felt nothing. They will not have pain and they will not grow old. We can remember them as they were. That is how I got through the slaughter in the early part of the war. I liked Lieutenant Giggs. Did you know he was a fine pianist? After the war he hoped to continue his studies."

I had been amazed that Bates knew that. I didn't. I knew, too that he was trying to make me feel better but it made me feel worse. Rupert had had a skill and a talent. My only skill seemed to be in shooting down German aeroplanes and I had not done that since the end of August!

We were grounded again by the weather for the next few days. We had been needed for the assault on Flers–Courcelette. But even Wing recognised the dangers of flying in such awful conditions. I would have preferred to be in the air rather than on the ground and brooding. Our replacements had not yet arrived but the thought of training the young men and then blood them too soon depressed all of the senior staff. We did have some interest in the battle however for it was the first time that the British Army used tanks. They were described to us as battleships for the land. They were impervious to machine gun fire and were heavily armoured and armed. Their drawback appeared to be their reliability and their speed. I, for one, thought it a good idea as it would prevent horses being used for the same task.

We managed to get into the air on the 17th September. That was a fateful and fatal day for us. It seemed simple enough when we were briefed. My flight was given the task of spotting for the artillery at Gueudecourt. We were still winning the battle in this sector but it was felt one more assault would tip the balance in our favour.

Ted's flight was sent to patrol the sector close to Longueval and the other two flights were sent to Bapaume to escort some BE 2 bombers. The brass wanted the communications through the valuable cross roads and supply depot disrupted.

I led my four aeroplanes back to the familiar land around Delville Wood. I felt nervous, which was not like me. The five of us were slightly closer together than was normal. We hoped that by concentrating our fire we could destroy the German defences. The five pilots were, to all intents and purposes, merely delivery men. It was the sergeants who did all the work. All that we had to do was keep the aeroplane in the air and watch out for enemies. We saw none and I breathed a sigh of relief as we headed back to the field.

Ted had already landed and was waiting for me. "I see you had no problems."

I shook my head, "And you?"

"Piece of cake. Perhaps it is getting too easy. My flight hasn't seen a German aeroplane for ages. I hope Gordy and Charlie were as lucky."

The irregular beat of a damaged Rolls engine told us that it had not been a lucky encounter. When I saw Charlie's aeroplane limping in almost sideways then I knew there was trouble. The Very flare confirmed it. Ted and I ran to the side of the airfield to help in any way we could. I saw Johnny Holt leading in Lieutenant Dodds but of the other aeroplanes in the flight I saw not a sign.

Charlie bumped his aeroplane down which showed that there was something wrong with both Charlie and his bus. Doc Brennan and his orderlies rushed to the aeroplane which just stood on the main runway. Charlie was wounded and he was helped from the Gunbus. As he was carried away on a stretcher I shouted to the gawking mechanics. "Don't just stand there! Get this bus off the runway. We have more damaged aeroplanes coming in."

Johnny and Lieutenant Dodds had just touched down at the end of the runway. I saw three specks appear in the east. It was Gordy's flight but they had lost a bus too.

When Johnny landed he taxied and parked his bus. When he climbed down Ted and I went to him. He took off his helmet and goggles. He looked distraught. "What a bloody massacre!"

"Calm down, Johnny, and tell us what happened."

"We had just bombed the crossroads and we had no problems. We let the eight BE 2s leave and then we turned to follow. Suddenly six Huns dropped from the skies. I had never seen them before. They were smaller than the Fokkers but, sir, they had two machine guns firing through the propeller and they must have been twenty miles an hour faster. We didn't stand a chance. Bamber, Foster and Rogers were all hit in the first pass from behind. Two of them just bloody blew up! Lieutenant Sharp tried your technique and led us up to them but they hit him and did the Immelmann Turn. If Lieutenant Hewitt hadn't arrived then we would have all been dead meat."

The three Gunbuses of D Flight were just rolling down the runway. I saw that Gordy had made it. That was something.

"How many did you hit?"

His voice was very quiet when he said, "None. We never hit one of them sir!"

As Gordy climbed from his aeroplane and walked towards us I knew that our days of ruling the skies were over. We had lost four Gunbuses and never even managed to hit one German aeroplane. The world was changing.

Chapter 19

Archie held a meeting of the pilots from A and D flight with Ted and I present. I could see from his face that he was regretting the fact that he had not accompanied them.

Gordy's hands were still shaking as he lit his cigarette. "I have never seen the like sir. We could always hold our own with Eindecker. The new Fokkers and Halberstadts were just slightly faster but this is… well you have to see it to believe it. It looks like a slimmer, smaller version of the Fokker. It is harder to hit because it is so fast. The two machine guns just tear thought metal. They managed to catch up with the BE 2s. They shot two down and damaged another two. I am not sure we even hit them once."

Captain Marshall said, "I will ring Wing and see what they have to say." He shrugged, "They may have heard of this new menace."

He left us. Gordy asked, "How is Charlie?"

I had checked with Doc Brennan before coming to the meeting. "The bullet went straight through his arm. That is the advantage of the steel jacketed bullets. Luckily it missed the bone otherwise he might have lost the use of it. We will be without him for a couple of weeks."

Gordy shook his head as he stubbed out his cigarette and reached for a second one. "Then he is lucky because if we go up against these lads then, one by one, they will get us. Mark my words."

Archie said, "Surely…"

"Sir, we have no protection at the front. How we managed to avoid losing a gunner today I have no idea. And we are so big and slow that they can fly inside us and use the Immelmann. They can drop beneath our rear and then we are dead meat."

"Then we will have to use the circle."

"With respect sir that isn't going to work against these buggers. They are too fast, small and agile. They can twist and turn inside the circle. We are beaten!" I had never heard Gordy so depressed.

Captain Marshall returned, "It seems that Wing has had reports of this new squadron. It is that ace of theirs, Boelke. He and Immelmann were the two top aces until we bagged Immelmann. The Kaiser pulled him out, gave him his choice of the best pilots and they are based thirty miles from here; Jasta 2."

A deadly and sombre silence descended upon the meeting. They were the best of the German best flying a superior aeroplane. Gordy was correct; we were in for a world of pain.

Archie smiled, "Right boys, go to dinner and have a good drink. I am grounding the whole squadron tomorrow and I will go with Captain Marshall to Wing. Until we know more we don't go up."

None of us were very happy about that. It seemed like cowardice. It made sense but it did not sit right. The meal was like a funeral and we drank just to get drunk. It was the worst night I had ever spent with my friends.

We spent the next day ensuring that all of our buses were repaired and then serviced. We knew that we would have to face this new menace and it was unlikely that we would emerge victorious but we had to ensure that we were as good as we could be.

Ironically the four replacement pilots and buses arrived during the afternoon. There was no question that we would be sending them up. If experienced pilots like Charlie and Gordy were finding it hard then the new boys would last minutes. In the mess, that evening, I could see the confusion on their faces. They had heard so much about our squadron and yet there was an atmosphere of doom and gloom.

The four of them sat together. I called Freddie over. "Go and have a word with the new boys for me Freddie. Explain what went on yesterday. They won't be flying operations until the end of the week."

Freddy looked relieved. "And that is a good thing sir. We have seen too many young pilots go west far too soon."

"So Bill, what do we do about these new fighters?"

I turned to Ted, "Why ask me?"

He shrugged, "You are the top pilot and you always have ideas about this sort of thing." He nodded towards Gordy who was staring into his glass. "We haven't faced them yet but from what Gordy said we have no chance."

"That's not true. People said that about the Eindeckers." I grabbed a handful of cutlery. I laid them out so that they progressively rose into the air. "From what Gordy said they were very hard and hard to see." Gordy heard his name and turned to look at what I was doing. "They dive down at a steep angle and go for the gunner and the pilot. Then they swoop underneath to rake the stern." I demonstrated with a fork.

Gordy gave an ironic laugh, "And how do we counter that?"

"Line astern with the last aeroplane in the flight lower than the previous one and so on. That way when they try to swoop down they will have to run the gauntlet of all the gunners firing at them. The lowest aeroplane will have to have their gunner on the rear Lewis."

Ted nodded, "That might help us to cut our losses but it still doesn't shoot down the buggers!"

"Don't be so sure. The Buckingham tracer makes shooting more accurate. The gunners will see how close they are. If these new fighters are diving then they can't use their guns. Our lads could wait until the last minute to fire."

Gordy smiled, "Well it is a plan, at least, but I am not confident."

Ted shook his head, "He is getting worse than me. He hasn't even told you his good news yet have you Gordy?"

Good news was always welcome. "What good news?"

He visibly brightened. He had forgotten. "You are right Ted. Mary has arranged the wedding. December the 2nd at St. Mary's church Tottenham. Your young lady, Beatrice will be there."

"That is great news and is something to look forward to."

"Aye, if we survive the next month. I have never prayed for November before but I am now."

Bates was particularly attentive the next morning. "The chaps were telling me about these new aeroplanes sir and the dreadful losses you suffered." He shook his head. "You take care, sir."

"I will but it is not as bad as the trenches. There is always a chance of getting back or even crash landing. I have been damaged and crashed before now and walked away. You always have to have hope. There is no point in giving up."

"If you say so sir."

"I will tell you something Bates. I nearly gave up once before when my whole regiment ceased to exist. Almost everyone I knew was killed or wounded. I found hope in the RFC. I found a calling in the air. I can't believe that I was chosen like this just to die needlessly. Just believe."

He smiled, "I will sir. You have such a positive life force that I believe you."

That belief almost evaporated when I attended the briefing. Captain Marshall looked visibly upset. That was not like him. "I have some bad news to impart. Major Brack died yesterday. He and his whole flight were shot down by this new German fighter." There were audible gasps from the older pilots. Major Brack had been a popular and charismatic leader; more than that he was a good pilot. "We now have a name for this menace. It is an Albatros D111. You may well meet them today."

Archie stood. "I know it will be difficult for us today. We are depleted in numbers. We can, realistically, only muster three flights today. I will lead the remnants of A Flight with D Flight. Bill you and Ted will patrol with your flights separately." He went to the map. We have three areas to cover. We will be spotting for the artillery again. I will have this sector over Ginchy. It is the one where the new Jasta is most likely to be." I saw Gordy wince. I knew that Archie would lead from the front and not put others dangers he should be facing. "Ted, you will cover Delville Wood. Bill, your flight will be to the north east of Delville Wood towards

Warlencourt. Your sergeants have your call signs. More than ever gentlemen, we need to watch for the Hun in the sun."

I noticed that Hutton's pockets were bulging when we headed for the bus. "What is that Lumpy? Grenades?"

He looked sheepish. "No sir. Sandwiches." He shrugged. "The last few flights we had I got used to nibbling in the air. I know we will be back before lunch but…"

I laughed. "A good idea! I am surprised you didn't bring tea and then you could have a picnic."

He reached into an inside pocket and pulled out a Dewar Flask. "Actually sir, I did!"

This time I burst out laughing so loud that the rest of my flight stared at me. "You really are the most resilient soul I know. Come on then Sergeant, once more unto the breach!"

He grinned, "That sounds like Shakespeare." He took the bugle from the cockpit and sounded charge. My flight cheered. It was little enough but it would do.

We took off and I hoped that the flight would remember my instructions. I had told Freddie to be as low as he could once we were on patrol. We would fly in line astern and keep within sight of each other. I had told them that if attacked we would go into line astern formation. Freddie had shown his maturity by asking what happened if we were attacked whilst isolated. I had been brutally honest, "Every man gets as low as he can and hedge hop back to the airfield. Until we have a better bus we avoid tangling with this Jasta 2."

Of course on the ground that seemed sensible but, as we crossed Delville Wood I wondered if I could leave my pilots to their own fate. I doubted it. I gave Freddie the northernmost area and I took the one to the south east. It would be the one most likely to be attacked. Once we reached our height Hutton began signalling the artillery. We were quite good at this now. Soon the shells were dropping on the German trenches. It was going well.

Suddenly I heard the chatter of machine guns and I saw the dreaded Albatros for the first time. There were four of them. They attacked Lieutenant Gerard. The poor young man had no chance.

I saw the front of the cockpit disintegrate and the gunner shudder as though he had St Vitus' dance. I watched in horror as he fell to the earth. Poor Gerard lasted a few moments longer. Even as his aeroplane plunged to earth I ignored my own orders as, I noticed, did Freddie. I banked to the left. "Lumpy get ready. Go for the pilot if you can."

"Righto sir."

The others appeared to be obeying orders and they both dropped like stones. I then saw their gunners standing with their rear Lewis ready to repel the enemy. They turned west. It looked like the Germans were ignoring me and were heading for Freddie who was bravely attacking them head on. His gunner must have been lucky for he managed to hit one of the Germans which began to smoke. His luck ran out when the next Albatros poured his bullets into the front cockpit. I saw Freddie grab his arm and then he too dived towards the woods. He had no rear gunner and he would die soon unless we could do something.

I aimed my bus at the first Albatros and I fired a burst. The range was too far but I wanted to attract their attention. It worked. As I headed north they swung around to fly in a line abreast at me. Hutton let rip at the one on the right and emptied one Lewis at the one ahead. I fired the second as quickly as I could. Their sudden turn had thrown their aim and we avoided serious damage. As they zoomed past us I shouted, "Get on the rear Lewis!" I saw that Freddie was as low as he could go and was heading west. I prayed that he would make it. By heading north I was taking the Albatrosses away from my flight.

I began to straighten up when suddenly it felt as though someone had hit the aeroplane with a bomb. The controls felt strange. I tried to turn and could not. Hutton shook his head as he said, "Rudders gone sir. And the ailerons too. Controls are shot to hell and back. We have no controls left, sir."

We were doomed to fly in a straight line. I could not turn. I gave the engine all the power I could. "We'll draw them away from the others eh?"

"That's the spirit sir, Nil Desperandum!" I saw him arm the Lewis. "Here they come, sir. For what we are about to receive…"

I actually felt the bullets as they struck the engine. They seemed to thud into my back. There was nothing I could do. I had to fly straight as I had no control over the aeroplane. I noticed that Lumpy was not firing. I knew he was not conserving ammunition; I had to trust his judgement.

I watched him as he mouthed, "Come on you bugger, a bit closer. Gotcha!" He gave a long burst on the Lewis and punched the air. "I hit his engine! There are just two left."

The next Albatros closed with us and I both heard and felt the bullets as they hit the Rolls Royce engine. Miraculously we kept flying with no loss of power but I knew that could not continue. The fuel gauge continued to fall. I had long ago given up any hope of returning to the airfield. We would run out of fuel and fall to earth. Hutton fired again. The Albatros suddenly zoomed overhead. He did not make the mistake of flying in front of my Lewis guns. I noticed that they were a small and neat aeroplane. It was a harder target.

The last one powered in and again hit the engine. As Lumpy emptied his magazine he shouted, "We have damage, sir! There is smoke coming from the engine. It looks bad sir."

I nodded. I could feel the power fading. I pushed forward on the yoke hoping that there would be some horizontal movement left. Miraculously the nose dipped a little. The Albatros which had just fired upon us zoomed overhead. As Hutton changed the magazine he shook his head and gave me a sad look. "Next time they come in sir, that will be it."

"I know. Still, we fight to the end eh?"

"Of course, sir."

We were now losing altitude rapidly. There was no point in looking for a safe place to land; we would have no choice in the matter. We would land when the engine gave out or the fuel ran out. I saw a wood directly ahead. We were going to hit it. All the enemy needed to do was wait.

"Sir!" Sergeant Hutton actually looked happy. "They are heading away from us!"

I could not believe it. They must either be short on fuel or ammunition. Either way we had been given a reprieve. "Better sit down quickly Lumpy and brace yourself. There are woods ahead."

He did not reply but turned and sat as quickly as he could. He had barely braced himself when there was the sudden silence of an engine stopping. We had no power. I was so grateful to the designers of the Gunbus. We had complained about the huge wing span but it saved us now. We glided gently down to earth. I had been worried we would nose dive but we kept the same angle of approach. Ahead of us I could see the trees. If we hit one head on then the effect would be the same as hitting the ground. It was maddening to have no control over the bus. My hands were still gripping the yoke but that was out of habit. The closer we came to the woods and the ground a little hope appeared. There were gaps between the trees. So long as we did not hit a tree square on there was a faint chance of survival.

I saw that Hutton had thrown his Lewis over the side and was braced against the cockpit frame. He would be the first to die if we struck a tree. I saw a gap and the Gunbus appeared to be heading for it. We were barely twenty feet from the ground. Would the undercarriage hit before we did? If it did so there was a danger we could flip over. I felt the undercarriage strike something but it must have been a bush for we did not flip. It showed me how close we were to the ground. I saw that the fuselage would just miss the trees; not so the wings.

As we struck there was a horrible tearing and crunching sound as the two wings on each side were ripped from the body and the undercarriage was removed. As the rudder had been damaged and the rear of the aeroplane was just air we were, effectively a cockpit and an engine slithering and sliding through the trees. The friction of the ground slowed us up.

I heard Hutton shout, "Bloody Norah!" and saw a huge tree looming up ahead of us. We were going to hit it. The weight of the engine and friction saved us. The front of the cockpit crumpled as we banged into the tree but when Hutton leapt out like a startled rabbit I knew he was uninjured. I climbed out and looked back. We were fifty feet inside the woods but, more importantly, we were alive. We had survived.

Chapter 20

"Are you alright Sergeant?"

He patted himself down. "I think so."

"Right we have no time to lose. Get your Lee Enfield and the Very Pistol." As he did so I jammed the maps into my greatcoat pocket. I took out my penknife and prised the compass from its mount. I patted my pockets. I had my Luger and my service revolver. There was nothing else I needed. I threw my goggles into the cockpit. I would not need them again and the helmet I jammed into my pocket.

"Right, let's get some distance from here." When we were thirty feet away I said, "All right Sergeant, burn her!"

He fired the pistol at the fuel which had been leaking from the fuel tank. The FE 2 caught fire and then I saw the flames racing back along our track. They reached the wings and they, too, began to burn. It would destroy the aeroplane but it would be a beacon for the Germans who would, no doubt, come seeking us.

Hutton stuck the pistol in his belt. "Right, sir," he said cheerily. "Which way?"

I pointed north. "Let's get out of the woods first and then we can work out a route home."

I led the way and I held my Luger before me. Hutton had his Lee Enfield. We would not be taken without a fight. I suspect that I was happier than Sergeant Hutton. I was a country boy and he was a city boy. I had played Zulus and Redcoats in woods like this on the estate. I knew how to read a trail and how to hide one. As soon as I saw the path, which headed north, I took it. It would be quicker and it would be safer. We would leave less sign. We had travelled no more than a mile when I heard the sound of an aeroplane engine. I stopped and held up my hand. We both ducked beneath the canopy of leaves.

I could not see it but, from the sound and its speed, it sounded like an old Aviatik. They would be spotting for infantry. As soon as the sound receded I led us off again. We had to put as much distance between us and the crash site as possible. It would take them some time to discover that there were no bodies. Then they would begin the hue and cry.

From the air the woods had not appeared to be extensive but a mile later and we had still to reach the end of them. I looked at my watch, which had survived the crash. It was two o'clock in the afternoon. We had six hours of daylight remaining. We needed to use that time to get as far north as we could and then march a little more under cover of darkness and find somewhere to hide out. Had they not been seeking us then the woods would have been perfect.

I smelled horses. I heard the jangle of bridles and tack. There was cavalry ahead. I looked around and saw a blackthorn bush. I pushed Hutton behind it and then arranged the grass to disguise our tracks. I put my finger to my lips and pushed Hutton to the ground. I hoped we would remain unseen.

I heard them talking as they rode up. They were German. The sound of their hooves came closer and closer and I pressed us deeper into the ground. I counted the horses as they passed. There were ten of them. I could hear them talking in German as they passed. As soon as they had disappeared from view I grabbed Lumpy. "Right, we have to move as quickly as we can before they come back. We run!"

I might not have been as fit as when I was in the cavalry but I was much fitter than Sergeant Hutton who huffed and puffed behind me. Luckily it was not as warm as it had been the previous week but even so, in our greatcoats we were both sweating. We did not have far to run. I almost fell out of the woods. There was a small road which ran alongside the wood. I pushed Lumpy back under the eaves and I lay down to gather my bearings.

I could see, to the left, horse droppings which showed the direction of the cavalry patrol's base. That made sense for the front was just ten miles or so in that direction. The road went to the right and I could see a village of some description. The problem was that we would stand out like sore thumbs in our brown uniforms during the hours of daylight. I came to a decision;

we would move in the woods but move towards the village. I wanted to see its size and if there was any possibility of moving through it unseen.

I signalled Lumpy and he picked up his rifle and followed me. The edge of the woods was covered in nettles and weeds. No one walked here. I saw that the wood ended a hundred yards away from where we were. We would have to find shelter there. There were spindly rowan trees as well as coppiced oaks; neither would be any use for shelter. There was, however, a small stand of hawthorn bushes intermingled with elderberry trees. They would be perfect. We hid within their cover. I was desperate to look at the map but I did not want to risk the white of the map being seen by the cavalry. We would wait until they returned.

We lay flat on our stomachs. Hutton reached into his pocket and pulled out two sandwiches. He offered one to me. The officer in me was going to decline but the rumble inside me made me grab it and nod my thanks. Bully beef had never tasted as good. Hutton finished his in record time and pulled out another. He mimed splitting it but I shook my head. I was still eating and his frame needed it more than I did.

He looked happier when he had finished and he pulled out his Dewar flask. It had a detachable mug at the top and he poured one and offered it me. I was still eating and I pointed to him. He drank it down as swiftly as he had eaten his sandwich and a look of contentment filled his face. I finished my sandwich and I too felt better able to function. He poured some tea in the cup and handed it to me. It was tea far sweeter than I would have chosen but it did the job. He had just returned it to his pocket when I smelled and then heard the horses as they came down the trail.

I did not need to tell Lumpy to be still. The patrol waited just inside the woods. Someone who looked like an NCO barked out orders and two men saluted and then dismounted. The rest of the patrol headed down the road. They were leaving guards to watch for us. It had been too much to hope that they would assume we were dead. We would need to wait until dark. I mimed for Hutton to get some sleep. I was forceful and he acquiesced. He was soon asleep. The map would have to wait.

As I watched the two Germans lit a small fire and appeared to be cooking some particularly aromatic sausages. The smell made my stomach ache for hot food. I began to plan our route home, in my head. There was no point in trying to cross the front line; we had seen it from the air. At best we would become prisoners and at worst we would die. The alternatives were to find an airfield, steal a German two seater and fly home. The other was to hike, what I thought to be, almost a hundred miles to the end of the trench system and try to get around the lines and back to the British positions. Neither prospect promised much chance of success. The only thing we had going for us was the fact that we would be travelling through French and Flemish people both of whom were, in theory, our allies. We just had to avoid Germans.

As night fell the Germans showed no sign of moving. I heard the sound of horses clip clopping up the road. They were changing the guards. This would be our best chance to escape. I woke Hutton and we slowly rose. We were well over a hundred yards from where they were. I could hear them talking. I knew that the horses would muffle any sound we might make. We slipped out of the woods and crossed the road. There was an alley leading up the back of some small rural cottages. We slipped along it. I had watched the houses as well as the Germans and knew that this lane went roughly north. It mattered not. I just wanted to pass through the village.

There were small houses on both sides of the alley and they had high walls. We were half way along when a dog barked. Hutton froze and I pushed him. I made a meowing sound. I pushed Hutton further down the lane. The dog barked again and then I saw a light as a back door was opened behind us and a French voice told the dog to shut up.

We hurried another twenty yards and then we reached the other side of the small village. The road headed north into the dark. I risked the road. We would both see and hear any vehicles. If the Germans had patrols out then we would hear their boots. It was a risk but we had to take it. As we disappeared into the night I was glad that Hutton had brought the food. There was little prospect of any more soon. We reached a crossroads. There was just enough light to read it. The road to the right went to Douai. It was in the east and would take us further from safety and deeper into enemy territory. To the left we would be heading towards Vimy and I knew that was very close to the front. We were left with one option, north and Lille. Lille was a large town. I remembered passing through it with the Yeomanry in 1914. I knew it was close to the front but it was worth a try.

I spoke quietly, "Right, Sergeant we will walk until we can find somewhere to shelter and sleep during the day. Are you up to it?"

His normally happy face suddenly looked very serious. "I won't let you down sir. I know I am not as fit as I should be but I will keep going."

"Don't worry, Lumpy. I have no intention of leaving you. We either escape together or…" I left unsaid the two dire possibilities which remained.

We trudged up the road. We stopped to relieve ourselves and when we heard vehicles coming along the road. There were very few. The couple of houses we passed appeared to be shut up for the night. When I looked at my watch in the moonlight I saw that it was gone ten o'clock. People in the country went to bed earlier than in the cities.

I could hear the struggle Hutton had to keep up with me. He was puffing and panting. I too needed sleep. I had had none while he, at least, had slept for an hour or two. As I put my watch away I saw, ahead, another crossroads and a large forest spreading east. The signs pointed west to Libercourt and Lens and east to Thumeries. I put those towns in my head. They would give us our location.

"Right Lumpy, into the woods. We need sleep and shelter."

We found a woodcutter's track and followed it. It did not look well used. I remembered on the estate, they had cut down wood for the fires when the leaves had fallen. The leaves had yet to fall. I gambled that the wood cutters would not be operating just yet. We followed the trail and I spied a hut. It was a rustic, homemade affair but there was a roof and a door. We approached it cautiously. I drew my Luger. I nodded to Hutton who pulled the door open and I peered inside. It looked empty. There were no windows but there was a crude chimney.

"I am going in. Tell me if you can see any light when I am inside." I closed the door and struck a match. There was a hay filled mattress, a crudely made chair and table. There also appeared to be an oil lamp. The match went out and I opened the door. "Well?"

"A slight glow from the bottom sir but you would have to be standing next to it to see it."

That decided me. "Right get inside. See if you can light the oil lamp. I'll have a look around outside." I closed the door and listened as the match was struck. He was right you could not see the light. I searched the back of the building. I found an old can. I shook it and something sloshed around inside. When I opened the top I could smell the fumes. It was fuel for the lamp. At the moment light was more important that food. We needed to know where we were. I also found a water butt. I did not doubt that it would be a little scummy but it would have to do. There appeared to be little else that we could use.

I carried the can back inside and saw that Lumpy had lit the lamp. "We have more fuel and there is some water outside."

Lumpy held up the Dewar Flask. "We still have cold tea and I have half a packet of fig rolls."

"You are a wonder, Lumpy. Right now that sounds like a feast." I took off my greatcoat and spread the map out while Lumpy divided the biscuits into two piles. He poured my tea into the mug while he ate the biscuits and then drank the last of the tea directly from the Dewar Flask. I looked at him, "I think I will save my biscuits for the morning. Food might be in short supply."

He looked crestfallen, "I forgot sir, I was so hungry…"

I laughed, "Never mind. Now come here and look at this map; just in case we get separated."

"No sir. I am not leaving you."

"We don't know what may happen so pay attention." I took out my pencil and drew a circle around the crossroads I had identified. "We are here." I scribbled a rough line from the Somme to Nieuport. This is the front line. We are going here." I drew a line from the crossroads to Ostend.

"That looks a long way, sir."

I shrugged. "We will walk at night and hide up by day. I am not sure we will find anything as good as this again but we can hope. I hope to get three nights of eighteen miles done and that will leave us with about thirteen for the most dangerous part: into Ostend."

"So we have four nights worth of walking?"

"I am afraid so."

"What about food?"

"We may not find any. Water should be easy to come by most of these French towns have fountains and the like. We will be using your flask to carry what we can. There is some rain water outside. We can drink some in the morning and then wash with the rest. Now we will have to keep watch during the day; four hours on and four hours off."

He gave me a determined look. "You let me sleep earlier sir so you get your head down and I will study that map."

"Right sergeant." I looked him in the eyes. "We can get through this just so long as we don't panic."

"I know sir and, sir?"

"Yes?"

"Put them biscuits in your pocket they are a sore temptation to me."

Laughing I pocketed them and then lay down with my great coat over me. I was asleep in an instant.

I woke when Lumpy shook me. "Time for your shift sir."

I looked at my watch. It was nearly noon. "I said four hours!"

"I know sir but you looked tired and I managed to stay awake." He pointed to the table. I found some blackberries, damsons and elderberries outside sir. I have had my share. They are all for you." He grinned. "We'll save the fig rolls for dinner eh sir? The water in the flask is clean sir. I filtered it through a handkerchief. It was a clean one sir, but it isn't now. Night!"

He lay on the now warm hay filled mattress and was snoring happily within moments. I drank some of the water and ate the fruit. I didn't like to say to Hutton that eating so much fruit might not be good for us but it was food and we needed fuel for our bodies. I risked a wander around outside. I knew that we had walked a mile from the road and I could dimly hear traffic trundling along it. I presumed that it would die down after dark.

I discovered Hutton's fruit bushes but, as I went deeper I discovered some cob nuts, wild garlic and mushrooms. I suspected that Lumpy would not know the difference between a mushroom and a toadstool. I was a country boy and I had been taught well. I filled my pockets with the bounty. The nuts were particularly plentiful and they would keep us going without causing problems of digestion. The mushrooms we would have to eat fresh.

Once back in the hut I had a rummage around and discovered an old blackened pan which the woodcutters obviously used. Using some stones I made a sort of tripod around the oil lamp. I put the pan on the top. The oil lamp was giving off heat. It would not cook quickly but it would cook over a period of hours. I cut up the wild garlic and mushrooms and placed them in the pan. Nothing much seemed to happen but I knew I just needed patience.

While I waited I examined the map again. We would have to bypass Lille. It was a large town and there would be police as well as Germans there. The problem was that it was not far from the front. Once we passed there we had the area around Ypres to contend with. I knew that had been heavily fought over and there were large numbers of troops on both sides. After that there was just Ostend and the problem of how to get back to our lines. It seemed even more unlikely now that we would manage to negotiate all of those obstacles.

I heard a hiss and realised that the mushrooms and garlic were actually cooking. I smiled. It was a small victory but we might actually have some hot food and that always made a difference.

Chapter 21

We both felt better after the mushrooms and garlic. I put some water in the pan with the juices and made a very thin soup which we drank. It was better than plain water and probably healthier. When it became dark we set off. We both had a spring in our step and, as I closed the door behind us, I silently thanked the woodcutters for their hospitality.

We had not heard any traffic for some time. I was confident as we stepped out along the road. I now knew our route and we both had an idea of how long it would take us. The road we travelled was lined with trees and we would have shelter should either a vehicle or people come along. Our greatest danger lay in German soldiers being sent to the front at night to avoid our air patrols. A column of German soldiers might well inspect the sides of the road more closely than a vehicle. We walked along the road without speaking. I had explained to Lumpy about noise travelling long distances at night. I knew he found it hard to curb his garrulous nature.

I was happy to walk in silence. It enabled me to marshal my thoughts. This was like the moment my regiment had all died. I had expected to die and yet I lived. We should both have died the other day and we had been spared. I resolved to make something of my life. I had Beatrice but I had nothing beyond the end of this madness. I spent the night working out what I might do after the war and where we might live.

We met no one on our walk save the creatures of the night which sometimes stopped as we approached and then scurried off into the dark. The houses we passed were all in darkness. All the way north I was acutely aware of the proximity of the war. We found the occasional burned out house; a victim of the early fluid days of the war. We were both tiring when I smelled the smoke from the wood fires and knew a town or village was close by.

Verlinghem was a tiny hamlet at a crossroads. We had reached the point where we needed rest. The hamlet itself was not suitable. We crossed the village quietly. Hutton pointed to the small dribbling horse trough. I nodded and watched while he filled our flask with fresh, hopefully, drinkable water. As he was filling it I saw another wood away to the west. I tapped Hutton on the shoulder and we made our way there. This was on a slight rise; it overlooked the village. We entered the woods and soon found a trail. I hoped that we would find another hut. We travelled a mile and a half and saw nothing.

The sun was coming up and we needed to be out of sight. The ground to our left fell away and I saw, in the first light of dawn, a small dell covered in spindly trees and undergrowth. It would have to do. We made our way down and I used my knife to cut some thin branches from a willow. I used them to make a crude shelter. I climbed back up and looked down. The sun was peering over the eastern horizon and I could see more clearly. It looked natural. The branches and leaves would die but by that time we would be well north.

Hutton was already making some fallen leaves into a bed. I spoke quietly, "Not exactly the Ritz but it will have to do. You sleep first, Sergeant Hutton, and I will keep watch for four hours." He looked as though he was going to speak. "This way I will ensure that we share the watch equally. I will wake you at ten. Now sleep."

He nodded and lay down. He was soon asleep and I laid my greatcoat over him. I took my Luger and left him. We still had nuts but we needed more food. Hunger and tiredness robbed a mind of the ability to function. I began to forage. I saw many rabbits but I was not willing to eat raw meat just yet and we could not afford a fire. Had this been spring then there would have been an abundance of bird's eggs but this was autumn. I found more mushrooms and a few hazel nuts. There were blackberries and even a stand of late fruiting raspberries. They would have to do.

I suddenly heard a noise. I left the trail and went to hide behind a large elm tree. The noise became conversation and I heard the voices of two teenage girls. They were coming to pick the fruit from the bushes where I had been standing a few minutes earlier.

209

They began to pick, chatter and giggle. I could not make out their words but I recognised the language. They were French. It seemed an age before they were satisfied with their haul. They turned and headed down the slope. I gave them a start and then followed.

The two girls headed for a trail and skipped along. My senses were attuned to the country once more. It had been a skill I had used when on a cavalry patrol. There was a ribbon of smoke rising from behind the trees. I moved cautiously and saw the girls enter a farmhouse at the very edge of the woods. It was less than a mile from our hide out. We had been lucky to avoid it. When the door closed behind them I made my way back to the dell.

Hutton was still asleep. I ate my half of the bounty of the woods and drank a cup of the water. Our diet would soon have an effect on our health. We had eaten neither bread nor meat for a couple of days and we had had more fruit and nuts than I had had in the last two months.

At ten I woke Hutton. I whispered, "There is a farm less than a mile away. Don't leave the shelter unless you have to. There is some food here."

He looked at the fruit and nuts, "I'll be looking like a bloody squirrel soon!"

"It is food and it will keep us going. We will have steak pie when we get home."

He grinned, "Now you are talking sir. With gravy and mashed potatoes!"

The thought of hot, rich food sent me to sleep. Hutton let me sleep for four hours and shook me awake. "It's getting warmer sir. I had to leave the shelter sir. Sorry but I have the shits."

I nodded, I had expected this. "Drink plenty of water."

"What if we run out?"

"We will get some more."

We left at dusk. I took a circuitous route to avoid the farm. As luck would have it I found a trail which appeared to head north. I risked a match to look at the compass and saw that it did lead north. It was not the direction I had intended to take but it would do. It was slower going than I would have liked but I could not see us meeting anyone. The path led across fields and through pieces of scrubby woodland. We were passing some cows when I saw some rabbits gathered close to the herd. They were getting milk.

"Hutton, come with me. Drink the last of the water. You need it."

The rabbits fled but the heifer continued to chew contentedly. "Give me the Dewar Flask and hold her head. Hum to her. They like that."

"Hum what sir?"

"Just a song, sergeant. I am going to milk her." It had been some time since I had milked a cow but you never forgot and we soon had a flask full. I poured a cup for Hutton and I drank some from the flask. I refilled the flask and we left across the field. The milk would counteract the effects of the fruit as well as providing nourishment.

We scurried through Quesnoy in the dark of night only pausing to grab a handful of water from the water trough. We were back on the road once more and, although we were making better time, we had to be more vigilant.

We were a few miles from Dadizele, our next stop when disaster struck. Perhaps we were overconfident or just careless; I don't know. We had left the road, which turned west towards the front, and were heading on a small narrow trail which led north. We were just negotiating a rocky downhill section of the path when I heard a sudden noise and a cry. I turned and saw Hutton sprawled at my feet. He was clutching his ankle and in some distress.

"Sorry, sir, I slipped on the rock and twisted my ankle. You leave me."

I shook my head. I told you Sergeant Hutton we do this together. This is not the spot to examine your injury. We will find some shelter. Here, I will help you up. You can lean on me and use the rifle as a stick. Go steadily and don't put any weight on that ankle. Your boots will stop it swelling."

We hobbled, gingerly down the slope. It seemed to take forever. I heard the intake of breath from Hutton when he caught his trailing ankle on the ground. We would be caught in the open soon. I saw that we were travelling over what must have been a farm at one time. There were field boundaries and walls but it was overgrown. It looked to be an enclosure for animals but there was no animal waste to be seen.

We followed the contours of the land and headed down. As the first faint rays of sun appeared I saw what looked like the deserted farm building. It looked to have a roof and a door. We had struck lucky once more.

The door was just ten yards away and a sanctuary beckoned. "Nearly there, Lumpy. Just grit your teeth and think of England."

"Funny sir I remember saying that to a girl once."

Just then I heard a growl followed by the ominous clicking of a double barrel shot gun being cocked.

Hutton looked at me and I felt a barrel tap me on the shoulder. I turned and saw an old man, pipe jutting from his mouth and he was pointing his shotgun at me. There was a sheep dog at his feet growling and looking ready to take a lump of English flesh from my leg. "English! We are English airmen."

The barrel lowered a smidgeon and he said, "Anglais?"

I nodded vigorously and said, "Oui." I mimed an aeroplane flying and then crashing.

He lowered the gun and smiled, "Avion?"

"Yes, an aeroplane," I pointed to Lumpy's leg. "He is hurt."

The old man nodded and he opened the door. He went inside and turned up the lamp. I could see, as soon as we entered that this was not a deserted ruin, it was his home. He had a room just like ours on the estate. There was a simple pot bellied stove, a table with three chairs and a bowl with a pitcher next to it. The chairs neither matched each other nor the table. He gestured towards the chair and, after uncocking his shotgun placed it in the corner. I noted that. He kept it loaded. Hutton sat down and I saw the relief on his face. I looked around the room and saw that there were just some family photographs and curious mementoes but the place above the fire was dominated by a picture of the Belgian king. This man was a patriot and that gave me hope that he might be on our side.

He barked a command at the dog which went outside. He poured some water into a pail and handed it to me. I took off the boot very carefully. I could see the pain which Lumpy had to endure. I dreaded taking off his sock and finding the ankle broken. I slowly peeled back the sock. I held his foot by the heel. It was visibly swelling and very red but it did not seem broken. I knew how to test for a broken limb but that would have to wait for a while. We needed the swelling to go down first. I lowered the injured foot into the water and the relief on Hutton's face was clear.

The old man nodded and took a frying pan. He began to carefully carve some thin slices of ham which he threw into the pan. He disappeared out of the back door.

"Do you reckon this is safe sir?"

"As safe as anywhere behind enemy lines is likely to be. You just rest. We take each day one at a time and deal with whatever we have to."

I glanced around and saw a photograph of the old man when he was younger. He was wearing a uniform of some kind. There was one of him and who I took to be his wife on their wedding day and there was a much more recent photograph of a young man holding a shotgun in one hand and a brace of rabbits in the other. The old man returned with a basket containing a clutch of eggs. He saw me looking at the photographs and continued to the stove. The smell of the frying ham made me begin to salivate.

The old man turned the ham and cracked a couple of eggs into the sizzling pan. He glanced at me; I pointed to the photograph I had just been looking at. "Your son?"

He looked puzzled and I struggled for the French word. "Er fils, votre fils."

He nodded and, after taking out the ham, cracked another two eggs. He looked at me with the saddest look I have ever seen.

"Il est mort." He said it slowly so that I could understand. I nodded. "Boche!" He mimed shooting and spat into the open fire.

I wondered if he had been a soldier too. It answered one question, however, the man was no friend of the Germans which made him our friend.

He took two old and slightly cracked plates from the dresser and put ham and eggs on each one. He placed them before us and took a stale piece of baguette. He tore it in two and gave it to us. He mimed eating and said, "Mange!" He took two bent knives and forks from a drawer and handed them to us. I wondered if he would eat too but I was too hungry to be polite and so I tucked in. There is something about the flesh of the pig which, when cooked, is almost divine. The yolk on the fresh eggs was the brightest yellow I had ever seen and oozed across the plate. The bread was stale but I didn't care and I mopped up every last piece of fat and yolk.

I sat back and noticed that the old man had been cooking some acorns on the stove top. I was curious. He took them off the heat and put them in a mortar and pestle. He began to pound them into a powder. He took the kettle which had boiled and poured it on the powder in the pan. Leaving the pan he took his own plate and sat down. He ate slowly and deliberately. He was not hungry as we were. It seemed to be something he felt he ought to do. There appeared to be little enjoyment.

When he had finished he stood, collected the plates and put them in the sink. He poured the hot liquid from the ground acorns into three mismatched and chipped cups. He handed them to us.

"What is it sir?"

"I have no idea but it is wet and hot. We should be grateful for small mercies." I sipped it. There was a slightly bitter taste which was not unlike coffee. "It won't poison you, Hutton, drink it."

He pulled his face when he sipped it but, like me, he soon became used to the taste. The old man mimed leaving and, what looked like, digging. I nodded.

"Nice old bloke sir." He pointed to his ankle which was still in the water. "Sorry about this sir."

"It can't be helped and we dropped lucky here. I reckon I'll give the old boy a hand." I took off my tunic and shirt.

"You ought to rest sir."

I shook my head, "You will not be going anywhere for a day or two. We will be sleeping here tonight. It is dry and warm. I'll see if I can talk to him."

"Is he French sir?"

I shrugged, "He could be French or Belgian but they speak their own dialect up here so my French which isn't brilliant to start with may not be much use. You keep your foot in the water."

I went down the short, narrow passage. I glanced to the left and right and saw two bedrooms. One looked to be the old man's and in use. The other had more photographs of the dead son and I assumed that had been his room.

When I stepped out into the light the dog growled. The old man snapped at him. He put his spade into the ground and reached into his pocket. He brought out some pork rinds. He gave me one and mimed giving it to the dog. Remarkably the dog sat and held out his paw. The old man smiled for the first time and I gave the pork rind to the dog. I knew from the estate dogs that I was now a friend.

The old man was digging out some potatoes. I saw a digging fork and I picked it up. I pointed to myself, "Je m'appelle Bill." I put my hand out.

He took it and shook it, "Albert."

I set to helping Albert. He watched me for a few moments to ensure I knew what I doing and then he jabbed his spade into the ground and began to pick some early sprouts. It looked like we were gathering dinner.

It had been some years since I had worked in a garden but I thoroughly enjoyed it. It was as though the war was on hold. I felt neither danger nor stress as the two of us toiled in the small holding. I could now see why we thought the farm had been derelict. The barn's door was hanging off. There were tiles

215

missing from what had been the sty and it was only this side, hidden by the house, which had been tended. He had a good supply of crops. He even had a few tomatoes left. I could see where he had used the plants and there were winter cabbages and cauliflowers in the newly cleared ground. The chickens clucked away happily in their hen house. He had given up on the world but not life.

He nodded happily and took the fork from me. We returned inside. The kitchen was immaculate. Hutton had cleaned it and washed all of the pots as well as the pans. He must have just sat down when we re-entered. Albert was moved and he shook Lumpy's hand.

"Lumpy, this is Albert. Albert, Lumpy."

Albert tried to pronounce Lumpy and it came out *Looompy*. We both laughed. The old man said, "Mange?"

Lumpy looked at me. "He asked if we are ready to eat."

Hutton grinned, "Always."

Instead of using the old bread, the old man went to the front door and there were three fresh baguettes there. While Albert took them in I said, "Did you hear anyone come and knock?"

"No sir. Sorry. I was busy washing up while you and the old boy were working in the garden."

"We were there three hours; we have been lucky. Someone came and they could have peered in and seen you. We had best stay out of sight."

The table was soon laid with a third of a baguette each, some cheese and some tomatoes. He picked up three ancient and huge glasses and a large stone jug. He poured out three healthy slugs of wine. He held his glass up, "Salut! Bon Appétit!"

The cheese was homemade goats' cheese and was delicious. The tomatoes were big, beefy and tasty. The wine was a little rougher than I was used to but was a perfect accompaniment to the cheese. After we had eaten he took out his pipe. I had not had the chance to smoke mine since the crash. I took out my pipe and offered him my tobacco. He chuckled when he saw the picture of the baby on the tin. He filled his pipe and we lit them with spills from the fire.

Lumpy lit a cigarette and looked longingly at our pipes. "I have always fancied smoking a pipe sir and looking at you two, well you look sort of matey."

"You are right, Sergeant and when I smoke mine with my dad I always feel close to him. Smoking his tobacco here with old Albert does the same."

"When we get back to Blighty I shall get one."

"We are going to get back then?"

"Of course sir. I was just feeling sorry for myself when I hurt my ankle."

Albert and I smoked our pipes in companionable silence. When we had finished he said, "Lapin?" and mimed shooting.

"What was that sir?"

"He wants to go rabbit hunting." I nodded. "Oui, Albert."

He picked up his shotgun and carried it open in the crook of his arm. He went to a cupboard and took out a single shot shotgun and offered it to me. I shook my head and picked up the Lee Enfield instead.

"Get yourself in the spare room, Lumpy, and get your head down; just in case anyone comes."

We went out of the back door and headed for the woods to the north. Albert waved his arm and the dog, whose name I had yet to discover, raced off. This was like going with my dad and George the estate gamekeeper. I had loved hunting. I suspected that if Old Albert hit anything with his gun he would be picking pellets out for a week. Just to the right of the woods was a grassy knoll. I could see holes erupting from it as though it had been struck by a giant shotgun. That would be a perfect place for rabbits. Albert, however, led us towards the woods. Suddenly four rabbits broke cover. The dog had started them. They were racing towards their burrow. It was too far for the shotgun but I dropped to one knee and squeezed one shot off. I chambered another round and took a bead on a large buck. I squeezed again and then fired a third. I stood.

217

Albert came and slapped me on the back, "Très bien, Bill."

As we walked up I saw that I had hit three. The last had been the worst shot and I had caught the doe in the hindquarters. The other two were clean head shots. The old man waved a finger at the dog and mumbled something I could not hear. The dog had started them too early.

I took out my knife and slit the first one up the middle. The usual stink greeted me. I put my hand inside and ripped out the guts. I quickly repeated it with the other two. Albert made the dog wait until I had finished before he allowed him to wolf down the gory mess of rabbit offal. He took out a piece of string and tied them around the necks of the three dead animals. He dropped them in his hunter's bag.

He led me to the woods and we began to forage for mushrooms. He started to speak to me as we did so. There was no need for silence. We were alone and in the woods. By speaking slowly, using mime and by my asking questions I came to understand him.

He told me I was a fine shot and I must be a good soldier. I told him I had been in the cavalry. The horse mime is an easy one. I mimed and told him that I was now a flier. Once again flying was an easy mime. He smiled and patted me on the back as though it was a good thing.

We had collected enough mushrooms and herbs. He led me to a dead tree trunk and we sat and smoked our pipes. It was there he told me that his son had been hunting when the Germans had come. They had seen the gun in his hands and shot him out of hand. He had been just twenty. It took some time and some elaborate mimes to tell the whole story. I looked at the old man and realised he had aged prematurely. He was barely sixty and yet he looked older. Albert's wife had never recovered and had died a month later. Since then he had lived alone. He kept waving his hand at the land and telling me how many animals he had kept. He had been a successful farmer. There were tears in his eyes when he had finished. He had given up on the world but the dog and his farm were all that he had left.

As we trudged back to the farm I realised that not all of the victims of war wore a uniform.

Chapter 22

When we woke the next morning I felt like a new man. Albert was a great cook and he had made a delicious casserole of the wild rabbits and mushrooms. He had served it with mashed potatoes and vegetables from the garden. The red wine sauce with wild garlic and thyme could have graced a posh London restaurant. The three of us had been able to speak much easier having made the breakthrough the previous afternoon. We all went to bed early. I let Lumpy have the bed and I slept on the floor. I felt much better the next day after a full night's sleep.

Although Lumpy was better than he had been he was in no condition to walk and we spent a second day much the same as the first. I don't think any of us was unhappy about the arrangements. Albert smiled more and laughed at Lumpy's jokes. I don't think he found the jokes in themselves funny but Lumpy's mimes were hilarious in themselves.

On the third day Lumpy was well enough to be able to walk around the garden with Albert's old stick. I nodded to Lumpy, "Albert, we can leave tomorrow."

"No, no, another two days!" He mimed a pig snorting and then shooting. "Cochon! Bang!" Albert seemed to have become younger since we had arrived. I think he had just lacked company.

Lumpy laughed when I told him he wanted to go hunting wild pigs. "You know, sir, we could stay here as long as we wanted."

He was right although I was aware that we might be noticed. The nearby villagers might be used to his shotgun but not the Lee Enfield. We had discovered that he left four eggs each day and the baker gave him the two or three small baguettes. It explained their miraculous appearance each morning.

It was in the afternoon when our idyll ended. We heard a vehicle on the road. It stopped. Albert frowned. The road was a mile away and we had heard vehicles but they had zoomed down the road and disappeared. We heard this one stop. He went to the door and glanced out. He said, "Boche!"

Lumpy and I dived into the room we had used for sleep. I handed my service revolver to Lumpy and took out my Luger. We both donned our uniforms. We did not want to be shot as spies. There was loud banging on the door. I heard guttural German. Then I heard Albert's voice. The voices all became louder as they entered the tiny cottage. We could not hear their words for Albert was speaking too quickly and we had no German. Suddenly I heard shouts; what sounded like a blow and then a barking. Two sounds happened almost together; there was the sound of a Luger firing quickly and then the blast of a shotgun! Then there was the sound of four single shots.

I leapt from the room with my gun levelled. I took the scene in quickly and was firing my Luger even as I looked at the devastation. A young soldier was staring at the bodies on the ground; the dog was dead and Albert was draped over the dead animal. My first bullet took the young soldier between the eyes. A sergeant was bringing his rifle around and I fired four times from the hip. He crumpled to the ground. The last man standing fired on an empty chamber and I emptied the magazine into his face.

I had just knelt down to see to Albert when the door burst open. It was the driver of the vehicle. Four shots cracked off as Hutton killed him.

"Take the Lee Enfield and check to see if anyone else is in the truck."

I put my hand to Albert's neck. He was dead. His chest had been riddled with bullets. His poor dog, which had died defending him lay dead beneath his body. The officer and the NCO who had been standing close together had been cut in two by the blast of the shotgun. This was now a house of death.

Lumpy came back in. "No-one outside sir." He seemed to see Albert and the dog for the first time. "Poor old bugger."

We had no time for sentiment although I felt like crying myself. Albert felt like family. "Get as much food as you can.

221

Use Albert's hunting bag to store it. We do no more foraging from now on. We need to be invisible." I waved my hand at the abattoir in which we stood. "They will search for us until they find us this time. We have to disappear from view. Get yourself the officer's Luger and as much ammunition as you can."

"Where are you off to sir?"

"To search their vehicle."

I took out my penknife and plunged it into the tyres. I opened the fuel tank and picked up a handful of dust and soil. I threw it into the tank. It was not vindictive. If they found the bodies and the vehicle they might try to use it to pursue us. I found some maps and papers on the seat. They were in German but I thought they might be useful.

I found a couple of German haversacks and grey greatcoats. I jammed them into the rucksacks. There was little else of value and I returned to the farm. I took one of the German haversacks and slung it on my back. I took the four undamaged water canteens. I shook them. They were half empty. I filled them with Albert's pitcher.

Lumpy slung the Lee Enfield across his back. "That's about it sir." I handed him the second haversack.

I stood over Albert. "I did not know you long, my friend, but I am honoured to call you a friend. I hope you and your dog sleep with your wife and your son now. I cannot bury you but I will remember you when I return to England. I will say a prayer for your soul." I suddenly noticed his pipe. It had been knocked from his mouth when he had been struck. I picked it up. "Here you are Lumpy, Albert's pipe. Smoke this and remember a kind and brave man."

He grasped it as though it was gold; his voice was thick with emotion. "I will sir."

I took two of the field caps from the German privates' shoulders and jammed those in the haversacks too. While Hutton sorted himself out I rifled the pockets of the dead Germans. I took all the money they had. Who knew when it might come in handy?

Finally I took two bayonets, their scabbards and their belts and gave one to Hutton. They might aid any future deception.

We left. I had not planned to leave so soon but fate had determined otherwise. We left through the back. Albert had shown me the track which led north and by passed Dadizele. The first half mile or so was over stones and would make tracking us difficult. We had about thirty miles left to go. Had Lumpy been fully fit I would have risked it in one hop but I did not want to risk his ankle. We marched for three hours before I rested. Albert's stick gave some support to Lumpy. We had left before dark but I knew that someone would come looking for the German patrol. I knew that it was my fault. Someone had either seen or heard us when we were hunting. Not all Belgians were of the same mind as Albert had been. There were some who would collaborate. They might not have known there were two airmen sheltering there but the crack of the Lee Enfield and the stranger wearing khaki would have been clues to my identity.

When we stopped we were just a half a mile from Rumbeke. There was a burnt-out barn in a field close to some woods and we took shelter there. I could see one or two lights in the village. It would be better if we were to lie up for an hour and continue later. When I looked at Sergeant Hutton's face it was drawn and pain ridden. This was doing his ankle no good at all but we had little choice in the matter.

I gave him a bottle of water. "Drink all of this. I have another three of them and we still have the Dewar flask full too. That will be our emergency supplies."

He nodded, too much in pain to speak. I grabbed Albert's hunter's bag and took out one of the cooked rabbits. I tore it in two and handed it to Lumpy with half a baguette. Both needed eating. I had nuts, fruit and some carrots which we could eat later. By my reckoning we had two days to endure and then we would be at the coast. I knew, from the maps, that if we headed across country we could be at the coast by dawn. The problem was we would have two armies, barbed wire and No-Man's Land to negotiate. We would go the long way.

When Lumpy had finished eating he looked much better. Some of the colour had returned to his cheeks and he was half smiling. He took out Albert's pipe. "Do you think he would mind me having this sir?"

"I think he would be delighted. He had no family and he liked us. I think he had been lonely for two years. He had his dog and that was his only friend. The baker didn't even speak with him. Did you not notice how he smiled and laughed more after that first day? No, he will look down and smile when you learn how to smoke it."

"You know sir I saw the way he looked at you. I think you reminded him of his son or at least how his son might have turned out if he hadn't been killed. I reckon we gave him a second chance and I am glad we met him."

I nodded. I think that Hutton was right. He had helped us and I liked to think that we returned the favour. I checked my watch. It was ten o'clock. "Come on, we'll risk the village."

After the incident with the German patrol we were wary and nervous as we slipped through. We could see lights further west. It was a larger town, Roeselare. We would avoid that. Our route would take us slightly north east and add to our journey but it would take us down quieter roads. We had just one scare before dawn when we heard the clip clop of a horse. We just made it into the ditch when the German horseman rode by. From the smell he had been drinking and I daresay we could have overpowered him and used his horse. However another missing German soldier would have pinpointed our position for the pursuing Germans. We let him continue along the road and disappear from sight.

The delay meant we would not get as far as I hoped. Torhout was the same size village as Dadizele and I wanted to avoid it. The map showed a huge forest just two miles north west of the town. We crossed the main road and headed across the fields. Lumpy was really struggling. I put my arm around his waist. "Put your arm around my shoulder and use Albert's stick. Keep your weight totally off your foot until we get to those woods."

He nodded and I felt his fingers tighten around my shoulder. His teeth were grinding together as he muttered, "I'll do it, sir, you'll see."

It was hard going over the fields. We had to scramble through bushes and clamber over fences. As dawn began to break we made the sanctuary of the eaves of the forest. We moved within its confines and I waited until I could see no more fields before I stopped. "Sit here while I have a quick shufti around."

I drew my Luger, now reloaded, and walked in a circle four hundred yards around Lumpy. I found a sheltered spot. A huge sycamore had been struck by lightning and fallen down. It covered a large area and there were lots of hiding places within it.

"Come on, Sergeant Hutton, just a few more yards and we can sleep." I helped him to the dead tree and while he lay down I made a rough shelter from the broken branches. When I was satisfied that we could not be seen I joined Lumpy.

"Now get some sleep and I will wake you."

He gave me a sceptical look, "Promise, sir?"

I smiled, "As an officer and a gentleman."

While he slept I reloaded both Lugers with fresh ammunition and cleaned the Webley. I was not certain we had finished with our weapons yet. I took out my pipe. I was tempted to light it in memory of Albert but good sense prevailed and I merely cleaned it. I took out the maps and examined them. I could not read much on the German map but it was interesting. I saw the skull and crossbones at various points and that meant minefields. I even saw some just off Ostend. They would be there to stop the Royal Navy closing with the shore and aiding the infantry. There were some German units marked including, tantalisingly, an airfield. I was not ready to risk that. I memorised the route and organised our options in my head.

After tidying the contents of the German haversack and the hunting bag I settled down to keep watch. I had much to occupy my mind from Albert and his sacrifice to Beatrice and my family. I had no doubt that I would have been posted as missing, presumed killed in action. We had many reconnaissance aeroplanes in that

225

area, it was not far from Ypres. The remains would have been seen. How would they react at home? I knew that mother would be distraught beyond words when she received the telegram while dad would be his stoical self. Sarah and Alice, too, would be upset. Our Kath lived too far away for her to find out immediately but what of Beatrice? I confess I did not know her well enough to really gauge her reaction. I suspected she would be strong. She would shed tears for me but they would be in private. The thought of that fine woman crying for me made me even more determined to get home as soon as possible.

I woke Hutton at one o'clock in the afternoon. He was not happy. "Sir, you said you would wake me."

"But I did!"

"You know what I mean. You will only get four hours sleep before we have to leave."

"Sergeant, you need the rest more than I do. I was being selfish. If you are fitter then I won't have to help you."

We left the woods before dark, at five. I was taking a chance but I wanted to be in Ostend in the middle of the night. We would stand out too much in broad daylight. I had a number of plans in my head but until we reached the port and the front line I would not make a decision. I elected not to tell Lumpy of my plans. I needed him to be flexible. I kept turning as we headed down the trail towards Ichtegem. He appeared to be walking well. The rest had worked. We had twelve or fourteen miles to go and we had nine hours to cover it.

We kept to the fields around Ichtegem and I was pleased we had done so. We sheltered behind a stone wall as a German cavalry patrol stopped in the village and began searching the buildings. It could have been a coincidence but I was convinced that they were looking for us. I checked my watch. It was seven o'clock. It would be dark in the next half hour. We waited to see which way they went. They headed for Ostend. That meant we could not take the main road. My map work came to my aid as I remembered a side road which went through Eernegem and brought us to the east of Ostend. It was a mile or so further but Lumpy's ankle appeared to be holding.

"Right we need to get across that road and head due north. Let's go before the cavalry returns."

It was the most nerve-wracking half a mile I have ever covered. It was dark and we were dressed in dark clothes but I was not certain if all of the Germans had gone. It was only when we crossed to the field on the other side that I knew for certain that they had not left a guard behind. We ran until we were two fields away.

When we found the road leading north we slowed down to catch our breath. "How's the ankle, Sergeant?"

"Holding up, sir. Albert had some foul-smelling liniment he applied. It seemed to work though."

Albert had been a godsend. I think we would have been captured if we had not stumbled upon him.

The road was the smallest we had yet used. I would have struggled to drive Lord Burscough's Crossley down it without scratching the coachwork. It made the journey more intimidating for there was nowhere for us to hide if we met anyone. Eernegem was a tiny hamlet of just ten houses. They were centred on a small square. We risked the centre. We had almost crossed it when the dogs began to bark. This was no time for an impression of a cat and we hurried on as fast as we could. We had just turned the corner at the edge of the village when I heard voices. I peered around the edge of a tree and saw huddle of people in the light from a door. I prayed that they were on our side and not the Germans.

Oudenburg was a nightmare. We were just half a mile from its eastern extremities. We could not use the road for even in the early hours of the morning there was much traffic on the road. Much of it was civilian but we did not know the loyalties of these people who were able to ply their trade in the hours of darkness. We had to resort to the fields again. However there were few hedges and we had to drop to all fours whenever we heard a vehicle in the distance. My plans to arrive during the hours of darkness looked doomed to failure.

We could smell the sea and we both picked up the pace for our destination appeared to be close. Then we heard voices. I knew there was a main road from the east which entered Ostend not far from where we were. The Germans had put a checkpoint there. We were trapped! The only solution appeared to be another dash across the road. It was not yet dawn but I knew it could not be far away. We would stand out if we tried that. We had to move east to avoid the German guards. Each step took us further from the beach and closer to daylight. Suddenly I spied hope. There was a large metal drain running under the road. It was obviously there to take excess flood water under the road rather than washing it out. I pointed to it and we scurried there.

Hutton looked at it, "I'll never get through there, I am too big. I will be trapped."

"Let's try. Take off your greatcoat and tunic." When he had done so I said, "Now put your arms in front of you and pull yourself through."

"If you say so, sir." He did not sound confident.

He entered the culvert and began to move slowly through. I gathered our bags and tied them together I entered the culvert. With Hutton it had been his waist which had been a tight fit with me it was my shoulders but I was able to move by wriggling.

"Sir I am stuck!"

Hutton's voice seemed unnaturally loud in the metal tube. "Ssh! Wriggle your shoulders. The tunnel doesn't get narrower; we got this far we should be able to do the rest. Relax. You are tightening up." I knew what he was feeling. It was claustrophobia. I too felt the tightening of the chest and the panic as the darkness seemed to close in. Hutton did appear to be stuck and I was contemplating trying to wriggle back when he began to edge forward again. Soon he was moving at a faster pace and I tugged our bags behind us.

As I popped out on the other side I felt joy at the release but when I saw the lightening sky my heart sank. Dawn was about

228

to break. I handed Hutton his clothes and he dressed. By my reckoning we had about two miles to go to the beach. We would have to risk it. Luckily the field in which we found ourselves was slightly below the level of the road and there were some scrubby bushes which afforded cover. Five hundred yards away from the road I felt that we could break cover. Dawn was not far away in the east but we, in the west, would still be in darkness. "Run. There shouldn't be anything before us until we reach the beach."

Our last obstacle was the coast road which lay before the dunes. I glanced left and right and there was nothing in sight. We sprinted across the road and flung ourselves into the safety of the dunes. We had made it. There, before us, lay the English Channel and, hidden in the darkness less than thirty miles away was England and home.

"You stay here and break out the food. I'll go and check the beach."

I made my way through the dunes. When I reached the last of them I peered down at the beach. As I had expected there were obstacles on the beach but there were also signs. Suddenly an early ray of sunlight lit up the sign which was just fifty yards from me. It was the skull and crossbones. The Germans had mined the beach!

Chapter 23

Poor Lumpy looked excited when I returned. He had the water and the last of the food laid out on his greatcoat like a picnic from before the war. "Well sir, are there any boats there?"

I shook my head. "They have mined the beach. We are stuck."

He nodded, "Right sir, then let's eat. You always think better on a full stomach and I am sure you will think of a way out of this."

His confidence was touching; it was misplaced but touching. I ate the last of the food and drank half of my water. Who knew when we might need water?

I looked at our options. We could head back to the airfield we had passed some miles ago and steal an aeroplane. That would mean hiding up in the dunes and enduring the ordeal of the pipe. We could head north east along the coast and find a part of the beach which was not mined or we could head into Ostend. Although I did not relish any of them the last one seemed to have the most chance of success.

"We'll head to the road and wait until dark. We will have to chance Ostend tonight."

"Righto sir," he said cheerfully, "I knew you would think of something."

We lay hidden in the dunes as close as we could get to the road without being seen. At about nine I heard the tramp of boots along the road. I bellied up to the top of the dunes and peered over. There was a company of German soldiers heading down the road towards Ostend. I watched as they approached, an idea forming in my head. I saw soldiers running towards the dunes and then rejoining some time later.

I slithered down. "Quick back towards the beach!" I did not want a peeing German to spot us. When we were hidden behind the next ridge of sand I watched and saw a German drop his trousers and relieve himself where we had just waited. I heard shouts from the road. The German shouted something and then, pulling up his trousers, ran to join his comrades.

"Follow me!"

We returned to the dunes near the road. We saw four men running along the road, trying to catch up with their comrades. I raised my head and looked along the coast road. There appeared to be another company marching towards Ostend. I made my decision. I threw Hutton one of the German haversacks.

"Take off your greatcoat. There is a German one in the bag." I threw him a field hat. "Put this on your head and put the hunter's bag and your greatcoat in the haversack. We are going to become Germans."

I slid down to the bottom to make the change easier. The greatcoat came down to our knees and the top of our boots. There was no khaki visible. I strapped the bayonet and the Luger around the outside of the coat. "Give me Albert's stick and you sling the Lee Enfield around your shoulders." I looked at Lumpy. He would pass inspection… at a distance.

We climbed to the top of the dune. The Germans were level with us. I saw two men running along the road to catch the column and, to our right, two men were heading towards the dunes.

"Right Lumpy, follow my lead. We have just had a leak. We will catch up with the Germans but not too fast eh?" As we stepped over the dunes and I feigned adjusting my trousers, I counted on the fact that the Germans would be used to this frequent call of nature. They would see two more comrades running along the road.

I saw that we would be about a hundred and fifty yards behind the column. A Feldwebel waved at us and shouted something. I waved and pointed to the stick. He urged us forward. We hurried for a few steps and he turned his attention to the two men who were leisurely walking from the dunes. He began to berate them.

We marched down the road. It was like that nightmare I had had when I first joined up. I was walking along a busy street and I was naked. That was how I felt; naked. We were passing houses on the outskirts of Ostend. We were nearing the port. As yet I had not worked out an escape but we were still free and we still had hope. The column ahead slowed up as we approached the intersection. The road from the left was the one we had followed. I saw another column of Germans coming along that road. The intersection was all confusion as the two columns met.

I tugged at Hutton's arm and led him along the left hand side of the column away from the prying eyes of the Feldwebel. Some of the Germans viewed us curiously and one said something, I feigned a coughing attack and managed to spit some phlegm into the grass verge. By then we were beyond the talkative German. I could hear raised voices at the front. There were officers and NCO's arguing. I grabbed Lumpy's arm and we pushed our way through the new German column. A couple of the soldiers shouted at us, I suspect they were swearing. I used the only German word I knew, "Scheiße!" We were pushed and shoved and even punched by one German but we erupted on the other side and found ourselves in an alley. We ran down it and turned right the first opportunity we had. We stopped to catch our breath out of sight of prying eyes.

"Are you all right?"

"Yes sir but that was a bit scary."

I nodded. The good news was that we were in Ostend. We could wander around, dressed as Germans and, hopefully, avoid any military police. I suspected that they would be at the exits from the town to search for deserters. The ones inside the town would be presumed to have permission to be there. "Don't talk and stay close."

We headed down the next alley and it brought us out, eventually, at a small square with shops and a market. There were a few German soldiers but it was mainly locals doing their daily shop. I slowed down to blend in. We paused at some stalls to inspect what they sold and then we wandered on. I wanted us to become invisible. Once we hit the centre of Ostend we were less visible as there were more soldiers and locals but we needed to get our bearings. There were some bars with tables and chairs outside at the harbour. I suspected that tourists and fishermen would have been their clientele before the war but now Germanic grey was the order of the day. I found a café which was close to the northern breakwater. It was relatively empty. Two other soldiers walked in before us. I took a table well away from them.

We took off our bags and sat down. The waiter slouched out with a sour expression on his face. He took the order of the two Germans. I listened. When he came to me I repeated the order and the waiter rolled his eyes as though we had all committed some enormous faux pas. A few minutes later he brought beers to us. I noticed that he waited for the other soldiers to pay. That was unusual. It demonstrated that the Belgian waiter was not happy about the Germans. He brought ours. I asked, "Combien?"

For some reason that did not displease him and he told me. I had no idea how much that was in German money and so I took out a note from the pilfered German wallets. It did not seem to worry him and he dropped some coins on the table. I waved my hand for him to keep the change and he smiled and left.

I took out my pipe and filled it. It would appear more natural. I used Albert's tobacco pouch which I had taken. It was a French tobacco and the smell would not appear unusual. I drank some of the beer. It was better than the French beer we were used to. I saw Hutton fingering Albert's pipe. I pushed the tobacco pouch and nodded to him. He began to fill it. I noticed him tamping it down hard and I shook my head and took his pipe from him. I began to loosen the tobacco with my penknife and then I handed it back. He nodded his thanks and then lit it. After a couple of puffs it was drawing well. I used my finger to push the tobacco down and nodded to him. I almost burst out laughing when the tip of his finger touched the burning ash. He would get used to that.

The café began to fill up but no one took the slightest notice of two soldiers smoking their pipes and drinking their beer. I glanced at my watch. It was getting on for noon. People were eating. Having nursed our beers for an hour or so I waved the waiter over. I held up two fingers and pointed at the beer. I risked some French. He seemed to appreciate it before. "Moules, frites?" I held up two fingers and he grinned and nodded.

Lumpy carefully put his pipe down. I could see that he was desperate to speak but to do so now would be a disaster. I had also ordered the food so that we would not have to speak to any garrulous German. The beer and the hot food took just ten minutes to arrive. I didn't wait for the bill, I just threw down a handful of notes. He took one and reached into the purse in his apron I waved it away and my new found friend grinned at me.

I am not certain if Lumpy had eaten mussels before and so I nodded to him and showed him how to eat them. His face lit up when he tasted them. He looked around the table for condiments. I smiled. He was looking for vinegar. To a northern working class lad vinegar and chips were synonymous. These might be called frites but we knew them as chips. When he had finished he looked at the cooking liquor. It was redolent with parsley, white wine, garlic and shallots. I took a piece of bread and dipped it in the juices. He nodded and tucked in. We washed it down with the beer and felt replete. I had noticed more senior officers arriving for a late lunch and I put a handful of coins in the ashtray and gestured for Hutton to follow me.

I headed not for the town but the breakwater to our right. I had observed people fishing from there. At the end of the line of shops and cafes was a hut selling accoutrements for fishing. I saw two crab lines. I pointed to them and to a pot of bait. The man gave me the price in French and I handed over another note. I was glad that I had taken the German money as it had come in handy.

I led Hutton to the end of the breakwater where there were the fewest people. I took off my haversack as did Lumpy. It was only when he laid down his Lee Enfield that I realised how lucky we had been. I should have taken the German rifles. We would ditch the incriminating evidence before we left. We loaded the lines and began to fish for crabs.

There was no one within forty feet of us and the water was crashing against the rocks we would be able to talk, albeit quietly. "Well done, Sergeant, you restrained yourself well back there."

He grinned, "It was hard. Mrs Hutton raised a noisy little bugger in me!" He glanced around. "So far so good sir, and the beer went down well. What was that we were eating?"

"Mussels and chips."

"Well it isn't cod and chips but it filled a nice hole."

I jammed my crab line between two rocks. I had been hot in the café with my greatcoat but the breeze from the sea meant I could wear it here without attracting attention.

"What now, sir?"

I pointed across the harbour. "We need to identify a boat we can steal and then sail back to Blighty."

He smiled, "Oh you can sail as well, sir?"

I shook my head, "I have never sailed in my life."

His face fell. "Then…"

"The way I figure it Hutton sailing a boat must be like flying an aeroplane. You want the wind from your quarter and you may have to steer a zig zag course to get where you want."

"How about a boat with a motor? We could work one of those."

"True but we are leaving at night and a boat with a motor would make a noise." I felt a tug on the line and I began to wind it up. I had caught my first crab. There was a little pool of rainwater next to me and I dropped the creature in it. It found a rock it could hide beneath and disappeared from view. I took the opportunity to stand and load the crab line with bait. Hutton stood too.

I gestured with my head, "See down there," below us was a ladder and a small wooden jetty. About ten yards away, there were four evenly spaced buoys. He nodded, "I am guessing that there will be boats which tie up there. They must be out at the moment. We wait until dark and steal one."

Hutton appeared to have the utmost faith in me and he grinned, "Sounds easy sir."

"It is anything but. There will be machine guns and guards at the harbour entrance. They will have patrol boats sailing across the middle and we have to learn how to sail without attracting attention." Even as I told him I contemplated abandoning the ridiculous idea but his words when we had first escaped, '*Nil Desperandum*' came to mind. Where there was life there was hope.

The afternoon dragged on. We relieved ourselves as the other fishermen did by using the sea. We caught four more crabs. Had we wanted we could have eaten like kings. A few of the Germans waved and shouted what sounded like goodbye as they left. We just repeated their words and it did not arouse suspicion. I worried that the four buoys were not going to be used as the sun began to set in the west. Then I saw the sails of two small fishing boats appear at the end of the harbour. One had a red sail and the other one which had been white a lifetime ago. They tied up at two of the buoys. I watched them approach and saw how the two crew on each boat handled the sails. It seemed they must have shared the fishing for they only had one small dinghy between them. They ferried their catch to the jetty and, after stowing the sail and fitting a tarpaulin to keep out the rain they left. They barely gave us a glance.

For the first time in many days I felt hope surge within me. I could see our transport home. Now we had to wait until dark.

The rest of the fishermen had gone and we were the only ones left. It was now a difficult time. We stood out like a sore thumb and I prayed for darkness. I kept watching the two fishing boats bobbing up and down in the water. Our escape was so close. Hutton pointed across the water. "Sir, a patrol boat."

It was small motorised boat about twenty feet long with a machine mounted close to the bows. That was a problem we would have to negotiate.

"Shall I get rid of the crabs now sir?"

"No, best leave them in case another fisherman comes to do some night fishing. It will add credibility to our story."

Darkness fell and I almost jumped for joy. We were, to all intents and purposes, invisible. We had been highlighted by the setting sun but now we were hidden by shadows.

"You can get rid of the crabs now, Hutton."

He had no sooner bent down to put his hand in the water than I heard footsteps and two Germans with a lamp appeared before us. One shouted something and held his hand out. They were military police and were obviously asking for papers. I caught Hutton's eye and gestured towards them. They came closer. I noticed that they had side arms but they were holstered. One held the lamp while the other had his right hand held out for our papers. I put my right hand inside my greatcoat as though looking for them. Hutton came to my right and the German barked at us again.

When they were just two paces from us Hutton threw three of the crabs at their faces. They just reacted, throwing their arms up. The lamp crashed to the floor and was doused. I whipped out the bayonet and slashed it across the throat of the barking German. Lumpy leapt on the other. He picked up a rock and pounded the man's head until it was unrecognisable as human.

"Well sir, that's torn it."

I quickly shinned down the ladder and threw off my greatcoat and tunic. I untied the dinghy and rowed to the two fishing boats. I tied the painter of one to the stern of the other and then towed them back to the jetty. It took me time. I clambered out and handed the ropes to Lumpy. "Keep hold of these. We will stick these bodies in the bottom of the boat with the white sail."

I clambered to the top of the ladder and I picked up the first soldier. It was not easy negotiating the ladder to the jetty but I managed it. I dropped it in the bottom of the boat with the dirty white sail and then repeated it with the second body. I pointed to the painter at the front of the red sailed boat. "Tie this rope to the stern of the other boat and wait for me."

I clambered up the ladder. It was not fair to ask Hutton to do this with his dodgy ankle. I grabbed the rucksacks, the Lee Enfield and the oil lamp and climbed back down. I put the bags in the front of the red sailed boat. I threw my tunic and greatcoat into the stern of the red sailed boat.

"Sergeant, sit in the middle and be ready to unfurl the sail and raise it."

He looked terrified, "How do I do that?"

"There is a rope there, untie it and then pull on this rope. It should come up. Just watch what I do on this other boat." I felt guilty. I had watched the fishermen bring the boats in; I just did the reverse of their actions.

I dragged one of the dead Germans to the stern and draped him around the tiller. I hoisted the sail. Reassuringly the boat began to move. I boarded our boat and I sat at the stern. The sail was hoisted but looked slack. The wings on our FE 2 were as taut as a drum. "Lumpy, pull the rope until it is tight."

As soon as he did so we began to move. The tide was on the way out. I pushed the tiller over so that we were heading for the middle of the harbour. We were now in a race against time. We had had no opportunity to observe the patrol boat and its route. We would have to take a chance and just try to avoid it.

"Lumpy, keep the Lee Enfield handy."

"Right, sir. We only have five rounds left."

"Then use them well."

I found I was shivering. I put my tunic and greatcoat back on and suddenly felt much warmer. We reached the middle of the river. The weight of the second boat was slowing us down but I was loath to lose it. I needed the confusion it could bring if we were discovered. The patrol boat was powered and could be on us in an instant. In the distance I heard its engine. It seemed to be on the west bank of the harbour. There was little point in worrying. If it saw us then I would worry.

"Keep the sail tight Lumpy."

"Sir!"

Every time I shifted the tiller slightly it affected the sail. Lumpy could not just sit there. He was constantly adjusting the sail and avoiding the boom as it came across. The harbour entrance beckoned. I took the German map out of my greatcoat pocket. I had it folded to the entrance of the harbour. I laid it before me. There was just enough ambient light for me to see where the minefields were. They might just be our salvation.

Chapter 24

Our luck held until the harbour entrance. A searchlight suddenly picked us out and a command shouted in German. "That's it Lumpy. Hit the man you can see and then the light."

As he cracked off the two shots I let loose the white sailed boat. The angle must have been perfect for it leapt ahead of us. I steered towards the gun, which they would not be expecting. I heard a cry and then the light went out.

"Keep the line taut and use your last three bullets on anything that moves."

The machine gun rattled out. I braced myself for the bullets to strike us but they hit the other fishing boat instead. I heard the whine of the patrol boat's engine as it used full power to reach this sudden danger. I knew that the minefield began half a mile from the harbour entrance and the safe channel ran north to south. I headed east towards the mines.

"Hutton, have you any grenades?"

"Two sir in my pack."

I reached in and found one. The gunner was still firing at the better target, the boat with the white sail. I turned the rudder to the end of the breakwater and the gun. We were safer here for the gun could not fire at us. We slowed a little but, as we came near to the wall I pulled the pin and lobbed the grenade in the air. When I put the tiller hard over, the wind caught our sails and we leapt across the water like a greyhound. The grenade's explosion filled the harbour with light and actually made us fly faster as the concussion spread. I saw the patrol boat. It was heading for the boat with the dead Germans. We had bought some time.

The light faded and I pushed the tiller in the opposite direction. We skidded around the end of the mole and into the open sea. I felt the difference in motion as soon as we did so.

The machine gun on the patrol boat barked and I saw the other fishing boat begin to sink. The patrol boat slowed and I saw a searchlight play along the water then it disappeared as we became hidden by the end of the mole.

"Hutton, watch out for mines."

"Mines!"

"Yes I intend to go through the minefield."

"Isn't that dangerous?"

"I think they are intended to stop big ships so with luck we should be able to sail through them. You just watch out for them. Shout when you see one."

I smiled as he crossed himself. The wind was pushing us along quickly now. We had no second boat as an anchor. Of course the Germans had an engine but they were four times the width of us. I would choose the narrower channels. I glanced over my shoulder; the patrol boat was half a mile behind and emerging from the harbour. The searchlight was playing around the area in front of the bows.

"Hutton, rifle!"

He passed me the gun. I leaned on the tiller to keep the same course and then I rested my elbow on the transom. I aimed at the searchlight. I was not helped by the fishing boat rising and falling. My first shot struck the bridge and elicited a scream of pain. My second hit the bow. I had one bullet left. I breathed slowly and, as the stern came up, fired and the searchlight shattered as it was hit. I began to turn and as I did a rogue wave hit us and the Lee Enfield slipped to the bottom of the channel. It had served us well.

"Sir, minefield ahead!"

I heard the patrol boat engine as it was gunned. They were following our last course. They could not see us. The red sail would be almost invisible at night. "I will head to starboard. Shout out when you see a mine."

This was like a game of Russian Roulette with the biggest bullets in the world. "Mine ahead!"

I turned the tiller the smallest amount I could and waited for Lumpy's next shout. Nothing came but the patrol boat's machine gun began to fire ahead. He was to our left. Suddenly a mine exploded. The little fishing boat seemed to rise in the air. In that brief instant the patrol boat saw us and began to turn.

I reached into Hutton's bag and found the last grenade. "Lumpy, what fuse is in these Mills Bombs?"

"Ten seconds sir."

"Thanks."

The patrol boat had slowed and I could see a man on the bow directing the captain. Had I a rifle I could have hit him easily. They fired ahead again. I jammed the tiller to the left, towards them.

"Mine ahead!"

I edged the tiller to starboard. The bullets struck another mine behind us and sent us on a little tidal wave as it exploded. I heard Hutton shout, "Shit!" I saw the prickly points of the mine less than a hand span away. The light from the explosion sent the patrol boat back on our tail. I pulled the pin on the grenade. I had one chance. If I failed then it would either be the prisoner of war camp or a damp grave for the two of us. I released the handle and counted to five. I threw the grenade as far in the air as I could.

"Hold on Hutton. This could get messy!"

The grenade exploded in the air just over the bow of the patrol boat. Whether it was shrapnel which hurt the captain or an instinctive reaction to the explosion I have no idea but the patrol boat veered into a mine and was thrown into the air. We were hurled forward. We had no control over our direction. If fate had a mine waiting for us then we, like the crew of the patrol boat, would be dead.

We almost crashed back into the water. "Hutton, let the sail go slack." I had worked out that a tight sail meant we sailed quickly. I needed time to think. The remains of the patrol boat burned behind me and I looked at the German map. If we headed due west we would be out of the treacherous minefield. I looked at the compass. I pushed the tiller over. We went through the mines slowly but we went through safely. When we reached the other side I grinned and began to laugh. "Now we just need to cross the English Channel."

"After that sir, it should be no problem!"

He was, of course, tempting fate. I took out a canteen and drank some water. Once that was done I took the compass and laid it on the thwarts before me. "Tight sail again Lumpy. We now need speed."

As we headed through the dark towards the invisible coast of England I filled and lit my pipe. We had done well. I knew we were not home, not even close to home but there was, at least, light at the end of this tunnel.

I saw Hutton lighting Albert's pipe. He made a better stab at his second effort. The compass showed we were still heading north by north west and we were on course. I glanced at my hand which was still covered in the blood of the man whose throat I cut. It was the first time I had ever killed with a knife. If I had thought about it I would not have gone through with it but I just reacted. I shuddered at the memory. War makes a man do things which are alien to his nature.

The wind picked up a mile or so off shore. "We'll be home in no time if this keeps up sir."

I looked up at the rag of canvas tied to the mast head. It had begun to veer alarmingly so that we were being pushed further north than north west. I glanced behind and saw that the waves were growing in size. This was where my inexperience could hurt us. Did I reduce sail? Did I tack?

"I am going to try to bring us further west Lumpy. Hang on this could get rough."

As I pushed the tiller over slightly a huge wave deposited an enormous amount of water into the bottom of the boat. I quickly put the tiller back to its original position. We were almost flooded to the sides of the boat. Lumpy's legs were under water.

"Blood hell, sir! Don't do that again or we will be in Davy Jones' locker!"

"Get bailing, Lumpy."

He found a tin mug which was used for bailing and I began to throw handfuls out with my free hand. My move had been a disaster. We were so heavy that we were barely making headway.

I looked behind and saw that the waves were now five or six feet high. A sudden storm had blown up. The rain began to fall too. We were in danger of being swamped. Lumpy could not reduce sail for he was desperately trying to bail us out and I had to hold a straight course or we would be sunk. I had felt so clever at outwitting the Germans I had forgotten that the sea was the common enemy. In addition we were now out of sight of land. I looked down to the compass. It had gone; washed overboard. With a cloud filled sky I had no means of navigating. We would have to go where the wind took us.

The wind was gaining in intensity but Hutton was bravely battling the water in the bottom of the boat and he was winning. It was now just below the thwarts.

"When you can, Lumpy, reduce the sails a little or we will end up with rags."

"Right sir. It is bloody tiring, I'll tell you that. I couldn't be a sailor!"

"I don't think the Royal Navy uses sailing vessels now."

"And I can see why!"

When the water was around his ankles he lowered the sail slightly. We still moved forwards but we didn't tip into the waves so much. After another hour of solid bailing we just had a little water slopping around the bottom. The canvas the fishermen had rigged at the bow deflected much of the bow water else we would have been sunk.

"See what we have lost."

I saw him rummage around the bottom of the boat. "We have the two haversacks sir. They are a bit wet though."

"We need to conserve some food and water. Bring me my canteen and divide the food up. You can be quartermaster. We are on rations from now on." He gave me a worried look and I shrugged, "We lost the compass. I have no idea where we are. When daylight comes we will know which way is the east and I intended to head due west. Until then we let the wind take us." I thought, ruefully, not that we could do anything about that.

243

We had some soggy, salty bread and the remains of the cheese. The nuts would last us a little longer. Lumpy found the last of his fig rolls and we had the last four there and then. They would not last another day of soaking. Washed down with the water it gave us some sustenance and I was glad that we had eaten in Ostend. Who knew when we would eat again?

It was a soggy red dawn which broke the darkness. The old adage of *red sky in the morning, sailors warning*, rang through my head. There was nothing to be seen and that in itself was worrying. British and German shipping kept close to the shore and the fact that we were alone meant we were miles from either Belgium or England. The wind had not abated and we were driven north. I assumed north from the position of the sun but we could be sailing north east or north west. Both would bring us to land but in which country? Poor Lumpy looked ready to drop.

"Sergeant, lie down on the haversacks and try to get some sleep."

"No sir, I'll be fine."

I pointed behind us. "With the wind in this direction there is little than you can do anyway. Get some rest and when you wake I'll show you how to steer so that I can get some sleep too."

That seemed to persuade him. "Very well, sir. I need a lie down and that's no error."

Like all good soldiers Lumpy could fall asleep as soon as his head hit the ground and his eyes closed. I set myself a target of four hours before I woke him. We had left the minefield in such high hopes and I had thought we would have reached the Thames estuary by dawn. In my mind we had sailed triumphantly into port to be greeted by cheers and the flash of the press; so much for that fantasy.

The salt made me so thirsty and yet I knew I must not drink the last of our precious water. I would have a drink when I woke Hutton. That thought would keep me going a little longer. The horizon kept rising and falling as we climbed the peaks of waves and crashed into the troughs. Sergeant Hutton slept all the way through it. My fingers holding the tiller were white with salt and I could barely feel them. The German greatcoat was now soaked. It did not keep out the wet like my own flying coat. We should have changed coats as soon as we could. I laughed. This would have been the first opportunity to do so and that would have been difficult with the precocious wind and waves.

I must have closed my eyes for a moment but the boat dipped alarmingly and I awoke. The wind had been easing a little but suddenly it seemed to attack us with renewed force. I suspect we had been in the eye of the storm for a brief moment. I was going to wake Hutton but I thought I would give him a little longer to rest. Suddenly there was a huge gust of wind. It seemed to whip the sail around and it must have woken Hutton. He lifted his head and was smacked hard by the swinging boom. I saw blood and he slumped, face down, to the bottom of the boat. I just reacted and I half stood. In doing so I let go of the tiller and the boat suddenly veered to port. The main mast and the sail had taken a lot of damage and I heard a crack and saw, to my horror the mast break and it came crashing down. I just reacted. I lifted my arm to stop it and I did. There was an ugly crack as my left arm broke and I fell backwards. I saw a trickle of blood dripping down my arm. The bone must have come through the skin.

The sail and the mast were dragged behind us. I later realised that had saved our lives for it acted as an anchor and kept the small boat stern on to the waves. Holding my broken arm before me I gingerly made my way to Hutton. I put my fingers to his neck and felt a heartbeat, he was alive. I saw the bloody wound at the side of his head but the bleeding appeared to have stopped. He was face down and there was water in the bottom of the boat and so I moved his head to the side. I did not want him drowning nor did I want him to choke on his tongue. I had done all that I could for him. I opened his haversack and took out his RFC great coat. I laid it over his unconscious form.

I spied Albert's stick. Hutton had fallen on it and broken it in two. I grabbed the narrow end and made my way back to the stern. The ropes holding the sails were useless now and so I cut six short lengths. I jammed the knife into the thwarts and carefully placed the broken piece of walking stick next to my broken forearm. I unwrapped my scarf from around my neck and wrapped it around the arm and the stick. Next came the hard and painful part. I took one of the lengths of rope and looped it around the arm. I knew how to make a one handed knot. I did not tighten it. I repeated it four times along the length of the forearm.

I took the other end of the broken stick and jammed it in my mouth. I had to do this quickly or I would not be able to do it at all. I tightened the knots as much as I could one by one. The pain was agonising. I closed my eyes with the pain and bit down on Albert's old stick. Shock waves seemed to race through my body but I persevered and as I tied the last knot I spat the wood out.

I took a swallow of water and ate a handful of the nuts I was saving. I needed something inside me. Finally I took the last length of rope and fashioned a sling to support my arm. Once the rope took the weight then the pain diminished slightly.

I had time to take stock. I saw that the wind was not as strong as it had been and the waves not as high. The freak wave had been nature's goodbye. I could still see nothing on the horizon but the sun above and my stopped watch told me that it was sometime in the morning. We were still heading north and there was nothing we could do about that now. I looked at the German map, my English one had been washed over too. By my reckoning they would find the dinghy with the two corpses somewhere off Norway; failing that it would be the North Pole.

I crawled down the boat and poured some water into Lumpy's mouth. It moistened it, that was all I could do. I put the stopper back in and made my way back to the stern.

I had done all that I could. I lay against the tiller with my right arm. I rested my broken arm on the top and I closed my eyes. Soon I was asleep.

I had a dream that I was flying high and being pursued by five Albatros aeroplanes. No matter which way I twisted and turned they stuck to me like glue and there were getting ever closer. Suddenly my Gunbus disappeared and I was falling down and down. The earth changed to the sea and the sea became a black hole. When I hit the sea I seemed to keep on falling.

Chapter 25

I was woken by a sharp pain. It felt as though someone had jammed a red-hot needle into my broken arm. I lifted my head and shouted. I saw that it was almost dark but, straight ahead I saw a light and could smell the smoke as a ship bore down on us.

"Help! Help! Ware ship!" I was aware that the noise of the sea would drown out my words but I shouted anyway.

I waved my good arm despite the waves of pain it sent down my broken arm. The bow of the ship, which was a warship, appeared to be just a hundred yards from us. I was certain that it would ram us and I was contemplating a watery grave when it suddenly veered to the side and slowed down.

A voice shouted down in German. Fate had really played a trick with us. I had thought we had cheated the Germans but they had found us.

"I am sorry but we are English I don't understand you."

A couple of faces appeared above us and a cheery voice said, "Sorry about that, we thought you were the Hun. Killick, get a couple of hands down there to secure the boat."

"I have a broken arm and there is an unconscious man here too."

"Righto. Get Meredith up here too." The officer grinned down, "We'll have you up in a jiffy. The German greatcoats threw us, old boy. Sorry about that."

"Don't mention it. I am just happy you found us."

A scrambling net was thrown from the side and two sailors dropped lithely into the boat. They cut away the wreckage and used the painter fore and aft to tie the boat to the net.

"I think I can manage to climb up but Hutton here will need help. He had a blow to the head."

"Right sir, go steady and if you get stuck we will give you a hand."

I put one foot in the net and leapt upwards with my right hand. I managed to grab hold of the net just three feet from the top. The warship was smaller than I had thought. Unfortunately the motion of the vessel caused my broken arm to hit the side and pain coursed, once more, through my body. I gritted my teeth. Safety was just a little way ahead. I took the weight on my right hand and threw my right leg as high as I could get it. I pushed down on my left leg and began to rise. My head appeared level with the deck. A sailor said, "You are a tough bugger sir." He leaned over and gripped my right arm. I saw that the muscles were knotted like a battleship's hawser. "Push with your leg sir. Jenkins watch his broken arm."

And then I was hauled, unceremoniously aboard. The seamen helped me to my feet. "We'll get your oppo for you."

The officer held out his hand. "Lieutenant Jonathan Reed, commander of this minesweeper, 'Black Prince'. Welcome aboard."

I held out my hand, "Captain Bill Harsker, 41 Squadron Royal Flying Corps and the other chap is Flight Sergeant Hutton."

He looked amazed. "You are a long way off course. Where were you based?"

"Close to the Somme."

"Then you have had a hell of a journey. You can tell me about it when we get your friend up."

As the sailors helped Hutton I gave a brief account of our journey. The sailors had rigged something up and Hutton was being safely hauled up. When he was on board the two sailors threw the haversacks and greatcoat on board and them clambered up the scrambling net.

"Right chaps, target practice. I want the fishing boat sinking." We began to move away from the little boat. When we were a hundred yards away the two pounder and the machine guns all fired at her. She sank within minutes.

"It seems a shame somehow. She had served us well."

"Yes I know but the thing is you are on the edge of a minefield. If she had drifted and set one off then we would have to send a ship to investigate. It was necessary old chap." He turned to a rating who was kneeling next to Hutton. "How is he, Meredith?"

"He'll live sir. Just a nasty blow to the head." He glanced at me. "Let's get that arm seen to eh sir?" Hutton was put on a stretcher and we were taken below decks to the tiny sick bay. There was just one bed within and Hutton was placed carefully in it after they had taken off his boots and coats. Meredith said. "He'll be all right for a minute or two but let's see to this." He took out a hypodermic needle. I hated needles. He laid it on a kidney bowl and then carefully took my coat off my right arm. He then cut the ropes holding the splint and then took off the scarf and the stick. The pain was excruciating.

He looked at me sadly, "There is no easy way to do this sir. I can give you something for the pain but not until I have your tunic off." He nodded to his assistant. "Undo the officer's shirt and be ready to get it off his broken arm as soon as I say."

He peeled my tunic slowly down to the elbow. With an apologetic look he began to straighten my arm. I squeezed the nails of my right hand into my palm as I felt the rough edges of the bones grate together. Like a magician with a table cloth he whipped the tunic off in one motion. "Now Jonesy!"

The shirt came off equally quickly. The sudden cold made me shiver. "Nearly done sir." Meredith injected my arm and the pain began to subside immediately.

Jones held a small glass to me. "Try this sir, it'll warm you up."

"What is it?"

"Nelson's blood sir. That'll put hair on your chest."

The neat rum worked and, together with the injection drove all pain from my body. I watched as Meredith aligned the ends of the broken bones so that they were straight. He looked at me apologetically. "Have to get this right if you want to use this again." Satisfied he said, "Jonesy, get me two metal plates." He glanced up at me, "You a pilot then?"

"Yes, doctor."

He laughed, "I am no doctor. Sick Bay attendant I am. That's why I am leaving your oppo there for a bit. I can mend broken arms but concussions are something else. I can do more harm than good there. We are heading for King's Lynn and we should be there in a couple of hours. They have a proper doctor and he will see to your sergeant."

He had me patched up within fifteen minutes. The plaster cast would protect my arm and I hoped that, when the rum and the painkiller wore off, it would not hurt too much. Jonesy helped me with my shirt and was going to do the same for my tunic, I shook my head. "I'll carry it over my arm."

"Righto sir." As he folded it he said, "Is this the Military Cross, sir?" I nodded, "And this one? I have never seen one of those before."

"That's the Legion d'Honneur. It is a French award."

He suddenly became animated, "Sir, are you the bloke who got his medal off the King?" I nodded, "I saw it in the paper." He turned to the sick bay attendant. "We have a hero on board."

Meredith smiled as Jones folded the tunic and laid it over my arm. "You should really lie down, sir, but this is the only bunk in sickbay and your pal needs it. Jonesy, see if the skipper will let this officer lie on his day bed."

Jonesy raced off. "There's no need."

"That's all you know. Shock has a delayed reaction. You look all in to me."

The skipper was more than happy and I found myself lying on a cot just aft of the bridge. After the fishing boat this felt like an ocean liner and the movement soon had me asleep. Jones woke me with a cup of hot tea sweetened with rum. "Here y'are sir. We are docking in an hour. And Billy Meredith says your oppo has come round."

"Thank you, Jonesy. I appreciate all that you have done."

He shook his head, "No sir, I read that bit in the paper about you again. You are a real hero."

The skipper put his head around the door, "What was that about a hero?"

I shook my head, "Too many people think that all pilots are heroes."

251

"Well you have to admit it is more glamorous than sailing this tin pot boat around the North Sea."

"I'll tell you this for nothing, out there in that fishing boat I would have traded places with you in an instant."

He nodded, "I have radioed King's Lynn. The local military commander will meet you there and we'll get back to the glamorous world of sweeping mines."

Having seen the effect of the mines he was sweeping I think he was underestimating his own skills. I finished the tea and made my way back to the sick bay. Hutton was sitting up and drinking tea. "Well you look better, Lumpy."

"Billy here sorted me out. Reckons I'll just have a bump and a scar to remember it by."

The sick bay attendant stood, "I'll go to the mess. It is just down the corridor. Yell if you need anything."

"Thank you."

Hutton looked at my arm. "What happened sir?"

I sat on the bed and told him the whole story. "I knew I shouldn't have slept."

"It might have been for the best. If you had been awake we might have sailed blindly on and missed this minesweeper. It is never over until it is over. You were right when we set off, Nil Desperandum."

When we docked in the tiny port I saw a car waiting for us and two soldiers. I shook the skipper's hand. "Thanks for everything."

"You are welcome and it relieved the monotony. You take care. I'll get my chaps to bring your things to the car."

We walked down the gangway. There was a hatchet faced sergeant there. He looked to be in his fifties which explained why he was not at the front. "Captain Harsker, is it sir?" He had an aggressive tone which I did not like.

"It is and this is Flight Sergeant Hutton."

"If you would get in the back of the car sir we will take you to Captain Ebbs."

"Thank you, sergeant."

We sank into the soft seats of the Bentley. I had forgotten what comfort was like. We drove a little way from the harbour and entered a small barracks. Captain Ebbs looked to have no more than a company under his command. The sentries on the gate looked as old as the sergeant and I realised that these were territorials.

"We'll get your bags, sir." The driver smiled a little more than the sergeant.

The sergeant led the way to a large office. I saw, behind the desk, a huge picture of the king and underneath it a painting of a stand of redcoats against the Zulus. A sergeant was seated at one desk whilst a young lieutenant was at the other. For some reason they both looked nervous.

When Captain Ebbs finally arrived I saw that he too was an older man. He was a small, neat little man with a neatly trimmed moustache. He was at least sixty and begged the question why he had never risen above that rank. He laid his swagger stick down carefully as though it was a precious object.

He sat down and stared at me. I don't know what I had expected but it was not this. "So Herr Harsker, you thought you could sneak ashore and spy for the Kaiser did you?"

I looked at Hutton in case this was some sort of dream. The other three soldiers in the room, the two sergeants and the lieutenant did not appear surprised. "I beg your pardon?"

The hatchet faced sergeant threw a German haversack, a great coat, a Luger and a German map on to the table. "These were found in your possession, you German bastard."

"But sir!"

Captain Ebbs picked up his swagger stick and slashed Hutton across the face. "Silence, you German swine."

I tried to rise but hatchet face had me pinned to my seat. "Sit down before I knock your bloody head off!"

I breathed slowly and gathered myself. I saw the hatred in Hutton's eyes. "We are two RFC air crew. We were shot down near to Ypres and we made our way to Ostend where we stole a boat and escaped. We were damaged in a storm and rescued by the Black Prince."

"A cleverly rehearsed story but you are dealing with a superior mind here. This is just the sort of trick the Hun would come up with." He tapped the swagger stick on the desk. If he tried to hit me with it he would find himself eating it. "I am having a firing squad convened and you will be shot at dawn."

The lieutenant who had been looking increasingly uncomfortable said, "Sir, don't you think we ought to telephone London to confirm his identity? He may be telling the truth. He does not sound German and his story makes sense."

"Nonsense Lieutenant White, you are too naïve and trusting. These two are spies and we will shoot them." He picked up the swagger stick. I had had enough. I pulled my right arm forward and elbowed the hatchet-faced sergeant between the legs. He went down as though pole axed. I whipped out my gun and held it to the forehead of Captain Ebbs. Hutton took out his Luger and covered my back. "Listen you pathetic excuse for an officer. I am Captain Harsker MC of 41 Squadron and in a moment I am going to leave here with Sergeant Hutton. I will happily shoot you or anyone else who tries to stop us."

"I'll have you court martialed for this!"

I laughed, "I have lived through one before and that was from someone just like you!" I cocked the Webley. "Perhaps I ought to do the world a favour and finish you now." He went white.

The lieutenant knelt down and picked up my tunic. He held it triumphantly in the air. "I thought I recognised you sir." He turned to Captain Ebbs "Sir, this is the officer who received the Military Cross from King George and the Legion D'Honneur." He pointed to the ribbons.

"I er, well, er I mean you can see why I..."

I holstered the Webley. "No I can't! A word of advice Captain... resign and find somewhere far away to hide. When this war is over I am going to come and get you."

"Are you threatening me?"

"Of course, I am, you pathetic little man." I grabbed the swagger stick and used it to lift the hatchet-faced sergeant to his feet. I put my face close to his. "And the same goes for you Sergeant. I have seen too many good men die. You pair are neither good nor men. Now out of my way." He limped to the side with hatred in his eyes. I handed the swagger stick to Hutton who snapped it in two and threw it towards the shocked and apoplectic captain.

"Lieutenant, you seem to have some sense. Could you get your driver to take us to a hospital? My friend here needs stitches."

Glancing at the captain who remained speechless he said, "I'll drive you sir, in my car. I am off duty now."

Once in the car I said, "Ask for a transfer Lieutenant before you become like him."

"I have been trying sir but he always refuses me permission." He sighed, "I wanted to be a pilot."

"Then ring General Henderson and say you spoke to me. He is desperate for young men who have something about them."

He brightened, "I will do sir."

"And get in touch with your headquarters and tell them everything that went on tonight. I wouldn't want you in trouble as well."

"Right sir, I will and thank you."

The hospital was in Norwich. When the doctor saw Hutton's face and heard our story he was appalled. The nurse took Hutton away to dress the wound and he looked at me. "You don't look too good either, captain."

The pain killer had worn off a long time ago and I was in pain. "I have to admit that I don't feel too grand, doctor."

I began to feel faint. He and the nurse caught me and laid me on a bed. He thrust a thermometer in my mouth. When it came out he shouted, "Get theatre ready! This man has an infection." He looked at me. "This should have been dealt with as soon as you landed. You are in danger of losing your arm."

A team of nurses swarmed over me. My clothes were removed, almost painlessly and an operating gown put on me. The doctor injected my arm. "Count backwards from ten, Captain Harsker."

I reached four and then all went black.

Epilogue

When I awoke there was a nurse standing over me. She smiled. "You are a lucky man, Captain Harsker. There was some material in the break in your arms and it was infected. A delay of an hour more and your arm would have had to be removed. As it is it is touch and go if you are out of the woods yet. The doctor is a brilliant man and you will be in good hands."

She turned to go and I grabbed her hand, "Nurse, could you do me a favour?"

"If I can."

"Get me a pen and paper please." As she went to the nurse's station I saw Hutton asleep in a chair. "How long has he been here?"

"Since you came out of surgery. He refused a bed and said he needed to watch over you. That is real loyalty, Captain Harsker."

I wrote down Beatrice's address and the hospital telephone number on the paper. "This is my young lady. Could you tell her where I am, she is a nurse."

"Of course Captain Harsker, it will be my pleasure."

As she left and the door slammed Hutton sat bolt upright in his chair. He grinned when he saw me sitting up. "I was right worried about you, sir. They were all flying around like chickens without heads."

"Well I am fine now so please use the bed they have given you. You were closer to death than I was."

He stood, stretched and yawned. "You look better sir, so I will. Goodnight."

"Goodnight, Sergeant Hutton, and thank you for caring."

"Where else could I get a pilot I have trained so well sir? It's in my interest to keep you healthy."

After he had left I tried to rise but another nurse came in. "And where do you think you are going to?"

"I was going to stretch my legs."

257

She wagged a finger at me. "Here, the doctor said to give you this. Take it and get some sleep. You need it!"

I did as I was told and the tablet began to work. I just closed my eyes and soon I was asleep. I had my falling dream again and wondered what it meant.

When I woke I could smell the nurse in the room. I opened my eyes and looked up into the smiling face of Beatrice. She leaned down and kissed me. "As soon as Matron heard you were wounded again she granted me compassionate leave and I caught the first train up here that I could. Until you are well I am not taking my eyes off you."

She kissed me again, "And that is the best medicine I could have. I will be looked after by an angel."

The End

Glossary

BEF- British Expeditionary Force

Beer Boys-inexperienced fliers (slang)

Blighty- Britain (slang)

Boche- German (slang)

Bowser- refuelling vehicle

Bus- aeroplane (slang)

Corned dog- corned beef (slang)

Craiglockhart- A Victorian building taken over by the military and used to treat shell shocked soldiers. Siegfried Sassoon and Wilfred Owen both spent time there.

Crossley- an early British motor car

Dewar Flask- an early Thermos invented in 1890

Donkey Walloper- Horseman (slang)

Fizzer- a charge (slang)

Foot Slogger- Infantry (slang)

Google eyed booger with the tit- gas mask (slang)

Griffin (Griff)- confidential information (slang)

Hun- German (slang)

Jasta- a German Squadron

Jippo- the shout that food was ready from the cooks (slang)

Kanone 14- 10cm German artillery piece

Killick- Leading seaman (slang-Royal Navy)

Lanchester- a prestigious British car with the same status as a Rolls Royce

Loot- a second lieutenant (slang)

Lufbery Circle- An aerial defensive formation

M.C. - Military Cross (for officers only)

M.M. - Military Medal (for other ranks introduced in 1915)

Nelson's Blood- rum (slang- Royal Navy)

Nicked- stolen (slang)

Number ones- Best uniform (slang)

Oblt. - Oberlieutenant (abbr.)

Oppo- workmate/friend (slang)

Outdoor- the place they sold beer in a pub to take away (slang)

Parkin or Perkin- a soft cake traditionally made of oatmeal and black treacle, which originated in northern England.

Pop your clogs- die (slang)

Posser- a three legged stool attached to a long handle and used to agitate washing in the days before washing machines

Pickelhaube- German helmet with a spike on the top. Worn by German soldiers until 1916

Scousers- Liverpudlians (slang)

Shufti- a quick look (slang)

Scheiße- Shit (German)

Singer 10 - a British car developed by Lionel Martin who went on to make Aston Martins

The smoke- London (slang)

Toff- aristocrat (slang)

V.C. - Victoria Cross, the highest honour in the British Army

Maps

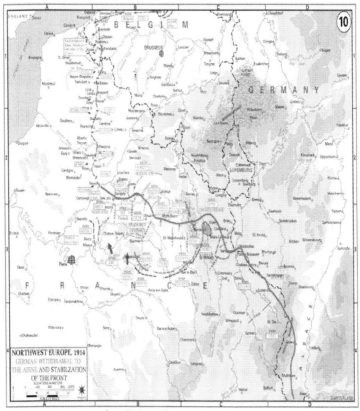

Map courtesy of Wikipedia

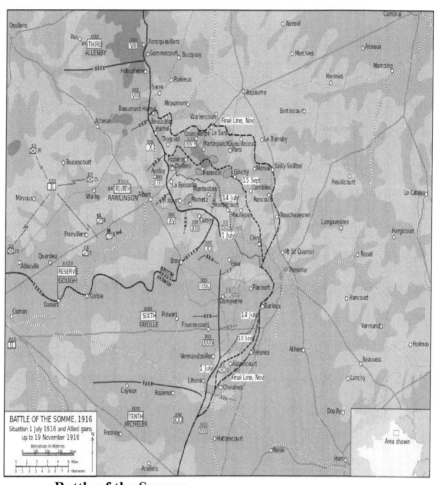

Battle of the Somme
Courtesy of Wikipedia –Public Domain

Map of the Somme battlefield, 1916, showing the frontline before the three major offensives of 1 & 14 July and 15 September as well as the final frontline at the end of the battle of 18 November. Based on a map from *A Short Military History of World War I - Atlas*, edited by T. Dodson Stamps and Vincent J.

Esposito, 1950. This work has been released into the public domain by its author, Gsl.

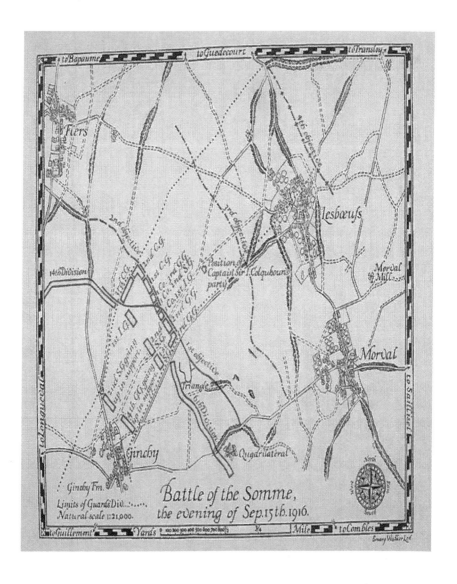

Historical note

This is my third foray into what might be called modern history. The advantage of the Dark Ages is that there are few written records and the writer's imagination can run riot- and usually does! If I have introduced a technology slightly early or moved an action it is in the interest of the story and the character. The FE 2 is introduced a month or so before the actual aeroplane. The Red Baron is shot down six weeks before he really was. I have tried to make this story more character based. I have used the template of some real people and characters who lived at the time.

The Short Magazine Lee Enfield had a ten shot magazine and enabled a rifleman to get off 20-30 shots in a minute. It was accurate at 300 yards. Both cavalry and infantry were issued with the weapon.

For those readers who do not come from England I have tried to write the way that people in that part of Lancashire speak. As with many northerners they say *'owt'* for anything and *'eeh'* is just a way of expressing surprise. As far as I know there is no Lord Burscough but I know that Lord Derby had a huge house not far away in Standish and I have based the fictitious Lord Burscough on him. The area around Burscough and Ormskirk is just north of the heavily industrialised belt which runs from Leeds, through Manchester, to Liverpool. It is a very rural area with many market gardens. It afforded me the chance to have rural and industrial England, cheek by jowl. The food they eat is also typical of that part of Lancashire. Harsker is a name from the area apparently resulting from a party of Vikings who settled in the area some centuries earlier. Bearing in mind my earlier Saxon and Viking books I could not resist the link, albeit tenuous, with my earlier novels.

The rear firing Lewis gun was not standard issue and was an improvised affair. Below is a photograph of one in action.

The photograph demonstrates the observer's firing positions in the Royal Aircraft Factory F.E.2d. The observer's cockpit was fitted with three guns, one or two fixed forward-firing for the pilot to aim, one moveable forward-firing and one moveable rear-firing mounted on a pole over the upper wing. The observer had to stand on his seat in order to use the rear-firing gun.

It is an artistic work other than a photograph or engraving (e.g. a painting) which was created by the United Kingdom Government prior to 1964. HMSO has declared that the expiry of Crown Copyrights applies worldwide.

An F.E.2 without armament

This image is in the public domain because the copyright has expired. *This applies to Australia, the European Union and those countries with a copyright term of **life of the author plus 70 years**.*

Baron Von Richthofen was actually shot down by an FE 2 during the later stages of the Battle of the Somme. In this novel it is Bill who has that honour. The Red Baron is portrayed as the pilot of the Halberstadt with the yellow propeller. Of course the Red Baron got his revenge by shooting down the leading British ace of the time, Major Lanoe Hawker VC. Hawker, was flying the DH2 while the Red Baron flew the superior Albatros D111. That is in the future. In this novel the best German fighter is the Albatros D1 and the Albatros D series gave the German superiority for the rest of the year.

The circle devised by Bill and Billy really existed. It was known as a Lufbery circle. The gunner of each F.E.2, could cover the blind spot under the tail of his neighbour and several gunners could fire on any enemy attacking the group. There were occasions when squadrons used this tactic to escape the Fokker monoplane and the later fighters which the Germans introduced to wrest air superiority from the Gunbus. It made for slow progress home but they, generally, got there safely.

The Immelmann Turn was named after the German Ace Max Immelmann who flew the Fokker E1. He was apparently shot down by an FE 2 although one theory is that his interrupter gear malfunctioned and he shot his own propeller off. I prefer the first theory. This is the Immelmann Turn as a diagram.

I have no evidence for Sergeant Sharp's improvised bullet proofing. However they were very inventive and modified their aeroplanes all the time. The materials he used were readily

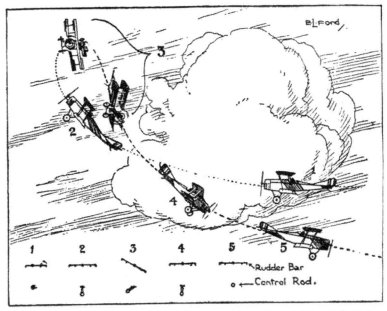

available and, in the days before recycling, would have just been thrown away. It would be interesting to test it with bullets.

The Mills bomb was introduced in 1915. It had a seven second fuse. The shrapnel could spread up to twenty yards from the explosion.

Hulluch was the scene of the first German attack with gas. The Bavarian regiment attacked the British near to Loos. They had some forewarning of the attack as a German deserter told them and rats were seen leaving the German trenches. (A sure sign of leaking gas bottles.) The Germans had nearly as many men incapacitated as the British but the inferior nature of the British gas mask meant more deaths amongst the British. The bombing raid is pure fiction.

General Henderson commanded the RFC for all but a couple of months of the war. The Fokker Scourge lasted from autumn 1915 until February 1916. It took the Gunbus and other new aircraft to defeat them. The BE 2 aeroplanes were known as Fokker fodder and vast numbers were shot down. There were few true bombers at this stage of the war and the Gunbus was one of the first multi-role aeroplanes. The addition of the third Lewis gun did take place at this stage of the war. The Germans had to react to their lack of superiority and in the next book the pendulum swings in Germany's favour when the Albatros DI11 and other new aircraft wrested control of the air away from the RFC,

More aeroplanes were shot down by ground fire than other aeroplanes and I have tried to be as realistic as I can but Bill Harsker is a hero and I portray him as such. He does achieve a high number of kills. Lanoe Hawker was the first ace to reach 40 kills and he died just at the end of the Somme Offensive. Bill is some way behind that figure.

The Somme Offensive July1st – 18th November 1916

The Somme Offensive was an absolute blood bath as the table lower down shows. However the RFC definitely won the battle of the air and dominated the battlefield completely. It helped that the Kaiser had withdrawn his best pilot, Boelke after the death of Max Immelmann but the superior aircraft the British and allies possessed helped. On July 1st Major L W B Rees attacked ten two seater German aeroplanes winning a Victoria Cross in the process. The figures given for the Newfoundland Warwicks casualties are accurate as are the appalling first day casualties- 1000 officers and 20000 men dead in one day. By the end of the Somme offensive in November 1916, the RFC had lost 800 aircraft and 252 aircrew killed (all causes) since July 1916, with 292 tons of bombs dropped and 19,000 photographs taken.

The South African Division did take Delville Woods in the British push to Pozières. The German defenders were dug in the woods. The South Africans took over 2,500 casualties. I do not know if FE 2s bombed the woods but this period of the war did see total dominance of the skies by the RFC. Until Boelke formed Jasta 2 in late August (The Red Baron was one of his younger pilots) flying Albatros D111 the RFC totally dominated the Somme. After that the Germans ruled the skies until Spring 1917. In September 1916 the RFC lost 167 airmen. Training standards did plummet as airmen were rushed to replace dead pilots. At the end of 1916 the life expectancy of a young pilot was three weeks.

The Buckingham tracer ammunition was introduced at the end of August. The fighting around Delville Woods saw the re-emergence of the German aeroplanes and they nearly swung the battle in the German's favour. Close contact between the aeroplanes and the ground repulsed the attacks and, by the 3rd of September they had secured the vital woods and surrounding area.

There was close cooperation between ground forces and the RFC. They used mirrors to signal and laid out sheets to mark their forward positions. Had the RFC not been so successful then there might have been less gains in the battle of the Somme.

Tanks were used for the first time but they were handled badly. They learned lessons which enabled them to be more successful at Cambrai in 1917. It is like the disaster of Dieppe in 1941 where the lessons led to the successful D Day landings.

Casualties in the Battle of the Somme
United Kingdom-350,000+
Canada-24,029
Australia-23,000
New Zealand-7,408
South Africa- 3,000+
Newfoundland-2,000+
Total British Commonwealth- 419,654
Total French-204,253
Germany-465,000
Killed and Missing
British Commonwealth- 95,675
French- 50,756
Germany- 164,055

Selected Specifications for the aeroplanes mentioned in the novel
FE2b
2 crew

47 feet wingspan

12 feet 6 inches height

Rolls Royce Eagle engine 360hp

Maximum speed 81 mph (up to 88 at higher altitude)

Ceiling, 11000 feet

2 Lewis machine guns and up to 517lb of bombs
AEG G1
3 crew

52 feet wingspan

11 feet four inches height

2 Mercedes 8 cylinders in line engines 100 hp each

Maximum speed 78 mph

Ceiling 7874 feet

2 machine guns
Aviatik B1/B11
Crew 2

Wingspan 40 feet

Height 10 feet 10 inches

Mercedes D11 Engine 99hp

Maximum speed 60 mph

Ceiling 16404 feet

1 machine gun
Fokker E1
1 crew

29 feet wingspan

9 feet 5 inches height

.7 Cylinder air cooled rotary engine 80 hp

Maximum speed 81 mph

Ceiling 9840 feet

1 machine gun (later variants had a machine gun firing through the propeller)

Arco DH2

1 crew
28 feet wingspan
9 feet 6 inches height
Gnome Monosoupape 10 hp Rotary engine
Maximum speed 93 mph
Ceiling 14,000 feet
I machine gun either fixed or moveable

Nieuport 11

1 crew
29 feet wingspan
7 feet high
1 Le Rhone Rotary Engine 80hp
Maximum speed 97 mph
Ceiling 15,000 feet
1 machine gun

Fokker D.1

1 crew
29 feet wingspan
7 feet 5inches high
Mercedes D 111 160 hp Engine
Maximum speed 93 mph
Ceiling 11000 feet
1 7.92 Spandau mg

Albatros D.1

1 crew
27 feet 10 inches wingspan
9feet 8 inches high
Mercedes D 111 160 hp Engine
Maximum speed 109 mph
Ceiling 17000 feet
2 x 7.92 Spandau mg

Halberstadt D111

1 Crew
28 feet 10 inches wingspan
8 feet 8 inches high

Argus As.11 inline 120hp engine
Maximum speed 99.4 mph
Ceiling 14764 feet
1 7.92 Spandau mg

I used the following books to verify information:
World War 1- Peter Simkins
The Times Atlas of World History
The British Army in World War 1 (1)- Mike Chappell
The British Army in World War 1 (2)- Mike Chappell
The British Army 1914-18- Fosten and Marrion
British Air Forces 1914-1918- Cormack
British and Empire Aces of World War 1- Shores
A History of Aerial Warfare- John Taylor
First World War- Martin Gilbert
Aircraft of World War 1- Herris and Pearson
Thanks to the following website for the slang definitions

- *www.ict.griffith.edu.au/~davidt/z_ww1_**slang**/index_bak.htm*

Bill and Lumpy will return with the fourth in the series 1917.

Griff Hosker September 2014

Other books

by

Griff Hosker

If you enjoyed reading this book then why not read another one by the author?

Ancient History

The Sword of Cartimandua Series (Germania and Britannia 50A.D. – 128 A.D.)

Ulpius Felix- Roman Warrior (prequel)
Book 1 The Sword of Cartimandua
Book 2 The Horse Warriors
Book 3 Invasion Caledonia
Book 4 Roman Retreat
Book 5 Revolt of the Red Witch
Book 6 Druid's Gold
Book 7 Trajan's Hunters
Book 8 The Last Frontier
Book 9 Hero of Rome
Book 10 Roman Hawk
Book 11Roman Treachery
They are all available in the Kindle format.

The Aelfraed Series (Britain and Byzantium 1050 A.D.-1085 A.D.

Book 1 Housecarl*
Book 2 Outlaw*
Book 3 Varangian*

The Wolf Warrior series (Britain in the late 6th Century)

Book 1 Saxon Dawn*
Book 2 Saxon Revenge*
Book 3 Saxon England*
Book 4 Saxon Blood*

Book 5 Saxon Slayer*
Book 6 Saxon Slaughter*
Book 7 Saxon Bane

The Dragon Heart Series
Book 1 Viking Slave
Book 2 Viking Warrior
Book 3 Viking Jarl
Book 4 Viking Kingdom
Book 5 Viking Wolf

Modern History
The Napoleonic Horseman Series
Book 1 Chasseur a Cheval
Book 2 Napoleon's Guard
Book 3 British Light Dragoon
Book 4 Soldier Spy
The Lucky Jack American Civil War **series**
Rebel Raiders
Confederate Rangers
The Road to Gettysburg
The British Ace Series
1914
1915 Fokker Scourge
1916 Angels over the Somme
1917 Eagles Fall
Other Books
 Great Granny's Ghost (Aimed at 9-14 year old young
people)
Carnage at Cannes is a modern thriller
Adventure at 63-Backpacking to Istanbul

For more information on all of the books then please visit
the author's web site at http://www.griffhosker.com where there is a
link to contact him.

Made in the USA
Lexington, KY
04 February 2019